T0013479

"The stories in *Dearborn*—by turns hilarious and heartbreaking, astute and absurd—capture such a vital, underspoken aspect of the Arab American experience, that sense of being not quite from the place you love and not quite loved by the place you're from. Ghassan Zeineddine has a talent for those very small details of Arab life in a place like Dearborn— the generational fatalism, the converted garage living room, the unlikely mash-up of cuisines at the neighborhood restaurant. These are wonderful stories from an exciting new name in Arab American literature."

—OMAR EL AKKAD,
author of *What Strange Paradise*

"These stories will stay with you for weeks and years after you've finished them, making you again laugh, wonder, and rage. *Dearborn* is masterful, gentle, wild, and full of heart."

—RIVKA GALCHEN,
author of *Everyone Knows Your Mother Is a Witch*

"*Dearborn* is one of the funniest, truest, and most heartfelt books I have ever read. Zeineddine writes with so much grace and understanding, so much love and compassion, so much mastery that these stories will become part of who you are."

—MORGAN TALTY,
author of *Night of the Living Rez*

"At once urgent and timeless, the stories in *Dearborn* are searing and unflinching snapshots of an immigrant community struggling to carve out space for itself, to find home in unfamiliar territory. The unforgettable characters slash through stereotypes as they navigate heart-wrenching and absurd situations, all the while grappling with identity and intergenerational tensions. The world Zeineddine creates is filled with beauty, brutal realities, and humor. I couldn't put it down."

—**ZAINA ARAFAT**,
author of *You Exist Too Much*

DEARBORN

DEARBORN

◆

Stories

◆

GHASSAN
ZEINEDDINE

TIN HOUSE / PORTLAND, OREGON

This is a work of fiction. All of the characters, organizations, and events portrayed in these stories are either products of the author's imagination or are used fictitiously.

Copyright © 2023 by Ghassan Zeineddine

First US Edition 2023
Printed in the United States of America

All rights reserved. No part of this book may be used or reproduced in any manner whatsoever without written permission from the publisher except in the case of brief quotations embodied in critical articles or reviews. For information, contact Tin House, 2617 NW Thurman St., Portland, OR 97210.

The lines of poetry that appear in "Speedoman" are written by Ulayya bint al-Mahdi and translated by Wessam Elmeligi in the anthology *The Poetry of Arab Women from the Pre-Islamic Age to Andalusia* (Routledge, 2019). Included by permission of the translator.

Stories from this collection have appeared or are forthcoming in the following literary journals, often in earlier form: "The Actors of Dearborn" (published as "The Citizenship Question, or, The Actors of Dearborn") in the *Georgia Review*; "Speedoman" in *TriQuarterly*; "Money Chickens" in *Pleiades: Literature in Context*; "Zizou's Voice" in *Prairie Schooner*; "In Memoriam" (published as "In Memory of Dearbornites") in *FOLIO*; "Hiyam, LLC" in *Grist: A Journal of the Literary Arts*; "Yusra" in the *Arkansas International*; and "Rabbit Stew" in *Michigan Quarterly Review*.

Front cover image: Postcard (circa 1930–1945) of the Ford Plant in Dearborn, Michigan / Boston Public Library; cropped and color-modified; https://flickr.com/photos/24029425@N06/8240927587

Manufacturing by Lake Book Manufacturing
Interior design by Beth Steidle

Library of Congress Cataloging-in-Publication Data
Names: Zeineddine, Ghassan, author.
Title: Dearborn : stories / Ghassan Zeineddine.
Description: Portland, Oregon : Tin House, [2023]
Identifiers: LCCN 2023016947 | ISBN 9781959030294 (paperback) |
ISBN 9781959030171 (ebook)
Subjects: LCSH: Arab Americans—Michigan—Fiction. | Dearborn (Mich.)—Fiction. | LCGFT: Short stories.
Classification: LCC PS3626.E353 D43 2023 | DDC 813/.6—dc23/eng/20230501
LC record available at https://lccn.loc.gov/2023016947

Tin House | 2617 NW Thurman Street, Portland, OR 97210 | www.tinhouse.com

DISTRIBUTED BY W. W. NORTON & COMPANY
1 2 3 4 5 6 7 8 9 0

For
my love, Rana, and our daughters, Alma and Mira,
my mother, Wafaa, and sister, Jana, and in
memory of my father, Ragheb,
and for Cleo Cacoulidis

CONTENTS

The Actors of Dearborn

Before arriving at Uncle Sam's house on the corner of Gould and Coleman Streets, Youssef Bazzi had been canvassing the neighborhoods in East Dearborn, Michigan, for over a month, knocking on doors throughout the day and late into the night, despite the heat or rain. His new job as census taker afforded him flexible hours, and at this point in his life, he preferred to be outdoors. He was thirty-one, and although tall and slim, he had grown a small belly since he had started canvassing in early August. He blamed his extra weight on the neighborhoods.

East Dearborn was predominately Arab, and among the Lebanese population, the Bazzi family was one of the biggest. Youssef was born and raised in the area and knew most of the people on each block, at least by face. Whenever a resident, quite often a fellow Bazzi, saw Youssef standing on their porch with his ID badge dangling from a lanyard around his neck, a census-issued laptop in his hand, and his census-issued briefcase hanging from his shoulder, they quickly invited him inside, sat him down in the living room, and brought him a glass of soda or lemonade mixed with orange blossom water, followed by a salty snack or perhaps a dessert and a cup of Turkish coffee. If it was around lunchtime or dinner, he was fed, and fed well. If Youssef had refused the food he would have offended his fellow Dearbornites.

After dusk, when the men and women sat on their porches or in their open garages to smoke a hookah, sip tea, and crack pumpkin seeds between their teeth amid the fireflies flickering in the air, Youssef was urged to take a seat and enjoy a puff from the hookah. The wind carried the scent of apple-flavored tobacco. Children ran across the lawns and rode their bicycles down the sidewalk in the streetlight filtering between the trees. Every so often, a car blaring Arabic pop music thundered past. The modest brick houses were built so close to one another that Youssef could simply cross a driveway and step onto the next person's property.

"I thought you were working for Ford," many folks told Youssef.

"I don't need Ford," he said, feeling emboldened. He had previously worked in the communications department at the Ford Motor Company, where he had languished for years in a cubicle until he was laid off in the latest round of cuts.

Youssef's new job was to verify addresses and update residents' information in preparation for the 2020 census, but he often went off script.

"Are you happy in life?" he'd ask. "Have you become what you've always wanted to be?"

"I didn't know the census was so personal," one resident said.

"I'm here to listen," Youssef said.

When Youssef came across his former high school classmates, they all greeted him as "Broadway Joe." Uncle Sam had given him this Americanized nickname back when Youssef was a teenager and dreamed of acting in Broadway plays. Youssef had starred in all the plays staged at Fordson High, sometimes even performing female roles. According to Mr. Emerson, his English teacher and theater director, his most memorable performance was as Abigail Williams from Arthur Miller's *The Crucible*.

"I don't understand this acting business," Youssef's father had told him after the opening night of *The Crucible*. Youssef's parents had sat in the first row, horrified at seeing their son dressed as a witch. "You're a man, Youssef. A man! Be like your brother."

At the time, Youssef's older brother was the starting fullback on the varsity football team and known as the "Lebanese Express" for his ability to plow through defensive linemen. But Youssef had no interest in sports and had never tried out for any of the teams. The head football coach could hardly believe that Youssef and his brother were related. "Guess there's only one express train in the family," the coach had said. All Youssef cared about was the stage, the spotlight hot on his skin, the wooden floorboards squeaking beneath his feet. The Arab boys in his class and in the neighborhood distanced themselves from him following his performance in *The Crucible*. They thought he was too girly.

Even now, Youssef missed wearing costumes and having the makeup artist highlight his face. But he had a new role, one that came with props and a revolving stage. He kept a makeup kit in his briefcase, and every now and then, before stepping out of his car, he powdered his cheeks and forehead and put on eyeliner.

That early afternoon in mid-September when Youssef arrived at the front door of Uncle Sam's house, leaves were starting to change color and fall. An American flag fluttered from a pole in the front yard. Banners sporting the logos of the Detroit Lions, the Detroit Tigers, the Detroit Red Wings, and the Detroit Pistons hung from the railing of the front porch, and there was even a banner for the Great Lakes Loons, a minor-league baseball team based in Midland, Michigan. After the attacks of 9/11, Uncle Sam had begun decorating his house with patriotic and athletic symbols even though he didn't care for baseball or football. He only knew that Americans were obsessed with their sports teams. He'd also changed his name from Samir to Sam.

The house was a one-story, and as he stood outside it, Youssef realized that all the window blinds—or at least all the blinds he could see from the porch—were closed. When he knocked on the door, Uncle Sam opened it and stuck his head out while looking side to side. He quickly ushered Youssef in and bolted the door behind him. He wore a gray Detroit Lions sweatshirt and matching gray sweatpants. His curly silver hair sat atop his head like a stormy sea. A short, pudgy man, his eyes were red and swollen. He and Youssef's father had grown up together in Bint Jbeil, a village in southern Lebanon near the Israeli border, where as boys they'd been inseparable, riding around town on the back of a donkey, taking turns with the reins. They'd even immigrated to the US together after the Israeli invasion of Lebanon in 1982, landing jobs at the Ford Rouge plant in Dearborn. After several years of standing on the assembly line and having to yell over the sound of churning machines, Uncle Sam had used all his savings to purchase a gas station on Schaefer Road. His business had prospered, allowing him to buy a house and start a family.

However, when his patriotic fervor blossomed following 9/11 and he began calling his wife, Hanan, "Hannah" and his sons, Abdullah and Nasser, "Abraham" and "Nicholas," and bought them all a Detroit Lions wardrobe; when he suspected that their landline was being tapped and that white men in suits walking in their neighborhood were either FBI or Homeland Security agents; when he nearly lost his mind, chewed his nails until they bled, could hardly sleep anymore, and spent every waking hour terrified that the government would accuse him of supporting terrorist organizations and then revoke his family's American citizenship and send them all back to Lebanon—or worse, to a black hole—his wife lost her hair from the stress he had put her under and asked for a separation. Uncle Sam ended up moving out and renting the house he now lived in. Since arriving in America close to forty years ago, he had always felt that the government had its eyes on him and his fellow Arabs. Back in the eighties he'd feared being mistaken for a hijacker. And then 9/11 had happened and his anxiety had skyrocketed.

Last night, Youssef had read on the City of Dearborn Facebook page that ICE had paid a visit to Uncle Sam's gas station. Two agents had burst through the door and demanded that Uncle Sam sign a document and hand over all his employees' paperwork. He refused, trembling behind the register. They yelled at him and threatened him with deportation. He didn't budge. He knew his rights. The agents left empty-handed.

Uncle Sam led Youssef into the dimly lit living room. Youssef sat on a couch in front of the fireplace, which had a wide-screen TV hoisted above it. A large family portrait hung from the wall. In the picture, Uncle Sam sat next to his wife with their sons on either side of them. They all wore matching Detroit Pistons jerseys.

Youssef opened his laptop.

"Your father told me about your new job," Uncle Sam said.

"It ends in October."

"Go ahead, ask me the question."

"Which question, Uncle?"

"You know which one, and you already know the answer."

"I'm here to confirm a few details for the census."

"Ask me the question!"

"Are you an American citizen?"

"Yes. And so are my wife and sons. Did you see them on your route?"

"Not yet," Youssef lied.

"If you do, can you tell my wife that I miss her? That I still love her. I hope she's watching her weight; she's got high cholesterol."

Youssef nodded. He had confirmed their information earlier in the week. It had been four years since Uncle Sam had moved out, and Hanan was now working as an office assistant at a local doctor's office. When Youssef had seen her, she'd looked happy, her black hair in a perm. She had been dressed in a tight-fitting yoga outfit when she answered the door. Abdullah and Nasser were both married and had long since moved out of the house.

Uncle Sam pulled out his smartphone and looked at the screen. His eyes widened. "Bismillah al-rahman al-rahim. Look what the president just tweeted." He got up from his chair and flashed the screen at Youssef.

We've got illegal immigrants in our country that have got to go! It's our duty as Americans to deport these rapist animals back to the hellholes they came from!

"Ignore his tweets, Uncle."

"But he's our president, and ICE is going to do what he tells them. They've been terrorizing us for over a year now."

"I heard about their visit to your gas station."

Uncle Sam bit his lower lip. "I think they were after Rocky. His tourist visa expired."

Rocky, Uncle Sam's nephew from Lebanon, had been living with him for the past three years. He worked at the gas station. Youssef had seen him a few times when he filled up his tank.

"Is he here?" Youssef asked.

"He's in his room, talking to his girlfriend from the internet." Uncle Sam shook his head. "I've never done anything illegal before. I was left with no choice."

Rocky, Uncle Sam's sister's youngest son, had arrived in 2016 at the age of seventeen, having flunked out of high school in Bint Jbeil. "Please try to save him, because Allah knows that my husband and I have tried our best and failed," Uncle Sam's sister had told him. At that point, Uncle Sam was living alone in his rented house. He had boxed up all his American flags and sports banners in the basement, thinking there was no need to show-case his Americanness when he had lost his family. But when he began to cook for Rocky, buy him clothes, and support his daily needs, which included making protein shakes for his weight training, he brought out the boxes and redecorated his house. He changed his nephew's name from Mohammed to Rocky.

"An informant must be working for ICE," Uncle Sam said. "I bet Iyaad Baydoun over at the Shell Station told them about Rocky. He's my fiercest competitor. The fucking rat."

Youssef checked the time on his watch. He still had a few more houses to visit before he could head home.

"I haven't offered you anything to drink or eat," Uncle Sam said. "How rude of me."

Before Youssef could respond, Uncle Sam went to the kitchen and began opening and closing drawers.

"I'm just having a bad day, baby girl," Youssef heard someone say in accented English from down the hallway. It must have been Rocky, who was now twenty. "You know I'm so hard for you. I mean, how to say in English . . ."

Uncle Sam returned with a tray bearing a glass of Pepsi and a bowl of mixed nuts and placed it on the coffee table next to Youssef. He peeked between the blinds before sitting down. He peered intently at Youssef.

"Are you wearing makeup?"

"No," Youssef said, blushing.

"What do you plan to do once your job ends?"

Youssef hadn't thought that far ahead. He had enough sav-ings to last a few months. He still lived at home with his parents and helped them pay the bills. In Dearborn, a single Arab man or woman left home only when they married. That's what Youssef's brother, the former Lebanese Express, had done. The one time that Youssef had attempted to live alone—when, after graduat-ing from university, he took a Greyhound bus out to New York

City to make it as an actor on Broadway—he'd returned from the Big Apple demoralized and with his heart in pieces. It was then that he'd applied for the communications position at Ford.

Youssef sipped his Pepsi, not bothering to respond.

"Have you met anyone?" Uncle Sam asked.

Youssef shook his head. He had gone on dates, including those that his mother had fixed through her matchmaking network, but nothing had materialized.

"You're stuck in the clouds—storm clouds," one date had told him, "and I'm not about to pull you down."

Since returning from New York and spending all those years in a cubicle, Youssef felt like he was living someone else's life, one that had been programmed for him. At least now, as a census taker, he experienced more spontaneity.

"Rocky's girlfriend lives out in LA," Uncle Sam said. "He hasn't even met her in person, but he says they're in love. I could never meet someone online. Not that I'd ever want to. Maybe my wife will come back to me. I know my sons won't; they hate me." He checked his phone and covered his mouth. "Look," he said, showing Youssef the president's most recent tweet.

The child-eating illegals are robbing our homes and spreading drugs and diseases into our American neighborhoods! The other day I saw one drinking the blood of bats! Report them!

Uncle Sam pulled at his hair. There was a knock at the door.

"Rocky, they're here!" Uncle Sam said.

Rocky sprung out of his room. "The pizza?"

The knocking turned to pounding.

"ICE!"

Rocky ran down the stairs to the basement.

Youssef stood up, his heart in his throat. He felt like a criminal, the same feeling he had experienced as an eighth grader in the fall of 2001, when he had gone on a school field trip to a farming town two hours north of Dearborn, and at a rest stop, a middle-aged white man with a crew cut had walked up to him, pointed at him, and said, "You're going to pay for what you did." The man started yelling at Youssef, his spittle landing on Youssef's face. "I was born here," Youssef wanted to say, but didn't dare speak. After this incident, Youssef no longer considered himself white, even though the census classified those of Middle Eastern descent as such.

Uncle Sam tiptoed to the door and looked through the peephole. "Praise be to Allah," he cried. He opened the door and paid a pizza deliveryman. Rocky had ordered three large pizzas.

♦

YOUSSEF JOINED UNCLE SAM and Rocky at the dining room table. He took a slice of pizza. After the false scare, both uncle and nephew were too anxious to eat. Uncle Sam, Youssef learned, had barred Rocky from leaving the house after ICE had visited the gas station.

"I'm under house arrest, bro," Rocky told Youssef.

He had arrived in Dearborn as a scrawny teen. But Uncle Sam put him on a diet of Rambo and Rocky films. Together, the two of them would stay up into the early hours watching either Sylvester Stallone machine-gunning down enemies or knocking out boxers in a ring. Rocky (then Mohammed) began lifting weights at the local gym. He rewatched the Rambo and Rocky films, memorizing lines, improving his English. A year later, he had a major growth spurt. He now stood well over six feet tall, his muscles bulging in his Detroit Tigers sweatshirt. His neck had widened into a block. When he spoke English, he tried to sound like Stallone. "How you doin'?" he greeted people on the streets.

"ICE is out there," Uncle Sam said. "Do you want to be sent back to Bint Jbeil?"

"Send me to Hollywood."

Youssef looked up from his plate.

"Hollywood?" Uncle Sam said. "You want to meet your internet girlfriend?"

"Her name is Lorrie," Rocky said. "And she believes in me. Says I've got the looks and talent to make it as an action hero in Hollywood."

Rocky reached for his phone on the table, swiped his thumb against the screen, and handed it to Youssef. "Check out my YouTube channel," he said.

Youssef cleaned his greasy fingers with a napkin and pressed play. In the video, Rocky stood bare-chested in the backyard. A red bandanna held up his black hair. He wore blue jeans over cowboy boots. His skin was glistening. He pulled out a pack of Marlboros and lit up, squinting in the sunshine. The camera zoomed in on his chest to capture his flexing pectoral muscles.

"I rubbed my body down with olive oil for that shot," Rocky said. "Check out the next video."

Youssef pressed on another clip. In this one, Rocky, still bare-chested, sat on the floor against the door in his room, his head in his hands. He was sobbing, which sounded like cats mating.

"The tears are real," Rocky said. "I thought of how much I miss Mama while I cried. Lorrie says I've got acting range."

"Let me see those videos," Uncle Sam said.

Youssef passed him the phone.

"What do you think?" Rocky asked Youssef. "These are my first films."

"They're not exactly films," Youssef said.

"But they can be. I just need Hollywood to discover me."

Youssef envied Rocky's blissful naïveté. He had been filled with the same unadulterated ambition when he boarded that Greyhound bus headed for New York. On the day he took off, he woke before sunrise, left his parents a note on his bedroom desk explaining that he was pursuing a career on Broadway, and sneaked out the front door, carrying a duffel bag on his shoulder.

He'd known his parents would have held him back if he'd told them his plans in person. They had ceased attending his plays after his performance in *The Crucible*, and had pressured him into studying business at the university. As the bus crossed into Ohio, Youssef was both terrified and thrilled at what he had done, and hours and bus transfers later, when the Manhattan skyline appeared in the distance, he had begun to grasp the magnitude of his decision and felt bile rise to his throat.

"Delete these right now!" Uncle Sam told Rocky. "We can't give ICE any more information about you."

"But how else will a film agent discover me?"

"You idiot! How do you expect to work in Hollywood if you're not legal?"

Rocky snatched his phone from Uncle Sam's hand. "I'm smarter than you think. By the way, I want you to stop calling me Rocky. I've got a new name now. A Hollywood name." He looked at Uncle Sam and then at Youssef. "Moe Mallone."

"You can't act in Hollywood if you're not legal," Uncle Sam persisted.

"I've got a plan for that."

"So you intend to abandon me? As if I haven't done enough for you."

"You're like a father to me. You know that."

Uncle Sam looked at Youssef. "Please knock some sense into my nephew. Tell him about your experience in New York."

Youssef's face darkened. He pushed his pizza to the side.

"What happened in New York, bro?" Rocky asked.

"I was once an actor—a stage actor," Youssef said. In college, he continued, he had performed in the local community theater, since the university didn't have a theater department. The theater had bad plumbing, peeling walls, and a frayed stage curtain. The backstage was infested with rats. But it was there that Youssef had trained as a method actor.

"What the hell is that, bro?" Rocky asked.

"It's when you breathe and live a character every waking hour."

◆

AT THE COMMUNITY THEATER, Youssef said, he realized he wouldn't be happy if he didn't become a professional actor, and so he'd tried his luck on Broadway. He rented a room in a four-bedroom apartment on 156th Street on the West Side. He could stretch his hand out his bedroom window and touch the brick wall of the neighboring apartment building with his fingertips. He shared one bathroom with three roommates, two of whom had their girlfriends over on the weekends. To pay his rent, he waited tables and worked as a part-time concierge at a condo building in Chelsea. He survived on baked beans and potatoes. In the afternoon, he auditioned for plays. It took him months to land a minor role in Anton Chekhov's *The Seagull*, which was staged way off Broadway—as in Trenton, New Jersey. Other roles came, sometimes in Manhattan, but never on Broadway. Youssef rarely had a day off and hardly knew a soul. He didn't bother calling home, as his parents had disowned him for abandoning them. New Yorkers were difficult to speak to, charging down the avenues and pushing their way into the subway. Winter seemed colder in New York than it did in Michigan, the icy winds burning his face. When he was feeling depressed, he took the subway to Times Square to converse with an Egyptian hot dog vendor who parked his cart on Forty-Fourth Street and played cassettes of Umm Kulthum from a portable radio. Youssef missed living among Arabs and seeing store signs in Arabic. He began to understand why so many Dearbornites shied away from leaving their hometown.

In his second year in New York, Youssef told Rocky and Uncle Sam, he was evicted from his room. The restaurant he waited tables at closed down, and after he failed to pay his rent, his roommates replaced him with someone they found on Craigslist.

He spent the next month sleeping in the back room of a mosque on the Lower East Side. The imam took pity on him and said he could stay for the time being, as long as he paid for his lodging in prayers. Although Youssef wasn't religious, he prayed in the early morning with the imam and listened to his sermons on Friday afternoons. When his part-time job as concierge turned full-time, he moved out of the mosque and into the basement room of a dilapidated brownstone in Brooklyn. He continued to audition for roles but was offered very few. He wondered if his talent as an actor, if he really had any, was only good enough for the community theater. On his walks down the streets of Manhattan, the collar of his overcoat turned up, the skyscrapers had taunted him. "This ain't your city," they said, arching over him. The honking of cars and the wails of sirens pulled at his nerves.

Youssef kept waiting for a lucky break, but by the end of this third year in New York, his spirit was broken. He hated the city, and it couldn't care less about him. And so he returned to Dearborn. When his mother answered the door and saw him standing outside with the duffel bag on his shoulder, his face sagging with anguish, she opened her arms. "Welcome home," she said, inhaling his scent.

◆

YOUSSEF SCRUNCHED UP HIS napkin. This was the first time he had shared his experience with anyone, though he had left out the part about his failed romantic relationship.

"Learn from Youssef, Rocky," Uncle Sam said. "The world outside of Dearborn is an ugly place. Besides, you can take over my gas station when I retire and you become legal."

"That's not what I want, Uncle."

Uncle and nephew turned silent. Youssef noticed how pale each looked. Uncle Sam reclined in his chair, barely able to keep his eyes open.

"You both should eat," Youssef said.

"I haven't been able to eat since the ICE visit," Uncle Sam said, yawning. He slung back his head and fell asleep.

"Follow me," Rocky whispered to Youssef, standing up from the table. Youssef followed him to his room. The walls were covered with Stallone posters.

"Can you teach me how to become a method actor?" Rocky asked.

"It takes years of practice."

"Give me a smash course."

"You mean a crash course?"

Rocky nodded.

There was no time to give Rocky an acting lesson, Youssef thought. He was already delayed. But he could easily make up for the houses he missed today the following morning, and besides, this census gig was only temporary. No need to take it too seriously. "Let's work on your technique first," he said. "In the videos you showed me, I can tell you're acting. You want to be natural. For example, you don't have to sob to show you're sad."

"Like this?" Rocky asked and frowned.

"You look angry. Like this," Youssef said, and pictured Halley, the woman who'd broken his heart in New York.

"Allah have mercy, you look miserable!"

Youssef removed his lanyard and placed it on Rocky's bed. He pulled out the ends of his shirt from his belt and rolled up his sleeves. "Wait, I need to get something."

He went to the living room and came back with his briefcase. He opened it and took out his makeup kit.

"Should I get the olive oil?" Rocky asked.

Youssef shook his head. "Sit down."

Rocky sat on the bed.

"Look up."

Rocky looked up and Youssef applied the eyeliner. He dabbed powder on Rocky's cheeks and then put makeup on his own face.

"Let's act," he said.

They acted improvised scenes in which Rocky was the hero and Youssef the villain.

"You're too stiff," Youssef said. "Use your body."

They tried another scene. Youssef's heart raced, reminding him of the thrill of being onstage. They acted until Uncle Sam came to the door, apparently awoken from his nap.

"Look," Uncle Sam said, showing them his phone. Youssef and Rocky read the president's tweet. *I just saw a Hispanic-looking man slaughtering a goat in the street! What's with these losers?! Poor goat!*

"America is crazier than I thought," Rocky said.

Just then a woman screamed out on the street. Uncle Sam dashed from the room, followed by Rocky. Youssef found them peeking between the blinds in the living room. He walked up to one of the windows and lowered a blind with his finger. A woman wearing a hijab was screaming in her front yard as an ICE agent led a handcuffed man toward a car parked at the curb. Other ICE agents stood on the sidewalk. They were all dressed in blue windbreakers.

"That's Fatima," Uncle Sam said. "The handcuffed man is her brother."

One of the agents turned in the direction of Uncle Sam's house. He wore aviator shades. His auburn hair was slicked back.

"Run!" Uncle Sam told Rocky.

Rocky fled to the basement, his steps pounding the stairs.

"Allah help us! Allah help us!" Fatima cried continuously.

"May Allah help us all," Uncle Sam said.

Youssef recited verses from the Qur'an that the imam in New York had taught him.

The agent with the shades said something to the rest of the group, who all turned to look at Uncle Sam's. He began to walk toward the house. Uncle Sam pulled away from the blinds, went around to the front door, and looked through the peephole. Youssef stepped back from the blinds, barely able to breathe. He heard footsteps approaching.

"What's he doing?" Youssef asked Uncle Sam.

"He's staring at my banners," Uncle Sam whispered. "Another man is coming."

"Can you believe this?" Youssef heard one of the agents say to another. "The guy's got a banner for the Great Lakes Loons."

The men chuckled and walked away. Youssef peeked through the blinds again. The agents were getting back into their cars. Fatima stood alone in her front yard. As soon as the agents drove off, neighbors came out of their houses to console her.

◆

YOUSSEF FOLLOWED UNCLE SAM down to the basement. Uncle Sam switched on the light and walked to a big wooden chest with a brass lock, stowed away in the corner.

"You can come out now, Rocky," Uncle Sam said.

Rocky opened the top and climbed out of the chest.

"I've got a plan to leave Dearborn," he said, his face red and sweaty.

"Take it easy. We'll think of—"

"You saw what they did to Fatima's brother! Listen to me, Uncle." He'd take a train out to LA, he said. He and Lorrie had decided to get married. She'd give him American citizenship. "She knows a good immigration lawyer."

"But she's from the internet," Uncle Sam said.

"There's no other option, Uncle."

"What if ICE agents capture you on the train?"

"Then I'll take a bus."

"They've been boarding buses and checking passengers' IDs."

"Then drive me."

"I can't leave my business. Things don't run well without me."

"I'll buy a cheap secondhand car and drive there myself."

"You don't even have a license. This is all crazy talk!"

"I'll drive you," Youssef said. Uncle Sam and Rocky looked at him. "We can leave in the morning."

"What about your job?" Uncle Sam said.

"I'm only a census taker."

Uncle Sam looked up at Rocky, his lips trembling. "At least eat a slice of pizza before you leave."

◆

IT WAS APPROACHING MIDNIGHT when Youssef and Rocky left Uncle Sam's house. Rocky carried two suitcases over to Youssef's Ford Focus, throwing them into the trunk. Youssef drove to his parents' house off Warren Avenue. His parents were asleep. He led Rocky down to the basement, which his father had converted into another living room with synthetic leather couches and a wide-screen TV hanging on the wall.

"We have to leave before my parents wake up," Youssef said.

Rocky nodded. Youssef left him in the basement and went upstairs to his room to pack a suitcase. Once done, he sat down at his desk and wrote a note to his parents.

An emergency came up and I had to drive a friend to LA. Won't be gone for long. Will call you later. Please don't be upset.

Youssef wondered if he had chosen the wrong coast to pursue his dream when he moved to New York. What if he was destined for film? He left the note on his desk and grabbed his suitcase and treaded softly back down the stairs to the basement. Rocky was sitting on the edge of the couch, picking at the cuticle on his thumb.

"I haven't left Dearborn since I arrived here," he said. "This city is a mini Lebanon; it's like a second home for me. LA is going to be different."

Youssef sat down next to him. He had felt the same anxiety when he left Dearborn years ago. "There are plenty of Arabs in LA. You'll make friends."

"I hope Lorrie will like me when she sees me."

"She must love you if you're engaged."

"We're not, bro. I lied to Uncle Sam. But Lorrie wants to see me."

"Have you told her you're headed out to LA?"

Rocky pulled out his phone. "I'm about to."

◆

YOUSSEF GAVE ROCKY HIS privacy and returned upstairs. He made a cup of coffee and sat at the kitchen table. He wished that things had worked out between him and Halley. They had met during Youssef's third year in New York. Halley was the prompter for an adaptation of *The House of Mirth*, in which Youssef played the role of Jack Stepney. She'd sit at a small table behind the curtains at stage left, the script open before her. She had long chestnut hair and wore black-framed glasses. One night after rehearsal, she had invited Youssef out for cheesecake at Saul's, the nearby diner. Over cake and coffee, Youssef told her stories about Dearborn, mentioning how the city was considered the capital of Arab America.

"I'd like to visit one day," she said.

"Please do."

Saul's soon became their favorite haunt. After they stepped out the front door one night and faced each other on the sidewalk in the soft glow of the lamplight, Youssef bent down and kissed her, tasting strawberry on her breath. Halley invited him over to her studio, where she taught him how to make love. They spent most nights together after that, and in the mornings, Youssef bought them coffee and bagels from the neighborhood deli. On their days off they visited the cafés and bakeries in Greenwich

Village and took the subway uptown to Columbus Circle and sat on a bench in Central Park to feed the pigeons.

In falling in love with her, he fell in love with New York. He now walked the avenues as if they had been paved for him. "Hey there, big guy!" the skyscrapers greeted him. He'd soon be the lead actor of a Broadway play, he just knew it, and he and Halley would marry and have children and raise them in this very city.

After five months of dating, he proposed to Halley.

"You haven't even met my parents," she said.

That night on stage, Youssef forgot his lines for the very first time. When Halley whispered the words, he looked to his left, searching for her in the shadows.

"I love you," he said.

"That's not the line," Halley said.

After the show, the director berated Youssef and threatened to replace him. He didn't care. All he wanted was Halley. She said she was feeling tired and wasn't in the mood for Saul's. She gave the same response the following night. When the play came to an end, Halley had held Youssef's hand, squeezed it, and told him goodbye. A month later, he left the city for good.

Youssef returned to the basement to check on Rocky.

"Lorrie said that I can stay with her until I find my own place!" Rocky said. "I haven't told her about my legal status—I don't want to scare her off—but I think she really loves me."

"I'm so happy for you," Youssef said with an aching heart.

♦

AT DAWN, YOUSSEF AND Rocky got into the Ford Focus.

"Let's eat some manakeesh before we leave," Rocky said.

Youssef drove to Rocky's favorite bakery in Dearborn. They ordered thyme pies and mint tea and sat down at a window table to eat their breakfast. The smell of baked bread hung in the air. On the suspended TV, an imam recited prayers in Arabic.

"At least it's warmer in LA," Rocky said.

"I hear Venice Beach is beautiful," Youssef said. He had packed enough clothes for a week. If he liked it out West, maybe he'd stay longer, try an audition or two. If Rami Malek, a fellow Arab American, could win an Academy Award for Best Actor, why couldn't he? Maybe he'd even meet someone in LA.

"I've never been on a road trip," Rocky said. "Can we visit the Grand Canyon?"

"Sure."

Although Youssef hadn't slept in over twenty-four hours, he was wide awake. Two men entered the bakery, dressed in matching blue windbreakers with ICE printed in block letters on the back. Youssef recognized the man with the auburn hair.

"Let me speak to your manager," the man with the auburn hair told the cashier.

"He at home. Sleeping, sir," the cashier said. Youssef knew him. He was a Syrian refugee named Mehdi. He had a thick black mustache.

The agent flashed his badge. "Let me see your ID."

"How come, sir? I do nothing illegal."

"What do we do?" Rocky whispered to Youssef.

"Act normal and eat your food. We'll make it to LA. I promise you that. You're going to be an action hero."

"I'm Moe Mallone," Rocky said, his voice breaking. Youssef held Rocky's hand.

The ICE agents turned toward them. The man with the auburn hair approached their table, looked at Rocky, and squinted.

"How you doin'?" Rocky said.

Speedoman

We were in the Jacuzzi when Speedoman entered the pool area and our lives. There were five of us, all sitting spaced apart, the warm water bubbling up to our hairy chests. Outside, it was gray and snowing, the roads icy. We came here, to the Ford Community Center in the heart of Dearborn, every Saturday afternoon to work out—intense cardio followed by weight training—and then relax our muscles in the Jacuzzi. It was the highlight of our week and we could hardly wait for the days to pass so that we could be together again. Our wives came too, and spent the entire time gossiping in a corner of the shallow end of the pool. We encouraged them to use the elliptical machines or the treadmills because, Allah knows, they could have stood to lose a few pounds. They ignored us.

The past week had been terrifying. ICE agents had arrested our poor brother Firas, dragging him from his home in handcuffs. The agents were everywhere, appearing at our workplaces and demanding that we submit paperwork on our employees or else risk deportation. We refused, knowing our rights. "We're Americans!" we cried. We told the white men in blue windbreakers that we had fled civil war in Lebanon and immigrated to Dearborn to reinvent ourselves. We'd worked the assembly lines at the Levy plant for several years before opening our own businesses: a convenience store, a gas station, a barbershop, a restaurant, and a halal butchery. The agents had rolled their eyes.

Now we were in the Jacuzzi, where we could forget our troubles. The community center was filled mostly with Arabs—all the brown faces had scared off the white folks. We were feeling confident—the kind of giddy confidence that comes after completing a hard workout. Then we saw a tall man in a pink robe, holding a thick book and towel, walk across the other side of the pool by the deep end. Our first thought: *What man wears pink?* His black hair was slicked back. He had a bushy mustache and long sideburns. Our second thought: *seventies porn star*, not that we watched porn, let alone seventies porn. That filth was haram; we were righteous Muslims. The man placed his book on a pool chair, draped his towel over the back, and put on a pair of goggles. He then turned to us—that is, everyone on the opposite side of the pool, including our wives, other swimmers, and the gym goers behind the glass barrier wall—and unloosened his robe. He wore a sky-blue Speedo. His package, his package was . . . He removed his robe and laid it on his chair, his chest still turned to us. He had broad shoulders and a small potbelly. His skin was too tanned for winter. He stretched his arms and twisted his torso from side to side before blowing into his cupped palms. He then strode down the side of the pool in the direction of our wives, walking with the haughtiness of a fashion model on a catwalk. "He better not get too close to our women," we hissed. He had a big nose with a bump at the bridge, an Arab nose, one that we all shared. Having arrived within a few feet of our wives, he turned around and headed back to the deep end. An image of a cedar tree covered the back of his Speedo. We looked at one another. Who was this stranger?

As Dearbornites, we are accustomed to encountering newcomers on a daily basis. Since the creation of Israel, our city has been home to refugees from the Arab world. We hear all kinds of Arabic dialects at the mosque and in the grocery stores and coffeehouses around town. With the violence in Iraq, Yemen, and Syria, the refugees continue to come, appearing on our shores like frightened children, just the way we were when we arrived in 1982 following the Israeli invasion of Lebanon. But in nearly forty years of living in Dearborn, we had never seen a newcomer like Speedoman, the name we gave him the moment he removed his robe. He was the first Arab—he must have been Arab—we had seen wearing a Speedo.

As for the cedar tree on his ass, we were reminded of the Lebanese flag sewn on the sleeves of our Cub Scout shirts, back when we were boys. We were born and raised in Bint Jbeil, a village heralded for its resistance against the Israeli Army, its roads lined with the portraits of martyrs. For a long time, the farthest we had ever traveled was to the coastal city of Tyre, where we saw the sea for the first time and wondered what lay beyond the blue expanse. When we learned we'd be camping near the cedars of Lebanon on our next scouting adventure, we jumped with excitement: we'd get to touch the same wood Noah had used for his ark.

On the day of departure, we boarded a school bus dressed in caps, black-and-white neckerchiefs, collared shirts with the flag and various badges sewn on the sleeves, and khakis. We sang folk songs as we drove north along the coast, passing through Tyre, Sidon, and Beirut. In Tripoli, we took a right and headed across the mountain ranges to Bsharri, where the great poet Kahlil Gibran was born. Our ears popped as we ascended the mountains. That night, we planted our tents in a daisy field at the crest of the Qadisha Valley and made a bonfire to keep ourselves warm as our counselors grilled skewers of chicken and shish kabob and a lone wolf howled in the valley's depths. The following morning, as church bells tolled, we took a twenty-minute drive to the cedars, meat still stuck in our teeth and the smell of burned wood in our hair. We were expecting a forest, but instead found only a handful of the majestic trees huddled together at the base of a mountain, like a group of forgotten philosophers. We walked down a dirt path that wound between them. To be cast in the shade of the cedars was to be graced by Allah.

Speedoman stood at the edge of the deep end. He raised his hands above his head, the sides of his thumbs touching, palms turned down. His underarms were waxed. Hell, his entire body was waxed. He dove into the water as if afraid to wake someone up from a nap by the sound of his splash.

◆

MASHALLAH. ALLAH HAS WILLED it. Our first utterance the moment we saw Speedoman enter the pool area. "Mashallah," we repeated, when he took off his robe and thrust his hips forward; "mashallah" when he turned around and showed us the cedar tree on his firm buttocks. He swam laps with the strength and precision of an Olympic swimmer—he didn't attack the water so much as glide over it. Our husbands in the Jacuzzi had their eyes locked on him. The lazy bums, they spent all their time in the hot tub instead of working out. Their version of lifting weights was for one of them to lie flat on the bench, barely lifting the barbell, while the rest stood around chatting, or laughing at some YouTube video on their smartphones.

Speedoman, for that was what we named him, climbed out of the pool and walked to his chair, dripping water. His bangs trickled over his face. He dried himself off with his towel, swept back his hair, slipped into his robe, and lay on his chair, where he opened a book as thick as the Qur'an and began reading. We were desperate to read the title of his book to get an idea of his literary tastes—we had a thriving book club—but we were camped too far away. Our husbands glanced at us; we immediately looked away from Speedoman. When we looked back at our husbands, they were staring at him, and so we returned our gaze as well to our well-endowed swimmer. He licked his finger to turn the page.

We asked about one another's children, if only to distract ourselves from the enigma in the pink robe. We hadn't seen a seventies man in years, not since we lived during that era. Our lives in Bint Jbeil had consisted of helping our mothers with house chores and attending school. Our parents were waiting until we graduated to marry us off. We expected to marry local men, because that's what our mothers and grandmothers had done. We only hoped that we wouldn't be married off to our unlikable cousins, though keeping the land in the family made sense. In those days most of the young village men had long sideburns and wore bell-bottomed pants and, in the evenings, they hung out in the main square, where they sipped Pepsi-Cola and smoked cigarettes. They boasted of being cosmopolitan men, though few had actually ventured north to Beirut. We would have loved to visit the capital, which travelers described as the finest city in Arabia, but we were bound to our homes. When the civil war broke out there in 1975, we thought we'd never get the chance to see it.

The only way to leave home was to marry. When our husbands came calling and asked for our hands, our parents gave them their blessings. We had no say in the matter. At least we were married off to our more likable (not necessarily desirable) cousins.

Speedoman was a man from the past, the kind of man we had imagined only lived in one of the great cities of the world. So why was he in Dearborn and not New York or Los Angeles? Was he chasing down a former lover? Was he escaping the law? Was he out for revenge? We attributed our line of questioning to the influence of Turkish soap operas dubbed in Arabic on Netflix.

When Speedoman walked toward us, we saw that he wasn't as young as we'd first thought. He was somewhere in his forties, with thick hair. Our husbands were bald.

We checked the time on the clock. It was half past five. We had a dinner reservation at Baba's Tacos and Shawarma at seven. It was our Saturday ritual—a workout followed by dinner with our lesser halves. But we didn't want to leave so soon, and neither did our husbands. Every so often, we noticed, one of them would pull himself out of the Jacuzzi and sit on the edge, and then dip back in. If we approached Speedoman to learn what he was reading, then they would accuse us of flirting with a stranger. *What Muslim woman does such a thing?* they'd surely ask. The hypocrites; it had been years since they'd last attended Friday prayer service.

The shorter way to the women's locker room was past the Jacuzzi. We took the long route. As we neared Speedoman, our hearts began to race. We could hardly breathe. We heard our husbands calling out our names. Speedoman licked his finger again to turn a page. We read the title on the cover of his book: *A History of the Byzantine State and Society*. Our man was a history buff. Interesting. Not once did he look up at us. Too bad, because we were wearing brand-new burkinis.

♦

AT BABA'S TACOS AND Shawarma, we sat at one end of the long table and our wives at the other end. We had arrived an hour late. After our workout, we'd rushed home to bathe—bathing together in the communal showers at the community center was a foreign idea to us. Only our wives saw us naked, and it had been a while since they had.

We ordered beef tacos, chicken shawarma, lamb chops, fried liver, tabbouleh, and bowls of guacamole, salsa, hummus, and baba ghanoush. Despite all the food, we had no appetite. We were only hungry for stories of our youth, and that's what we exchanged at dinner, remembering the days we'd hunt and camp in the woods and swim in the Litani River. We had been happy back then, before we were married with children. We wanted to be scouts forever! But when we turned eighteen, we sought to make a living. Some of us worked in the shops in the main square and others took up jobs in construction. One summer, a villager who had immigrated to Dearborn returned to tell us that there were plenty of well-paying positions in the factories there. We had no interest in leaving our beloved village, and after we married and began having children, we thought we'd never leave. But the Israeli invasion changed things; fighter jets bombed our land and decimated our houses, schools, and mosques, killing our loved ones. We left with thousands of others. The first time we and our families got to see Beirut was when we drove up to the airport to leave the country. By that point, most of the city had been destroyed.

We were easily susceptible to bouts of nostalgia. A song by Fairuz, the smell of home cooking, a Lebanese film on TV could trigger our melancholy. Our wives complained that our favorite pastime was to reminisce about the past. They preferred our lives in Dearborn because the city, with all its Arabic restaurants and grocery stores and mosques, reminded them of home while having the conveniences of America. But an imitation of home was inferior. We wanted the real thing.

Speedoman had unlocked something deep inside us, we realized that evening. We were reliving our memories, not simply remembering them. We could feel the neckerchiefs around our necks, hear the crackle of pinewood in the bonfire, smell the holy cedars. We felt young and free again.

We were interrupted from our thoughts when our wives asked us to pass the lamb chops. We had been furious at them for approaching Speedoman, but instead of chastising them, we asked if they had caught the title of the man's book. They shook their heads, as if they hadn't even noticed the stranger in the pink robe.

As we forced ourselves to eat, we heard our wives smacking their lips and licking their greasy fingers as they wolfed down the chops. They were licking a little too greedily. Were they, we wondered not for the first time, our true soulmates? Was there even such a thing as a soulmate? Allah bless our wives, they looked after us and had raised our children. But had we ever been in love with them—the mad kind of love we saw in the movies?

◆

WE LIVED A FEW blocks from one another in East Dearborn. While our husbands were at work, we managed our online business and later prepared dinner. We sold handmade jewelry and purses we crafted ourselves or commissioned other women to make. Our children were either in university or had married and started their own families.

That Wednesday afternoon, several days after we first saw Speedoman, we met at Salma's house to discuss our latest book club selection, Danielle Steel's *A Good Woman*. We had torn through the book like the rest of Steel's novels, but just then, as we sat in the living room sipping tea, we had no interest in discussing romance literature. We were three days away from another Saturday. Would Speedoman be at the community center? What were the chances that we'd meet again at exactly the same time? Was he a new member or had he just paid for a day pass?

It had been months since we'd last had sex. When we did, our husbands lasted as long as it took to boil a single rakweh of Turkish coffee. We never suggested improvements because they had fragile hearts.

What would happen if our husbands waxed their bodies and actually lifted weights? Would we ravage them in bed?

Later that night, as we lay under our covers while our husbands snored, we messaged one another in our WhatsApp group, the "Smokin' Entrepreneurs." If Speedoman returned on

Saturday, what color Speedo would he be wearing? Would he have finished his book on the Byzantine empire? Was he that voracious a reader? Was the man married? Had anyone noticed a ring on his finger?

We decided on a name for Speedoman's blessing between his legs: the Beast from the Middle East, aka BME. We messaged until we fell asleep.

◆

AT AROUND THE SAME time as the previous Saturday, Speedoman entered the pool area. He was in his pink robe, with a book and towel in hand. The book was slimmer than the one from the previous week. He placed his items on a chair and then looked up at the ceiling, which caused us to look up at the lights—ah, there was a trapped bird. It hovered over a spotlight before perching on a beam. How had we not noticed it before? When we looked back down, Speedoman had already removed his robe. His Speedo was pinkish gold, the color of sunset. He began his walk down the side of the pool, in the direction of our wives. We eagerly waited for him to turn around to see the image on his ass. When he did, we reached for our hearts. Beirut's Pigeon Rocks covered his rear, the two towering rock pillars with grassy peaks rising from the sea. He walked slowly enough for us to discern the features of the scene: a couple stood at the railing of the Corniche overlooking the Pigeon Rocks, facing the horizon.

After the civil war ended, in 1991 we had returned to Lebanon to visit. We had followed the news of our country's self-destruction from abroad, wondering if the violence would ever end. A hundred thousand Lebanese had been killed. We spent most of our time upon returning in Dahieh, a Shiite suburb of Beirut, because it was too dangerous to stay in Bint Jbeil, which, like the rest of southern Lebanon, was still occupied by the Israeli Army. One day, we hired a bus driver to take our families into Beirut to tour the city. Many buildings were pockmarked with mortar shells and bullets. Downtown was a wasteland of crumbling walls and streets overgrown with weeds. Our children whined about how much they hated Lebanon and wanted to return to Dearborn. We fed them ice cream to shut them up.

We took a long walk down the Corniche. The fronds of palm trees lining the promenade swayed in the wind. Fishermen stood at the railing with their lines cast out to sea. On a stretch of rocky shore below us, young men smoked cigarettes and sunbathed, their skin slowly darkening. We walked up a steep incline that plateaued at the Pigeon Rocks and stood there gazing at the sea, remembering the first time we saw the Mediterranean as boys and wondered about the world beyond our shores. When the sun dipped into the water and the stars emerged, we returned to the bus.

Back by the pool, melancholy coursed through us. Damn Speedoman! How was it possible that a stranger knew what heart strings to pull? Was he some kind of informant or spy working for ICE? Had he wiretapped us?

At this point, he had finished his laps and was now reading on his chair. We were determined to discover his identity. When we noticed the time on the clock, we realized that if we didn't leave the Jacuzzi now, we'd be late to our dinner reservation at Ali's Famous Sushi and Kabob. Our wives called out our names, pointing to the clock. *We know*, we gestured. *Calm the hell down.*

But we couldn't extract ourselves from the bubbling water, not until we understood what Speedoman was up to. Should we approach him? If we did, our wives would see us conversing with him and think that we were infatuated with the man. We just wanted an explanation for the images on his Speedos. It had been nearly an hour now, sitting there watching him, and the heat was starting to get to us. We climbed out of the Jacuzzi and sat on the edge. Our chests were nearly dry when we saw our wives walking past Speedoman. They paused when they arrived at his chair—his face was buried in his book—and then continued on to the locker room. Feeling cold, we dipped back into the water. Now was our chance to question Speedoman. We were five, he was one. The numbers were on our side. If one of us faltered in his questioning, there was someone else to step in. All for one and one for all! Why were we even hesitating? For God's sake, we had survived seven years of civil war and an Israeli invasion. We had stood up to the ICE agents, and before them, back when the towers fell, we stood up to FBI agents when they started surveilling us because we happened to be Arab. There was nothing that could hold us back, and if we didn't get out of the water now, then—Speedoman stood up, put on his robe, gathered his book and towel, and left the premises. We looked at one another. He was headed to the locker room. We left the Jacuzzi.

Our lockers were in different aisles, the space we gave one another to change in privacy. But now we congregated together, towels draped over our shoulders. We hadn't spotted Speedoman in any of the aisles. We headed over to the communal showers and saw him under one of the showerheads, his back turned to us. The paleness of his ass stood out in contrast to his tanned body. He was singing a ballad by Hafez Abdel Halim about the irrepressible flame of love. His voice was more passionate than memorable. We had grown up listening to Abdel Halim on the transistor radio and had seen all his Egyptian films. We began to hum along, which got Speedoman to turn around and look at us. He smiled. His package, his package was . . . We fled the showers and retreated to our respective aisles.

◆

Poems by Ulayya bint al-Mahdi. The title of the book Speedoman was reading the second time we saw him. The title was in Arabic.

Our man was a reader of diverse interests. Over dinner at Ali's Famous Sushi and Kabob, we pulled out our smartphones and ordered copies of the book, which we unanimously chose as our next book club selection. We opted for overnight shipping. We spoke in whispers as we did this so as not to attract our husbands' attention, but they were adrift in melancholy. They had barely touched their food, and we knew they loved sushi.

Days later, we met at Lamise's house to discuss Ulayya's poems. We each took turns reciting our favorites from the book, and ended up reciting the following poem together:

I hid the name of the loved one from all people,
And repeated my yearning in my heart.
O how I long for an empty sanctuary,
Where I can call the name of my love.

We imagined Speedoman as the speaker of the poem. Intoxicated, we suddenly arrived at the same question: Why not work out at the community center during the week? We all rushed back to our homes, packed our gym bags, and waited for Lamise to pick us up in her minivan. She drove like a getaway driver, swerving between the cars, honking her horn.

"Faster!" we cried. We still had to process online orders and make dinner for our husbands.

We changed into our burkinis and hopped into the Jacuzzi. After half an hour, another group of hijabis came over and complained that we were hogging the hot tub. We reluctantly got out and sat in our regular corner of the pool. We waited another hour but he didn't appear. Before leaving the community center, we visited the reception desk and asked the young woman behind the counter if she had any information about a new member. The young woman sat in a swivel chair, chewing bubble gum as she texted someone. She had spiky black hair and wore a nose ring. We described Speedoman as a seventies man, leaving out his Speedos but mentioning his pink robe. The woman popped a bubble. We just want a name, we pleaded. Without bothering to look up from her phone, she said it was against company policy to disclose membership information.

We returned the next day, but still no sighting. The following day, we decided to cook dinner in the morning so we could spend more time at the community center before our husbands came home from work. We were in the Jacuzzi when Speedoman appeared in the afternoon. On the back of his Speedo was an image of a woman standing on the balcony of a French colonial-style building, lowering a basket down to a man on the street. We had seen a very similar sight in Beirut. We couldn't stand the heat of the Jacuzzi anymore—how did our husbands tolerate it?—and moved over to our corner in the pool. Speedoman never acknowledged us, absorbed in his book—a new book, by the looks of it, with a red cover. Or was that part of his ploy? He knew we were there; he must have recognized us, even though we had never exchanged words. He was luring us, the bastard. But why? When it was time to leave, we stopped in front of his chair to read the title of his book: *Introduction to Quantum Mechanics.* He was reading intensely, as if we didn't exist. His robe was fastened over his body, his feet extended. We recited our beloved poem: *I hid the name of the loved one from all people . . .* He looked up at us and completed the poem. He had a soft, deep voice. We couldn't quite place his Arabic dialect. Did this mean he wasn't actually Lebanese? He opened his robe like the door to a secret treasure. Mashallah, the BME was awake and swollen.

"You've come alone today," he said.

Our eyes traveled up to his face. We were about to ask him for his name, for his story, when our hearts got caught in our throats. We shouldn't be here. Other hijabis might spot us and tell our husbands we had gone astray.

"Would you like to pull up some chairs?" he asked, making eye contact with each of us.

We hurried to the locker room, nearly slipping on the tiles.

That night in bed, over WhatsApp, we contemplated our stage fright, for that was what it truly was. We had missed a golden opportunity.

"We'll talk to him tomorrow," Lamise texted.

"Inshallah," we responded.

But Speedoman never appeared the next day.

◆

WE ATTENDED FRIDAY PRAYER service at the mosque. We stood in line next to one another among dozens of men and followed the imam's prayer, bending down and touching our foreheads to the floor. For days, we'd been unable to shake off our melancholy. We missed Bint Jbeil like never before.

We were also ashamed. Even though he hadn't appeared the previous Saturday, we couldn't stop thinking about Speedoman and we didn't know what this meant; we were afraid to dig deeper into our thoughts. We had all seen his package, which made each of us feel worse about our own. We considered our baldness, our flabby arms, our round bellies, our stubby feet. Perhaps we needed to hire personal trainers. Maybe then our wives would look at us with the same hunger as they did Speedoman.

We prayed that Allah would guide us down a righteous path. We prayed and prayed, even after the imam and congregants left the room. In less than twenty-four hours, we'd be back in the Jacuzzi, and this terrified us. We were at an age where such emotional turmoil wasn't good for our health. If only Allah would answer our prayers.

◆

SPEEDOMAN WORE AN IMAGE of Bint Jbeil on his buttocks. There was no mistaking the communal spring in the main square, in the shade of a weeping willow tree. We couldn't talk to him with our husbands looking over our shoulders, and this killed us. We'd have to try again during the week. Or so we thought, before he put his book down, removed his robe, and walked over to the Jacuzzi and asked if he could join. Our husbands made room for him. Not wanting to miss a word, we climbed out of the pool and walked toward them. The men were all silent. Speedoman looked at us, grinning. We were worried he'd mention our previous encounter, which would get us in trouble with our husbands, but he was a discreet man. Our husbands gave us the stink eye. We gave it right back to them. We were all too nervous to speak.

"I'd like to show you all something," Speedoman said in Arabic. "Meet me out front in the parking lot in an hour." He got out and walked to the locker room. He was that confident.

An hour later, we and our husbands found Speedoman standing outside in a faux-fur coat, gym bag in hand. He wore fingerless gloves and a beaver hat with earflaps. The sun was setting, an orange ray breaking through the gray sky.

"Follow me," he said.

We followed him to a broken-down Volkswagen van, the kind that hippies once drove. He had an Arizona license plate. He opened the trunk and removed a cardboard box.

We looked at one another, and then at our husbands.

Speedoman extended the box to each of us. We reached inside and pulled out a calendar with Speedoman on the cover, dressed in a Speedo. We flipped through the pages. For each month, he wore a different themed Speedo, all evoking our homeland.

"You're a model?" Lamise asked him.

"I'm a peddler. Just like my father and his father before him. My product is available for a limited time."

We asked for the price.

"One hundred and fifty dollars per calendar."

That's robbery! we thought. But we kept looking at it.

Our husbands asked him if he accepted credit cards.

Speedoman took out a card reader and plugged it into his smartphone. We demanded our own copies. Our husbands each bought two.

"God bless," Speedoman said. He closed his trunk, got in his van, and drove off.

That would be the last time we saw him. But we didn't know that then, standing there in the cold. We still needed to shower and get dressed for dinner if we wanted to make it in time for our reservation at Aunt Hinda's Pizza and Falafel Shack.

We exchanged glances with our husbands, trying to understand what had just happened, what had happened to us for the past several weeks. At dinner, we (our husbands included) perused the calendar. There was no website or name, nothing to identify Speedoman. We took out our phones and plugged key words into our search engines to see if he'd surface online; there was no trace of him.

When the food came, we (our husbands included) put the calendars away so as not to smear them with grease. At our side of the table, we reprimanded ourselves for not hounding Speedoman with questions. He had tricked us into buying his calendar. How many others had he duped?

When we asked our husbands to pass the falafel down the table, they looked at us with mournful faces. We were at a loss as to how to console them because we didn't know how to console ourselves. The calendar would, no doubt, add to our collective pain. And yet we couldn't wait to return to its glossy pages.

Money Chickens

S ome folks store their money in safes; Baba used chickens. I was six the first time I saw him shove a Ziploc bag filled with bills inside a chicken in the kitchen of our two-bedroom house in East Dearborn one evening back in 1988. He sat at the table, wearing yellow rubber gloves that reached halfway up his forearms, a cigarette dangling from his lips. The chicken lay on the cutting board. A small man with small hands, Baba had no problem thrusting his fist into the bird's bowels. He then sheathed the body in plastic wrap and placed it in the freezer. He slipped off his gloves, dropped them in the sink, and sat back down at the table to finish his cigarette.

I reached inside my pocket and pulled out my pack of candy cigarettes. I loved the first puffs because I was able to produce smoke made of powdered sugar, smoke that merged with Baba's in a ghostly swirl that hung over us like a shared thought.

Police sirens wailed in the distance. Baba looked out the window. "Bismillah al-rahman al-rahim," he said.

I repeated his prayer, looking at his reflection in the window-pane—the plump bags under his eyes, his thick mustache with curled tips. His face sagged with exhaustion. I had those very same bags under my eyes, giving me a somber, contemplative look for a boy so young. I'd been named after Baba's father, Ali.

"There's trouble in Detroit," Baba said. He had a loud voice, developed from years of yelling over the sound of machines at the Ford Rouge plant, where he worked. Detroit was a few blocks east. "We have to hide our money from the thieves across the border."

I removed my cigarette from my mouth. "Are we safe here, Baba?"

"We'll be safer once we return to Lebanon. That's what the money chicken is for: to build ourselves a house back home."

The money Baba made at the plant was barely enough to keep us afloat back then, not with the mortgage and the recent arrival of my baby sister. For the past month before her birth, he had been working odd jobs on the weekend to make extra cash, mostly as a handyman. But I saw him solely as a carmaker. Whenever I spotted a Ford sedan or truck on the road, I suspected Baba had had a hand in its making.

The only home I knew was Dearborn, where I was born and raised. My parents had immigrated to America in 1982, seven years into their home country's gruesome civil war. That evening in the kitchen with Baba, I was too young to point out this fallacy: How was Lebanon safer than America when Lebanese were killing one another in the streets?

Mama entered the kitchen, holding my sister in her arms. Her long black hair was parted down the middle. She wore her hijab over her shoulders like a shawl, always prepared to wrap it around her head in the event that a male neighbor came calling. She was a tall, big-boned woman who towered over Baba and me. She sniffed the air. "I smell raw meat."

The cutting board was still on the table.

"I found a new hiding place to safeguard our money," Baba said, and explained his stuffing. Mama's eyes widened. She opened the freezer and looked inside.

"Allah have mercy!"

"Don't worry, the chicken is halal. We can keep your pearl necklace and gold bracelets inside of one."

"I prefer the bank's safe."

Baba looked at me, telling me through his tired eyes that this chicken business would remain a father-son affair. We communicated in a private language similar to the one used between lovers. I looked back, telling him I understood. We reached for another cigarette at the same time.

♦

IN JUNIOR HIGH, I sold cigarettes to the white students in West Dearborn. Every Friday after school, I'd take the crosstown bus and get off on Michigan Avenue and stand outside the Blockbuster, the comic book store, or the local hamburger joint, waiting for boys and girls my age who were itching for a smoke. The houses were bigger and more spread apart on the west side, the streets lined with oak and maple trees. I kept cartons of cigarettes in my backpack and charged fifteen dollars for a pack or two dollars per cigarette because I could. Baba bought me the cigarettes.

"The money will go toward our house in Lebanon," he said. He still worked at the plant then, but had given up his weekend jobs to manage his cousin's car wash part-time. I understood that our cash businesses were tax-free because we didn't report our earnings. The real thief, Baba told me, was the IRS.

I was obsessed at that time with Kurt Cobain, who had shot himself in the head the year before, breaking my heart, and I sometimes used my earnings to buy CDs. If I had possessed a grungy voice or known how to play the electric guitar, I would have aspired to die young as a musical genius. But my talent was hustling.

"Care for a smoke?" I'd say to the students my age. I had become a smoker myself by then.

They'd look at me suspiciously. Who was this undersized teen with baggy eyes and a mustache, they wondered. It's true, even at that age I had a full-grown mustache. What I lacked in size I gained in hirsuteness. My fingers and forearms were becoming increasingly furry.

I'd remove my backpack from my shoulders, open the zipper, and let them peek inside.

"Holy shit!" one would say.

Whenever I spotted cops my heart raced. I always remained in place for a few seconds after seeing them, daring them to catch me, feeling more alive than I ever had before. I was sure that Baba felt the same thrill outfoxing the IRS.

On Sunday nights, Baba and I sat at the kitchen table to stuff our earnings into a chicken. I wore plastic gloves just like him. As he smoked, I craved nicotine, but I didn't dare light up when Mama was home, as I knew she would yell at me and then blame Baba for encouraging my bad habit. Whenever our chickens began to smell or turn greenish from all the freezing and defrosting, we exchanged them for new ones.

Baba bought a chest freezer, which we kept in the basement to store our money chickens. If a burglar ever cared to open the freezer, I wondered what he'd make of all those wrapped birds. We assigned a number to each chicken—we wrote the numbers over the plastic wrap with permanent ink markers— and recorded the amount of cash it contained in our account book. To save space in the chickens, Baba would exchange his small bills for hundred-dollar ones at banks outside Dearborn. He rotated the banks he visited in the suburban towns of Livonia, Plymouth, Northville, and Canton, so that no bank teller would recognize him or find his exchanges suspicious.

Whenever a trusted friend or relative planned to visit the old country, Baba would send with him or her stacks of cash, which the confidant would then give to Baba's father in Lebanon. Jidu Ali would deposit the money into a bank account in Baba's name.

One day, I hoped, my bank account would be filled with millions.

After we'd finished with our chickens one night, Mama and my sister, Danya, who was then eight, joined us at the kitchen table. We were all sipping tea served with pine nuts—Mama bought the nuts from Greenland (aka Al Mustafa's), a grocery store on Warren Avenue that sold imported products from Lebanon. More Lebanese had begun moving from the Southend to the east side of town, and as a result, more Lebanese grocery stores and restaurants had started opening up in the area. Houses in our neighborhood now displayed Arab designs, such as arched windows and entryways with pillars. Men and women sat outside on their porches to smoke hookahs. A few neighbors put out lion sentinels made of concrete on their front stoops to let others know that they had made it. Baba never cared to flaunt in this way because he didn't want to waste money on what he considered to be our temporary home.

"The tea tastes of Lebanon," Baba said, slurping the warm liquid. He licked the drops off his mustache. Years later, my wife would make me aware of my own slurping sounds when I sipped coffee or tea. I wasn't even conscious of them until she gently pointed it out. From then on, I would slurp my hot drinks only when no one else was around, not wanting to bother anyone but also not wanting to lose the memory of Baba's habit, which made whatever he was drinking seem extraordinarily delicious.

That night at the table, it was 1995. The Lebanese civil war had ended and the country was now in the midst of rebuilding itself from the ashes of its own fires. The only contact I had with my ancestral land was in the long-distance telephone calls Baba made to Jidu Ali and other members of my parents' families, who all lived in the village of Aynata, near the Israeli border. The calls were always filled with static, as if the distance between the continents were almost too vast for telecommunications to overcome. I would yell into the receiver to be heard, and Jidu Ali's questions would be invariably the same: *Are you eating well? Are you studying? You're not giving your parents any trouble, are you?* I wasn't self-conscious about speaking Arabic because we spoke Arabic only at home. I had a village accent like my parents.

Before immigrating to America, when Baba was still single, he had helped Jidu Ali run the family grocery store in the main square. One day, Mama had come in to buy a Pepsi-Cola. She was the tallest woman in the village and had been teased in high school because of her height. Baba had been bullied because of his small size. He had graduated a few years ahead of her, though he knew of her and saw her at the summer festivals. No one in Aynata thought Mama would find a man to marry her because Arab men were of average height—what man would want to spend the rest of his life looking up at his wife? But on that day in the grocery store, after Baba had popped off the cap of the soda bottle, handed it to Mama, and peered up at her—a black lock had escaped from her hijab and was hanging down the side of her face, tempting him to reach for it—he felt protected standing next to her, as though no one would ever bully him again. As for Mama, Baba was the most adorable man she had ever seen, though she thought his mustache could use a trim. They got to talking and married later that spring. When the Israeli Army rumbled in with their tanks and troops in the summer of 1982, Jidu Ali urged Baba to leave for America, where they had relatives in Dearborn. Mama was pregnant with me.

Baba rose from the table, saying he had a surprise for us. He left the kitchen and returned with a roll of paper, which he unfurled on the tabletop. It was the blueprint for a house.

"This is our future house in Lebanon—once I can afford to build it," he said, beaming. "We'll use limestone and red tiles for the roof."

"You'll each have a room," Mama told Danya and me, pointing them out. Danya and I were then sharing the same room in our current house. We slept in bunk beds, with me on the bottom.

"We're American," Danya said in English. "I'm not going anywhere."

"You're Lebanese before anything!" Baba said.

Danya rolled her eyes.

Baba waited for my response. When I was younger, he'd told me bedtime stories of his days growing up in the village. My favorite stories were about the Iraqi nomads, who passed through town every summer in their caravan of pickup trucks, the beds laden with wares and medicinal herbs for sale. I wanted to meet these nomads, and climb up the olive trees during the October harvest and whack the branches with a metal rod and watch the olives fall onto blankets laid out on the ground. I wanted to sip ice-cold water from the communal spring and hunt birds in the valley and one day meet my future wife in a grocery store. But as much as I had enjoyed Baba's stories, how could I agree to his plan without ever having set foot in Lebanon?

"See, Ali doesn't want to go, either," Danya said.

"Is that true?" Baba asked me.

"We can have two homes," I said. "One here and one over there."

Baba gave me a stern look, and then rolled up the blueprint and left the table. He didn't speak to me for the remainder of the evening. Fearing he'd never speak to me again, the next morning I woke him up and told him I wanted to live in the limestone house with the red-tile roof.

"May Allah always bless you, son," he said, his stale breath wafting over me.

◆

I STUDIED ACCOUNTING AT the state university in Dearborn. During my sophomore year, months after the attacks of 9/11,

Baba left his job at the plant and took out a loan from the bank to purchase his cousin's car wash on Warren Avenue. He refused to draw from our money chicken fund, which he considered sacred. By that point we had amassed nearly a hundred thousand dollars in savings. Baba's cousin decided to sell his business at a cheap price after he was interrogated by FBI agents under the suspicion that he was funneling money to Islamic fundamentalist groups in Lebanon. He was held captive in a nondescript prison for two weeks and denied any contact with his family or a lawyer. Upon his release and the sale of his car wash, he packed up his belongings and returned to Aynata.

"America has betrayed me," he said on the day he gave Baba the keys to the car wash.

Baba and I feared the FBI and their undercover agents, who had infiltrated our mosques. We feared the white men from out of town who drove through Dearborn to hunt for Muslims. Whenever they spotted our women in hijabs or our dark-skinned men with beards walking down the streets, they yelled, "Go back to your home." Once, a man in overalls walked up and down Michigan Avenue brandishing a skewered pig head.

But now Baba and I had our own family business, and since we were in East Dearborn, among Arabs, we felt relatively safe. Baba erected a billboard at the car wash that read MAHMOUD AND SON.

"What about me?" Danya asked when she saw the billboard. The four of us stood on the pavement looking up at it. Like Mama, Danya now wore a hijab. She was the tallest girl at Fordson High and starred as the center on the basketball team. I was as tall as Baba and sported a goatee. My body was covered in black fur, my chest hair curling up to my throat.

"This is a man's business," Baba told her.

"That's terribly sexist," Danya said.

"He's speaking the truth," Mama said.

Danya turned to Mama. "Stop reinforcing the patriarchy!"

"Bismillah al-rahman al-rahim," Baba said, clutching his heart. "This girl makes no sense to me."

"We'll soon leave this country," Mama told him. "That's all that matters."

Mama understood the importance of owning the car wash. Since most transactions were made in cash, Baba would be able to transfer a sizable portion of his earnings to our money chickens. But he had to be careful not to transfer too much, he told Mama and me, because that would raise red flags and the IRS would pounce on him. I never had the heart to tell him that he was too small a fish for the IRS to care that much.

The car wash prospered. When I wasn't in class or studying at the library, I was at Mahmoud and Son. Baba worked the register while I helped our employees wash the cars—I was meticulous about cleaning interiors. At the front desk Baba offered complimentary maamoul cookies that Mama baked from scratch.

Baba ordered us electric-blue bomber jackets with our names sewn on front. Baba wore the jacket off-hours, too—to the grocery stores, Fairlane Mall, the mosque. I was too embarrassed to wear my jacket to campus, not wanting others to know where I worked.

With so much cash flow, we needed more chickens. Or at least bigger-sized birds.

"What if we use turkeys?" I once asked Baba as we sat on the front porch, sharing a hookah. Baba had caved in and purchased lion sentinels, which stood on either side of the steps leading up to our house. We were working our way through a six-pack of Aziz, nonalcoholic beer that tasted of tangy apple. It was a warm spring evening, and children were out playing on the sidewalks and their front lawns in the streetlight. Our neighbor sat back in her swing as she listened to Fairuz from a portable radio. Baba took a long pull from the hookah, the water bubbling in the urn, and released a dragon's puff of scented tobacco. I had never seen him look so relaxed. The former factory worker was now a prosperous business-man, and I was proud of him and yearned to one day experience his feeling of accomplishment. When he handed me the hookah stem and I put my lips over the wet mouthpiece, I tasted his saliva.

"I never liked the taste of turkey," he said.

◆

AFTER COLLEGE I GOT a full-time job as an accountant but continued helping out at the car wash whenever I could. I still lived at home, though now I had moved into the basement, giv-ing my sister and me much-needed privacy. Like most of my Arab friends, I had no experience when it came to women. It was challenging to date with the community watching over us.

"Dearborn is so fucked up," Danya once told me. She had stopped wearing the hijab not because she didn't believe in God but because she had worn it only to appease Mama. She could do whatever the fuck she wanted to do with her body, she told Mama. "We live in a dai'aa." A village.

We were stuck in a time warp—our parents, and most of our friends' parents, had brought their customs and traditions from southern Lebanon across the sea and ocean to Dearborn. I understood what Danya was saying. But this was the only life I knew. I had never traveled outside of Michigan.

One evening, I attended a banquet in celebration of Arab American entrepreneurs. I'd been hesitant to go, as Dearborn banquets are eternally long affairs, but my boss was receiving an award and I felt obligated to attend. The same was true for Sara Nasrallah, who worked at a title company. We got to talking at the dessert table during the speeches.

"You went to Fordson," she said. "You were a year ahead of me."

She wore a bright-colored hijab, a long-sleeved blouse, and slim pants. In heels, she was much taller than me. I didn't rec-ognize her.

"You sold me cigarettes outside the comic book store on Michigan Avenue," she continued. "You charged me two dollars for every one of them. That was robbery!"

I pulled out my wallet and reached for two single bills. "Here," I said, extending my hand.

She smiled. "Keep it."

I learned that Sara's parents were also from Aynata and that, like me, she had never left town and couldn't see herself ever leaving Dearborn, despite the city's gray and icy winters and its dai'aa feel. Before we returned to our tables, we exchanged business cards.

Throughout the evening, I kept straining my neck to catch sight of her. When she turned her head and looked at me, I quickly glanced at the stage, where a stocky butcher famous for his kafta was being awarded "Butchery of the Year."

I returned home to find Baba at the kitchen table, stuffing. He was now stuffing once or twice per week. I sat across from him and lit a cigarette. He recounted an incident he had had at the car wash with a white man in a suit, whom he suspected was a Homeland Security agent.

"The man asked me whether I had any connections with Hezbollah," Baba said.

I didn't respond, still picturing Sara in heels, reliving her charming forwardness. The only intimate experience I'd had with a woman prior to that point had been with a white girl from my finance class during college. We were studying for an exam in an empty classroom late one Friday afternoon, sitting side by side at the table. Without warning, she reached over and kissed me. Her breath tasted like cinnamon. I kissed her hungrily, sloppily, and when she placed her palm on my chest, I came in my pants.

"Ali, did you hear me?"

I nodded.

"The government is surveilling us. I even hear the FBI has hired informants. You never know, your best friend might be spying on you."

"Okay."

Baba pulled his hand out of the chicken and stared at me. "What's her name?"

"Baba, I—"

"Give me her name!"

"Sara Nasrallah."

"She's an Aynata girl." He slipped off his gloves, stood up from the table, held my face in his hands, and kissed my forehead. "This is the best news I've ever heard!"

Mama and Danya entered the kitchen.

"Why're you yelling?" Mama asked Baba.

"Ali's in love!"

♦

SARA AND I MARRIED a year later and bought a modest bungalow two blocks up from my parents' house. Danya moved out to Portland to work at a nonprofit organization. In her words, she just wanted to "get the fuck out of the dai'aa."

I still visited home to help Baba with the stuffing. With the money and interest he had accumulated in his Lebanese bank account, he bought a piece of land in Aynata. He and Mama had started taking short trips to Lebanon to oversee the building of their house. Although they urged me to join them for a visit, I gave the excuse that I didn't want to leave Sara alone and that I had to look after the car wash while Baba was gone. The truth was, I had lost interest in the old country. As we smoked and shoved our hands into chickens, I communicated to Baba in our special language that I was now a married man with a house of my own, and that Lebanon wasn't in my plans. He understood with a pained heart.

48

A couple of years later, I opened my own accounting firm. Before moving back to Lebanon, Baba put the car wash in my name and sold his house. I inherited his lions and the chest freezer. I promised him that I'd continue stuffing to support us all.

At the airport, we embraced. We were both wearing our bomber jackets, which smelled of stale cigarettes. In that moment, I didn't care if anyone associated me with a car wash. Baba wept into my chest. And then he was gone.

◆

ON A SUNDAY EVENING, I was sitting at the kitchen table stuffing a chicken, a cigarette in the corner of my mouth. Snow flurries stuck to the windowpanes. A police siren drifted on the wind. When Sara came in and saw me with my sleeves rolled up to my elbows, my hands in plastic gloves, she said: "What the fuck?" I told her to sit down. She sat across from me, eying the Ziploc bags packed with bills.

I explained that first night I'd seen Baba stuff a chicken. Hearing my own voice, I realized I was sentimental about the notion of chickens as safes, despite its impracticality. It was something Baba had devised, and which I owed him the honor of continuing.

"It's for our future," I said.

"It's illegal."

"I'm not hurting anyone. And one day we'll need a bigger house for our children. They'll need funds for college. That's what the money chickens are for."

"We don't even have children."

Six months later, Sara was pregnant. She gave birth to our daughter in the spring. She never questioned me again about the chickens.

The recession pounded us in 2008; I thought I'd never stuff another chicken. Sara was laid off and my accounting business faltered. Every day, I received over a dozen calls from frantic clients asking about their finances. When I didn't return their messages, they barged into my office. They had families to raise, they cried, mortgages to pay off. Those in manufacturing and construction begged me to find them employment elsewhere, as if I were a recruiter. I tried my best to calm them, but in some cases I suggested they file for bankruptcy. Many lost their homes. My clients' anxieties and fears exacerbated my own, for the car wash was losing money. People opted to wash their own cars to save a few bucks, and it didn't help that more Arab-owned car washes had opened in town, giving me stiff competition. When the automotive companies threatened to close up shop, we all descended into a state of hysteria. How could we survive without Ford, GM, and Chrysler? They employed tens of thousands of Arab men. Baba wouldn't have made it in America without Ford. As the decade slouched toward its end, I worried that Dearborn and its people would share Detroit's fate—a city of abandoned buildings and broken spirits.

I had trouble sleeping, hearing my clients' voices in my head. The bags under my eyes swelled. I lost my appetite, shedding the little fat on my body.

"We should sell our house and move in with my parents," Sara said.

"But I love this house." As small as our bungalow was, it had hardwood floors and a birch tree in the backyard. Baba had killed himself at work so that we could have a roof over our heads—a roof he owned. He had never failed us, and I wouldn't fail my family. I refused to be homeless.

"Stop being sentimental," Sara said. "It's just a house."

"It's more than that!"

Our shouting matches left us bitter for days.

We couldn't afford our health insurance and were forced to cancel our policies. I started using our money chickens to pay for groceries. I sold Baba's lions for a pittance at a yard sale. If our daughter, Amal, who was a toddler, had become seriously ill, I wouldn't have been able to pay her medical bills. When we missed two consecutive mortgage payments, the bank threatened to foreclose on our house. That's when I sold the car wash for half of what Baba bought it for, bringing my chicken stuffing to an end. At least I still had my bomber jacket.

◆

SOMEHOW, WE SURVIVED. Whenever I lost confidence in my business acumen, I blamed my previous failures on the recession. *Hustlers never quit*, I told myself. But it had been a while since I'd felt the thrill of hustling. Sara found another job as an administrative assistant at a clinic and became pregnant with our second child. It was around this time, in 2011, that a business opportunity presented itself to me. Ahmed, my friend from high school and also an accountant, offered me a share in a pharmacy he planned to purchase. He wanted me to run the books and keep an eye on the place, as he'd be too busy managing other businesses. An aspiring business mogul, Ahmed was already in negotiations with other partners to open a hookah lounge and a frozen yogurt shop. His ultimate goal was to build a Muslim orphanage in his parents' village in southern Lebanon. "The orphans need our help," he told me, "and I'm going to be the one that saves them."

I spent most of my time at my accounting firm, but once or twice a week I began visiting the pharmacy to sit in the back office and process the accounts. I became familiar with the pricing of medications and the daily transactions with insurance companies and pharmaceutical manufacturers. Once in a while a patient would neglect to pick up his or her prescription. When this happened, I'd reimburse the insurance company and send the drugs back to the pharmaceutical manufacturer. One late night in the office, I realized that if I didn't follow these steps, we'd be able to keep the insurance money for ourselves without actually selling the medicine. The pricier the medicine, the more money we'd make. It wouldn't be that risky, unless we were audited—in which case, we'd almost certainly be discovered. I rose from my desk and began pacing the room, filled with jittery excitement. When I delicately broached this subject with Ahmed, he said it was worth the risk. "I'm thinking of the orphans, bro," he said.

My scheme proved successful. Though it did not bring in much money, it did not cause any trouble, and we likely could've continued without incident for many years. It soon became apparent, however, that Ahmed was desperate for more revenue to cover his other businesses' expenses, his luxury car leases, and his mortgage on a new house in Dearborn Heights. One night I drove out to the Heights to meet him at this home. He lived on a block of recently built brick mansions with manicured lawns on Beech Daly Road. The houses resembled overlarge jewelry boxes sparkling in the dark. His neighbors on either side were also Lebanese Americans from Dearborn: a real estate mogul and an Islamic hip-hop and R&B producer. None of the houses were decorated with lion sentinels.

An Escalade and a Mustang were parked at the top of Ahmed's gravel driveway. When Ahmed opened the front door, he released a pool of golden light. A crystal chandelier hung in the foyer, reflecting off a double marble staircase. As I followed Ahmed up the stairs to his study, I paused at the top to admire the view below, imagining Sara answering the door to welcome guests. Although we could have afforded a more spacious house then, I was apprehensive about taking out a big mortgage. What if another recession hit us? I still drove a Ford Taurus that I'd bought when I started my first job.

In his study, Ahmed reclined in a leather armchair behind an oak desk, propping his feet up on top. He wore snakeskin cowboy boots. He was a collector of cowboy boots and every year made a trip down to Houston to buy more. Like me he was a small man (in boots he was about three inches taller than me), but he had a bulldog face that even as a boy gave him the appearance of someone much older. In high school I had gotten better grades, and yet now he was more successful than I had ever dreamed of becoming.

"You should move out to the Heights, bro," he told me. "There's more space out here. The Iraqi refugees have turned East Dearborn into Little Baghdad. Soon it'll be a dump."

This kind of talk bothered me, though I often heard it on the streets. The Iraqis were fleeing war just as my parents (as well as Ahmed's parents) had, and so I felt for them. But I kept my thoughts to myself.

"We need to think of another scheme," Ahmed continued.

Ahmed's words were like electricity running through my blood. I was eager for a new challenge. If I stayed put, I'd never be able to afford a house like Ahmed's. *Hustlers think big,* I told myself.

The two-part scheme we came up with wasn't too complicated. To begin, we'd send false prescriptions to the insurance companies, who'd pay us for drugs we wouldn't dispense. The second part involved getting the pharmaceutical manufacturers to pay for patient coupons for prescriptions we'd also not dispense. In either case, we'd use fictitious patients. The only ones getting hurt would be the insurance and pharmaceutical companies, and we both thought these multibillion-dollar corporations deserved it. To keep the auditors at bay, I'd be sparing with the amount of prescriptions and coupons I issued.

Over the next few years our new plan brought in tens of thousands of dollars, inspiring Ahmed to purchase another pharmacy. We implemented the same schemes and made even more money. Whenever I checked our business mail, I was filled with both dread and excitement at the chance of finding a notice from the IRS, the insurance companies, or the pharmaceutical manufacturers, and when nothing came, I was somewhat disappointed. I was prepared to defend our accounts.

In any case, I traded in my Taurus for an SUV and bought a new car for Sara. Sara left her job to stay at home to raise our children—our second child was also a girl. I was thirty-four and starting to feel like a success story, but I wasn't ready to relocate to the Heights, not until I had more money in my bank account. This was when I came up with my grand scheme.

Back in Ahmed's study, I explained the following: we'd defraud the pharmaceutical manufacturers by submitting reimbursement claims to co-pay assistance programs for medications we'd neither purchase nor dispense. We'd continue to use false patients. But here was the catch: the pharmaceutical manufacturers would certainly audit us, and we'd only be able to ignore them for so long. My solution: we'd close the pharmacy and open up a new one in someone else's name before the auditors caught up with us. In order to make this work, we'd need to recruit people we could trust into the scheme.

Ahmed sat up in his chair. "This is some serious shit, bro. If we get caught, we could go to prison for this."

"We won't if I'm managing it. And we'll stop once we've made enough money."

Ahmed folded his arms across his chest.

"Think of the orphans," I said.

Ahmed formed a team of accountants and business owners who were either his relatives or close friends. We all met at his place to discuss the plan in detail. Including Ahmed and myself, we were ten—seven men and three women, all from Dearborn.

"Aren't the co-pay assistance programs set up to help patients who can't afford expensive medication?" someone asked.

"What's your point?" Ahmed said.

"I think we're crossing a moral line."

"We're taking advantage of the pharmaceutical manufacturers, not the patients," I said. We'd never harm the patients, I wanted to add, but didn't when I saw all eyes on me. I advised the team not to ever discuss our plans over their personal phones or via email. We'd communicate only through burner phones that we'd dispose of every two weeks.

"Where do we get such phones?" a realtor asked me.

"I've got them right here," I said, and opened my briefcase. I felt like I was the hero in a thriller movie.

Months later, the money was pouring in.

"You're a crafty Muslim, aren't you?" Ahmed told me in his study as we went over our accounts. He had recently returned from Houston and was sunburned. "I got you something," he said. He reached at the side of his desk for a paper bag and handed it to me. I pulled out a heavy cardboard box and opened the lid to find a pair of glossy snakeskin cowboy boots.

I took off my shoes and slipped my feet into the boots and stood up. They were a bit loose, but they'd do just fine if I wore thick socks.

"Howdy," I said.

"There's something I've been meaning to tell you for a long time now," Ahmed said. "Don't take this the wrong way. You're like a brother to me and I want what's best for you."

"Tell me."

"Have you thought of getting a body wax? I get one twice per month, and let me tell you, it's changed my sex life." He removed a card from his breast pocket and gave it to me. "This is the best waxing studio in town."

A week later, I returned home feeling like a plucked chicken. My skin was pink and cold. Sara and the girls didn't notice anything out of the ordinary, not even my hairless hands. That night, as Sara was reading a magazine in bed, I approached her in my bathrobe, wearing my boots. I was naked underneath.

"There's something I need to show you," I whispered.

"Why're you whispering? And since when do you wear cowboy boots?"

I removed my robe, letting it fall to my feet. She gasped. I made a three-hundred-and-sixty-degree turn. She sat up on the edge of the bed and rubbed her palms over my chest. "You feel like silk."

We fucked harder than ever before, biting each other's lips and breaking blood. We howled as we came together. I didn't leave a single hair on her sweaty body.

"What's gotten into you?" she asked me as we lay naked under the sheets.

"Let's move to the Heights," I said. I was now a millionaire.

◆

THAT SUMMER, WE RELOCATED to a brick mansion in Dearborn Heights. The girls each had their own room, and there was a huge backyard for them to play in. Sara converted a spare room into a space to practice yoga. I had my very own study. Occasionally, when Sara took the girls out and I had the house to myself, I'd stand in the foyer, and in the light of our crystal chandelier, I'd belt out the lyrics of Nirvana songs, imagining myself on stage as I played air guitar like a maniac and headbanged until my neck was sore.

It wasn't too difficult to leave Dearborn because many of the grocery stores, restaurants, and hookah lounges in the city had started opening up other branches in the Heights. We were living in the new Dearborn, and I was one of its rising business stars.

When my parents visited us from Lebanon, Baba asked me if I really needed a palace for a family of four. "You could have saved your money for a summer home in Aynata," he said. But then they began visiting the States every summer. "I really miss America," Baba told me as we smoked cigarettes in the backyard. After Michigan, they were headed to Portland to visit Danya, who now ran her own nonprofit organization. She was also dating a white guy named Chris. They had been seeing each other for two years and Chris had recently suggested they move in together. Danya had kept Chris a secret from our parents, knowing they wouldn't approve of her dating a non-Arab or non-Muslim. She planned to tell them on their visit.

"They're going to lose their shit," she told me over the phone, "but it's my life, Ali."

I had donated Baba's chest freezer to Goodwill. Baba didn't ask me about it. He was happily retired, living off his social security and money chicken savings.

I could now afford to send my girls to summer camps and fund their college tuitions and future graduate studies. I donated money to charities and mosques and in 2018 I was awarded the "Arab American Entrepreneur of the Year." Sara and I sat with our girls at a table at the same banquet hall where we had first met.

"I'm proud of you," Sara told me when I returned to the table after receiving my award and giving a speech. But the way she said it, with a particular look in her eyes, told me that she did and didn't know about my schemes. We both knew it would be impossible to give up this life, not after we had tasted it. I continued with the body waxes.

My life as a millionaire lasted four years. My team and I opened and closed twenty-two pharmacies over the course of this period. We made nearly fifty million dollars, which we split ten ways. (Ahmed finally built an orphanage in southern Lebanon, visiting the old country for the inaugural opening.) Our ruse ended on a cold December afternoon. The FBI had been investigating us for the better part of a year. They had already been investigating Ahmed's other business ventures when they discovered my scheme and got the DEA involved. A federal grand jury indicted us for insurance fraud, pharmaceutical fraud, mail fraud, wire fraud, and money laundering. If convicted on all these counts, each of us who had participated faced over thirty years in prison.

The news broke in all the local TV stations and newspapers, including the *Dearborn Post*. My name was listed with the nine others. That's when Sara and I lost all our friends. Parents stopped sending their children over to our house for playdates. As I awaited trial, for fear of being recognized I wore a baseball cap whenever I walked the streets. The news reached my parents in Lebanon, and when Baba phoned to speak to me, I was too embarrassed to answer his calls.

"You know I love you," Danya told me over the phone, "but what you did is fucked up."

She was the most courageous person I knew, I told her, reluctant to discuss myself. She and Chris were engaged, despite my parents' threat to disown her if she married him.

One day Sara burst into tears. "What if you're convicted?" she asked me. "How will we survive?"

I hired Amer Sidani as my criminal-defense attorney, one of the best in town, who negotiated a plea deal that left me with heavy fines and three years in prison. I lost most of my money and our mansion. Sara and the girls moved in with her parents. I moved into the Central Michigan Correctional Facility, where I shared a cell with Billy Shanklin, a man from Lansing serving a sentence for armed robbery and aggravated assault.

For three years I kept to myself at the prison, terrified of most inmates and more than a few of the correctional officers. The sound of electronic buzzers when cell doors opened and closed, the thick, bland walls, the clanging of ankle chains, prisoners jeering and cursing at one another, the occasional fight in the yard or in the chow hall, the dim light in my cell, the lack of fresh air, my nightmares of someone slitting my throat with a razor or raping me in the shower; these were my reality. I only had visits from Sara and the girls to look forward to, and even then, my heart ached at not being able to watch my girls grow up.

At the beginning of my sentence, my craving for nicotine left me with a pounding headache. Billy offered me his contraband cigarettes under the condition that I massage his big, flat feet that stank of sour cheese. My fur sprouted with a vengeance.

Sara and I grew apart from each other as the months passed, and I could only hope that once I was released we'd be able to mend our wounds. I figured she was sticking with me for the sake of our girls. But I was a doomed man. Who would hire me now? I'd never be able to run my own business, not with my record. These thoughts tormented me day and night, and now that I had so much time on my hands, I feared their onslaught.

Baba visited me one summer. We only had half an hour to talk in the visiting room, where the metal tables and chairs were bolted to the floor. We sat by a barred window, the sunlight falling on Baba's face, making him squint. His hair had turned gray. He could barely stand to look at me. This was the first time he'd seen me in my orange jumpsuit. He kept peering out the window, into the sun, as if plotting my escape from prison. He asked me a few basic questions about my daily life and then went silent. I wondered if he blamed himself for what had become of me. After all, he had taught me how to deceive the IRS. I had enjoyed every moment.

Whenever chicken was served in the chow hall, I savored every bite, for the meal took me back to the days when I hustled the streets of West Dearborn, humming a Nirvana song as I waited for buyers. I'd eat the meal with my head down, not wanting to be interrupted, wishing I could return to my childhood, if only for a moment.

"Once you get out of here," Baba said, locking eyes with me, "you and Sara and the kids should move to Aynata. You can live with us. There's a decent school for the girls; they'll be able to improve their Arabic. I'm thinking of opening a grocery store, like the one I used to run. Something to keep my mind busy. You can help me manage it. It'll be a fresh start for you—for the entire family."

After all these years, Baba hadn't given up hope of my moving to Lebanon.

"This is my home," I said.

"Listen to me, my son. I beg you."

Our time was up. I returned to my cell, where Billy was lying on his mattress, his hands clasped behind his head.

"Want a smoke?" he asked me.

I sat at the end of his mattress, propped his feet up on my lap, and began to massage them.

Marseille

It's early afternoon and it's been snowing since dawn. The young journalist from the *Dearborn Post* sits in the armchair before me, in the corner of my living room next to the frosty window, sipping from a mug of coffee that my caretaker made for him. His tape recorder rests on the side table between us. The neighborhood street and the roofs of the brick houses are powdery white now, turning this part of East Dearborn, where I've lived for most of my life, into a scene from a charming holiday postcard.

I light a cigarette with the one still burning in my mouth and put out the stub in the ashtray next to my glass of water. My gnarled hand trembles. The journalist seems surprised that a woman my age, one year shy of a hundred, is smoking. His name is Ibrahim and he's writing a profile of me, a survivor of the *Titanic* sinking in 1912. Although eighty-six years have passed since the disaster, the majestic ship has been on everyone's mind since the release of the new film before Christmas. I haven't seen *Titanic* and don't intend to for two reasons: one, I leave home only to visit the doctor; two, I'd rather not relive the horror of the sinking. I haven't seen the 1953 or 1958 films about the wreck, either.

"I'm ready when you are, Madame Ayda," Ibrahim says. His dark bangs are brushed to the side in a floppy arc. He wears silver-rimmed glasses, a wool blazer, and corduroy pants. He removed his bulky boots in the entrance so as not to dirty my carpet. There's a hole in his argyle sock, revealing the pink skin of his big toe.

I look at the recorder. My voice is deep and guttural. My Arabic accent clings to my English words like a stubborn child. The last time I tried to tell my *Titanic* story, I was in my late twenties, married with two children and pregnant with a third. My eldest daughter's fourth-grade teacher had invited me to visit her class to share my experience. They were learning about the ship and wanted to hear my firsthand account. I stopped halfway through my presentation to the class; my memories became too painful. I didn't want to break down in front of nine-year-olds, including my daughter. I grabbed my purse and walked back home.

But there's another story I plan to tell Ibrahim, not the one he's expecting. It's a story I've never told anyone before, one that I've carried with me since I was fourteen, my age when the ship sank in the icy waters of the North Atlantic. I tell Ibrahim to press record.

♦

I WAS BORN IN 1898 in Sofar, a Druze village in the high reaches of Mount Lebanon. There was a train station in our village, not too far from the Grand Sofar Hotel. The trains passed back and forth from Beirut to Damascus. Every time I heard their mournful wails, I imagined myself on one, headed elsewhere. I had only visited the neighboring towns and dreamt of going west to Beirut and seeing the sea up close. Don't get me wrong, I loved Sofar, loved walking down its narrow roads lined with limestone houses with red-tile roofs. In summer I'd play with my siblings and cousins in the pine forest. We'd creep into terraced gardens to pick fruits—our village had the most delicious plums and apricots. When we got thirsty, we'd hike down to the main square to drink from the communal spring. But the trains made me wonder about what lay beyond the mountain ranges.

A few of our village men had left for the Americas in the late nineteenth century in search of fortune. One such man, Ameen Fayyad, returned from Buenos Aires with hemp sacks overflowing with gold and his skin blistered by the sun. No one knew how he had made this money, but with it he built an Arabian mansion with marble floors and arched windows.

I was the eldest child of five. My family rented a one-bedroom house down from the main road. My parents slept in the bedroom and my siblings and I in the living room, on thin mattresses we rolled out at night and laid side by side. At the age of seven I had already become a chain-smoker. I see the look on your face, Ibrahim. Let me explain. You see, at the time I suffered from severe nosebleeds—I bled so much that my parents feared I'd bleed to death. The doctor in our village failed to cure me. That summer, my parents took me to a nomad camp in the woods for treatment. An herbalist rolled me a cigarette and told me to smoke it. I coughed with every puff, and my eyes watered. The herbalist rolled me more cigarettes and instructed me to smoke them all. My nose never bled again. From that point on, I kept a pouch of tobacco, rolling papers, and matches in my dress pocket.

My brothers and sisters would beg me for a puff, but I told them to bug off. "I've got a medical condition," I'd explain.

My father worked the fields as a hired hand, and I helped Mama clean the house and look after the younger children. I say the younger children even though I was a child myself. But back then girls my age were forced to become adults. At school, I was allowed to smoke only during recess. My classmates avoided me, saying I smelled like a stove. When I had free time, which was rare, I went to the train station and sat on a bench by the tracks and smoked alone.

My first husband arrived by train. I was fourteen and had already dropped out of school to work. I could sew, crochet, and even build things, like cabinets. Sometimes I cleaned houses. One day in early spring, as I was sewing a table cover for a customer, there was a knock on the front door. Baba was out in the fields and Mama was cooking in the kitchen. My siblings were at school. I rested my cigarette in the ashtray and answered the door to find a tall man in an overcoat and suit. His black hair was parted down the middle. He had a thin mustache and was clutching a handkerchief.

"Hello," he said. "Hi." He wiped his hands with the handkerchief. "Um, Ayda?"

"That's my name. Who are you?"

"Nabil Fayyad."

"Are you related to Ameen Fayyad, the millionaire?"

"I wish."

Mama came to the front door. Nabil introduced himself to her without shaking her hand. He seemed embarrassed about his own hands, the way he kept fiddling with his handkerchief.

"You and your brother went off to America, correct?" Mama asked.

He nodded. "We live in a city called Dearborn. I'm here on a short visit."

Mama looked down at me and then up at Nabil. "Please, come in."

We sat in the living room. I put an extra log of wood in the stove to warm up the room. Nabil kept looking at his shoes, afraid to make direct eye contact with us. Through his awkward small talk with Mama, I learned that he worked with his older brother at a dry goods store in America. He was twenty years old.

Mama understood what he was after, as did I: a wife to take back to Dearborn. You may wonder, Ibrahim, why a man with some money to his name would be interested in me. You can't tell now, but I was a looker in my youth. My hair was black and reached down to my waist. I had the body of a grown woman. Even then my voice was husky. Some men like husky voices. Word of my looks must have reached Nabil long before he arrived at our front door.

He stayed over for dinner to meet my father and the rest of the family. Before greeting Baba, I noticed that he wiped his hand with his handkerchief. Mama served lentil soup and bread. Nabil was quiet throughout the meal, and he spoke only when Baba asked him questions about his work and life in America. My siblings couldn't stop giggling. Once Nabil left, Baba said that he liked the man, though he thought Nabil had a weak, clammy handshake. "Felt like I was grasping a fish," he said.

Later that night, Mama asked me to join her for tea in the kitchen.

"We'll be blessed if the American asks for your hand," she said.

I sucked hard on my cigarette. Many girls my age had already been married off, mostly to their cousins. No one had shown interest in me because of my family's poverty. It didn't matter to me—I would have been fine with no husband. All I wanted from life was to ride the train every now and then.

"You can support us better by marrying him," Mama continued. "You understand?"

I stubbed my cigarette in the ashtray and pulled a new one from my pocket and lit up.

"If Nabil comes back, don't smoke in front of him. It might put him off."

On Sunday, Baba's only day off from work, Nabil appeared with his parents. He carried a bouquet of wildflowers and handed them to me as soon as he saw me.

"Flowers!" he said, as if I didn't know what they were. He laughed nervously, which I found endearing. Here was a man six years my senior who had sailed halfway across the world and was anxious in my presence. Did I have that kind of effect on men? I wondered.

In the living room, my family and I sat on one side and Nabil and his parents on the other. After an exchange of blessings, Nabil asked my father for my hand. Details were then worked out. The wedding would be held in a week, and two days later, Nabil and I would sail for America. As soon as Nabil and his parents left, I lit a cigarette and didn't stop smoking until dawn. My future had been arranged without my consent, and yet I couldn't blame my parents. At least I'd get to travel. I smoked on my mattress, surrounded by my siblings.

"Please don't go," one of my sisters said. "We'll miss you too much."

"Have a puff," I said, and let them each smoke. They all coughed. It was easier this way, distracting them.

I spent the next few days sewing myself a long-sleeved satin wedding dress. Mama sat next to me; since Nabil's proposal, she had become my shadow.

"I've never been in love before," I told her.

"There's no such thing as love, ya binti. There's only obedience. You need to cook for Nabil and wash and iron his clothes; you have to wake up in the mornings before he does to prepare his breakfast; you have to smile and never question anything he asks you to do; you have to pray for him; you have to accept him into your bed when he's in the mood; you have to bear him children. Do you understand, habibti?"

I nodded.

On the eve of my wedding, Mama could hardly look at me. When she did, her eyes filled with tears.

"Don't worry," I told her. "In a few years' time, I'll return from America with more gold than Ameen Fayyad. I'll build you the biggest house this village has ever seen."

The next day, I waited in my wedding dress for Nabil to arrive with the male members of his family. According to Druze custom, Nabil would take me back to his house for the wedding. My family wouldn't be in attendance. The groom's family was now responsible for the bride's well-being; they had to be trusted.

I heard the beating of drums from the living room. I peeked out the window and saw Nabil at the top of the road, perched on his father's shoulders. He was surrounded by a ring of dancers stomping their feet, their scimitars glinting in the sunshine. Nabil's arms were raised high; he was snapping his fingers. He looked handsome in his white suit, even though his movements were forced.

On our way to Nabil's house, he and I sat on the back of a mule, me up front. A relative held the reins and directed the beast of burden down the road. The troupe led the way, singing and dancing and beating on their drums. Villagers stepped out of their homes and onto their balconies and showered us with rice and rose petals and blessings and ringing ululations. At one point, I tilted to the side and nearly slipped off the saddle before Nabil caught me by the waist. He kept his arm around me for the rest of the journey. I hoped he'd always catch me when I fell.

In Nabil's bedroom later that night, we lay next to each other on the bed, under thick blankets. I was wearing lingerie that Mama had packed in my suitcase, along with dry foods.

"The first time will hurt," Mama had said. "Pretend to enjoy it. A few moans will do."

Apart from the winter room, which had the stove, the rest of the house was icy cold. A kerosene lamp cast everything in shadowy light. We had to get up early in the morning to take the train to Beirut. From Beirut we'd sail to Marseille, and from Marseille, we'd take a train up to Cherbourg. We'd board the *Titanic* at the port there. There was then a brief stop in Liverpool before making our way across the Atlantic to New York City.

"Mind if I smoke?" I asked Nabil.

"Not at all."

I lit up. He asked me when I had started smoking, and I told him about the herbalist and my nose bleeds.

"Do you think your nose bleeds would return if you ever chose to quit smoking?"

"You want me to quit?"

He shook his head.

"Good," I said, and lit another cigarette.

We didn't kiss that night, let alone make love. I was terrified to undress in front of him, but I wouldn't have minded a kiss. I was curious about how his mustache would feel against my lips.

"I'm a married woman," I thought to myself before drifting off to sleep. I could hardly believe it.

◆

I HACK UP PHLEGM and spit it into a wad of tissues. Ibrahim stops the recorder and combs his fingers through his bangs. He tells me he's seen the film three times. "Just breaks my heart," he says. I take a sip of water, adjust my false teeth, and continue my story.

◆

MY PARENTS AND SIBLINGS, as well as our neighbors and a handful of villagers, met us at the train station in the morning to bid us farewell.

"Send us gifts from America," my siblings said.

When Mama and I embraced, we spared each other the agony of making eye contact. If we had, we would have lost ourselves.

As sad as it was to leave my family, the train ride to Beirut was marvelous. I sat by the window, looking out at the passing landscape. At a bend round a mountain, I glimpsed the blue sea. We were sitting in the second-class carriage. Perhaps Nabil didn't have as much money as I thought, but I didn't mind. Traveling with us was a contingent of villagers also headed to America. We were all taking the same route.

"Is there a sea near Dearborn?" I asked Nabil.

"There are lakes—they call them the Great Lakes. I'll take you to Lake Michigan, which is so big that it looks like a sea."

I turned away from the window to look at him. He smiled.

"You have zaatar stuck in your teeth," I said.

He immediately cupped his mouth, and then reached inside his coat pocket and removed a metal container of toothpicks. He covered his mouth with one hand as he worked the toothpick between his teeth.

We got off the train in Mar Mikhaël, on the east side of Beirut, and took a horse carriage to a boarding house up from the port. The weather was much warmer, so I removed my winter coat. By the time we'd checked in at the boarding house and dropped off our chest and belongings in a communal bedroom, it was dusk. We had supper with our fellow villagers and boarders in the dining room. Instead of going upstairs to bed, I wanted to see the sea up close.

Nabil took me down to the port. The streets smelled dusty, as if they hadn't been washed in years. The air was humid and salty. We walked through pools of lamplight and arrived at the Mediterranean. Our ship, the *Lotus*, was docked in the harbor. It was too dark to see the horizon, but flickering lights dotted the calm waters. Nabil told me those were lanterns swaying from fishing boats. We strolled down the boardwalk. I inhaled the smell of fish and seaweed. Stars glimmered above. In the distance the silhouettes of mountains loomed large. Somewhere up there was my family. I hoped I'd see them again.

It took a little under two weeks to reach the port of Marseille. Those first few days on the *Lotus* I was green with seasickness. I could hardly speak or eat I was so sick. How strange, I thought, to spend my first week with my husband feeling like I wanted to die. He, however, was used to the rocky waves. When I felt my stomach turn, I pushed him aside and ran for the toilet.

We shared a third-class cabin with three other couples from Sofar. There were four bunk beds in the room. I slept on the bottom bunk, Nabil on top. When I started feeling better, I joined our roommates in games of backgammon and cards. We sat in a circle on the floor. At night, we snacked on salted pumpkin seeds and exchanged stories. I was the youngest in the group, but no one knew my exact age except for Nabil. On my official documents it said that I was eighteen. I rolled cigarettes for the men, noting that I'd have to buy more tobacco and papers in Marseille.

Nabil didn't participate in the games and remained on his bunk, reading. He loved American poetry; Walt Whitman was his hero. He had told me he once tried growing out his beard to look like Whitman, but couldn't stand getting food caught in his facial hair. Our roommates kept pestering him to at least play a hand of cards, but he refused.

"My wife will play on my behalf," he said.

My wife, I thought to myself. It still sounded strange to me.

During the day I sat on deck, gazing out and enjoying the sun on my face. I could look at the sea for hours, letting my thoughts roam. Nabil would sit next to me, his nose buried in Whitman. I wondered if he was more interested in the poet than me. But then I'd catch him staring at me, and when our eyes met, he'd quickly look away.

Having to share a room with others, Nabil and I had had no time to ourselves. Believe it or not, we still hadn't kissed yet. It would have been haram, improper, to kiss in public.

Especially when we were surrounded by our fellow villagers and countrymen.

We arrived in the Vieux-Port de Marseille on a cold, stormy day in March. The pounding rain reminded me of the winter rains in Sofar, which was now thousands of miles away. Nabil took two umbrellas from our chest and opened them on deck. We had to yell over the sounds of the storm to hear each other. The port was massive, with all sizes of ships and boats. Warehouses towered over the water.

Customs officials came on deck and set up a table to check our papers. Once our papers were stamped, we were permitted to walk down the plank and step foot in France. Before we disembarked, Nabil instructed me to wait on deck with the other women while he and the men went to look for a carriage to take us all to the Syrian Inn northeast of the port. The Syrian Inn was owned by a Beiruti man who had immigrated to Marseille years earlier—as you must know, Ibrahim, back then there was no Lebanon; our land was called Syria. Almost all Arab voyagers stopped at his place en route to sailing west.

An hour later, Nabil and the men returned. They carried our luggage down to two carriages and then came back for us. They were all drenched, despite the umbrellas. It was too rainy to see anything clearly through the carriage windows. We were wet and shivering.

We shared a room with the same Sofar villagers at the Syrian Inn, which was old and made of brick with creaking wood floors. The cramped room held several bunk beds and an old chiffonier. After we arrived, the women and I took turns bathing in the women's restroom while the men did the same in theirs. By the time I bathed, the water had turned lukewarm.

That evening, we sat in the lobby, waiting for supper. A man played sonatas on a grand piano. The walls were decorated with framed landscape paintings of the Levant. I would have preferred to tour the city, but it was still raining hard and none of us wanted to risk getting sick. We were scheduled to spend two nights here in Marseille before taking the train north to Cherbourg, on the English Channel.

Nabil and I barely spoke that day. We were cold and exhausted after our sea voyage. We waited and waited, listening to the pianist. Finally, we headed to the cafeteria, where we were served a terrible roast beef; we were too hungry to care. I remember dipping pieces of a stale baguette into watery gravy.

The following morning the sun was shining and the sky was bright blue. I told Nabil that I wanted to see Marseille. I wasn't interested in spending the day in the lobby playing cards, which was what our group intended to do. They preferred to rest up before the long train ride. Nabil and I needed time alone together, I thought to myself. We still hardly knew each other. Thankfully, he agreed to tour the city.

We asked the receptionist for tourist recommendations, explaining that we only had the day. He suggested we head a few blocks west and walk down La Canebière, the city's main avenue.

It was chilly outside, but with the sun out, it was perfect weather for a stroll. The air was fresh and smelled of budding trees. We walked down the pavement in search of a café. I lit a cigarette and raced to keep up with Nabil's pace. He had big strides; I took three steps for each one of his. The buildings reminded me of the ones I had seen in Beirut.

Nabil must have been nervous by our silence, because all of a sudden, he said he had a joke for me. "What did the wall say to the other wall?"

"Tell me."

"I'll meet you at the corner."

I laughed sympathetically.

"You're laughing to make me feel better," he said.

"You're right. That was a lousy joke."

We stepped inside a café. The floor had black-and-white tiles, wooden tables, and wicker chairs. The garçon dropped off paper menus. I had learned French in school and still remembered it.

"Do you read French?" I asked Nabil.

"Only English and Arabic. But I can say 'croissant.' I feel like having a croissant."

"Me too."

When the garçon returned to our table, I ordered croissants for us and two black coffees. The croissants came with strawberry jam and creamy butter. We devoured them.

"You've got jam stuck in your teeth," I said, leaning back and lighting a cigarette.

"Get used to it," he said, and smiled.

Beads of sweat glimmered on his fingers. When he saw me looking at his hands, he put them in his lap.

"No reason to be embarrassed," I said. "You're my husband. We're supposed to tell each other everything. Or something like that."

"I wouldn't know. This is the first time I'm married."

"Did you ever have a girlfriend in America? Tell me the truth, I won't be jealous."

"No."

"How come? You're a handsome man, Nabil."

He blushed. "You're beautiful."

More people started to enter the café, mostly businessmen.

"I've always been shy around girls," he said. "I'm shy around everyone."

"Because of your hands?"

"Yes. They sweat constantly, since I was a boy. Whether I'm happy or anxious, they drip with sweat. I can't help it. My underarms and feet also sweat uncontrollably."

"Who cares if your hands sweat?"

Whenever he was forced to shake someone's hand, he said, he'd notice how they'd then wipe their hand against their thigh, as if they were disgusted. He dreaded social occasions where the shaking of hands was required. He had avoided participating in the games of backgammon and cards on the boat because he didn't want to touch the game pieces with his sweaty hands.

"I have a smoking problem and you have a sweating problem," I said.

He looked at me intently. "I'm glad my hands sweat and not yours."

Nabil paid the bill and we continued down the street until we reached La Canebière. The wide avenue was bustling with horse carriages, men in suits and hats, and some women in crinoline dresses. I had never seen such dresses in Sofar and wondered how they were made. Shops, cafés, bakeries, saloons, and restaurants lined the avenue on either side. The columned buildings were massive, the sun reflecting off their windows. We walked down the pavement, looking up at this new world like the obvious tourists we were. We came across theater houses, grand hotels, and historic churches; shoeshiners, barbers, and beggars. Vendors pushed carts of dry goods and merchandise. We bought fresh orange juice from a stand and stopped at a tobacconist so I could replenish my supplies. We heard French, Italian, Spanish, and Arabic being spoken. A woman in a long black coat stood on a wooden box and sang patriotic songs in French. A metal bowl lay at her feet for tips. We sat down on a bench to rest our feet.

"The winters in Dearborn are gray and cold," Nabil said. "But summers are beautiful."

"Are there Arabs in Dearborn?"

"There's a small community. We all live in an area called the Southend with other immigrants."

"Do you have many friends?"

"A few. I'm not as social as my brother. He can walk into a room and capture everyone's attention. I'd rather cower in a corner." He looked at me. "Maybe now you regret marrying me."

"I didn't have a choice." When I saw the concern on his face, I said that I was trying to be funny. He didn't laugh.

I asked Nabil if I could work at his and his brother's dry goods store. I didn't care to be a housewife.

"We need an accountant," he said. "Are you good with numbers?"

"I can learn."

"I'm sure you won't have any problems adapting to America."

"What was it like for you?"

"Terrible. I was only ten when I left Sofar. I cried myself to sleep every night, missing my mother. I had to sob into my pillow, because if my brother heard me, he'd yell at me and accuse me of being a sissy. I didn't continue my schooling and instead worked with my brother. When I was seventeen, I found comfort in the poetry of Whitman. I read him every night before I went to sleep. I even tried to write free verse myself, but everything I produced was horribly sentimental."

"I'd like to read your poetry."

"It'll only make you seasick again."

For lunch we ate cheese sandwiches from a street vendor and then had coffee and chocolate éclairs at an outdoor café. As we were sipping our coffees, Nabil revealed that he remembered his former life—you may not know this, Ibrahim, but Druzes believe in reincarnation. It's one of our main tenets. I grew up listening to stories of family members who remembered their previous lives and, in some cases, had reconnected with their loved ones from them. It's said that one remembers their former life if they had died tragically.

When Nabil was a toddler, he kept telling his parents that he wanted to visit the white house with the pomegranate trees. His parents had no idea what he was talking about and suspected he was remembering his former life. Some days he'd weep and weep, and no matter what his mother did to comfort him, he couldn't stop crying. Over time, his family came to understand that he was weeping over the loss of this past life.

With each passing year, Nabil's visions intensified. He saw himself climbing up a pomegranate tree, brushing a young woman's hair, playing with a pistol in a shed. In each vision he remained a boy. The visions continued while he was living in Dearborn. He wrote letters back home asking his parents to survey the neighboring villages to determine if any boy who had lived in a white house with pomegranate trees had been tragically killed around the time Nabil was born. His parents asked around but came back with nothing. Whatever had happened to the boy, whoever he was, his soul now belonged to Nabil.

"Do you remember your past life?" Nabil asked me.

"No. I must have died an old woman."

We crossed the avenue and made our way in the direction of the port. As the sun started to set, the streetlights came on, and La Canebière lit up. Pedestrians flooded the pavement. I was sad that our day was coming to an end, and that tomorrow we'd be leaving Marseille.

We dined at a bistro in a narrow alleyway off La Canebière. The tables were packed next to one another. We both ordered steak and potatoes. Nabil also asked for a bottle of red wine. I had never had alcohol before. When I took my first sip, it tasted terribly bitter. But the more I drank, the warmer I felt. I poured myself a second glass. In the dim light, I noticed that Nabil's hands were dry. When I pointed that out to him, he looked down at them and a moment later they began to sweat.

"It's that quick," he said.

I extended my own hands across the table. "Hold them."

"No."

"It's me, your wife."

He held my hands.

Nabil ordered a second bottle, and we drank it down. We stumbled out of the bistro and into the cold, laughing hysterically— over what I can't remember. We held on to each other so as not to lose our balance. Under a streetlight, Nabil stopped, held my face in his hands, and kissed my lips. We kissed with hunger while pedestrians walked around us. Our breaths tasted of wine.

We strolled down to the port. The icy wind coming off the sea was refreshing. To the east was the Levant, to the south Africa, and to the west the opening to the Atlantic.

"Can we come back to Marseille?" I asked. "I love this city."

"Yes," he said.

Back at the inn, we tiptoed into our room. Our roommates were asleep and snoring. Nabil crept into my lower bunk. Under the covers, in that darkness, we kissed in silence. And then we made love. I bit Nabil's shoulder so as not to cry out in pain and in pleasure. When we were finished, he soon fell asleep. I kept my palm on his chest, feeling his heartbeat, the scent of his skin on mine.

The next morning, my feet were blistered and sore. We slept for most of the train ride up to Cherbourg. When we were awake, we could hardly keep our hands off each other, despite Nabil's sweaty palms. I ached for him.

We spent two nights in Cherbourg, and on the third day we boarded the *Titanic*.

◆

IT'S STOPPED SNOWING. The plow trucks will come out soon, disrupting the picturesque scene. And yet I'm not in Dearborn. I'm in Marseille, with Nabil, walking down La Canebière.

Ibrahim sits at the edge of his chair. "Are you all right? Do you need to rest?"

"I'm fine," I say. Eighty-six years have passed since that day in Marseille, and yet it still feels like yesterday. How's that even possible? Are my memories to be trusted?

"Where were you when the ship struck the iceberg?" Ibrahim asks. "What happened to Nabil?"

We were asleep in our third-class cabin when we heard the commotion, I say. When people found out about what had happened, they began to scream and push one another. It was mayhem. Somehow Nabil and I made it up top to the deck. It was pitch-dark and cold. Only women and children were allowed to board the lifeboats. Officers were shooting men who tried to get on. I refused to go without Nabil, but he promised he'd follow me in the boat for men. He was standing on deck as I climbed down to the lifeboat and put on a life jacket. That was the last time I saw him.

We were on the lifeboat, freezing, as I saw the ship sink into the frigid waters, its stern up in the air. Hours later, we were rescued by the *Carpathia*. The seamen provided us with blankets and hot tea, but I couldn't stop shivering. I've felt cold ever since then.

I was never able to board a ship again, let alone approach a large body of water. I haven't seen my family since I left them all those years ago. Most of them are dead now. God rest them.

I ended up working at Nabil's brother's store on Dix Avenue, in the Southend. I lived with Nabil's family in a bungalow. I was given Nabil's room, which still had his clothes hung up in the closet, his socks and underwear in the cabinet drawers. A stack of books lay on his desk. I asked Nabil's brother and his family for their stories about him. I asked neighbors. They all mentioned his painful shyness, his long silences, his love for reading, his kindness. I craved these stories, always wanting more.

When I was twenty-six, I married a Lebanese man and moved to East Dearborn, to this house, where I raised three children. My second husband knew that my first husband had died in the sinking of the *Titanic*. I didn't mention Nabil's name and he didn't ask any questions. When my children were old enough, I told them a brief version of my story, hardly mentioning Nabil. I wanted to keep my memories of him to myself. But there were times when I was overcome with sadness and withdrew to my room. My husband and children knew to leave me alone.

My children are now all grandparents and live in Michigan. My eldest daughter resides nearby and keeps insisting that I live with her. I prefer to remain in my house.

◆

I ASK IBRAHIM WHEN he intends to publish the article. In two days, he says. He'll go back to his office and begin typing it up.

"I'm sorry for your loss," he tells me on his way out.

I doubt he'll have enough space in his article to capture the story that I've told him. But I'm glad that I've shared it and that Nabil will live on in Ibrahim's recording, for anyone who cares to listen to it.

◆

MY CARETAKER MAKES US dinner and then retires to her room. I sit by the window and sip tea. My children call to check up on me. We have brief conversations, as I'm in no mood to talk. I light a cigarette and look out onto the snowy lawn bathed in yellow streetlight.

For years, I often pictured Nabil's reincarnation appearing at my front door in Dearborn and asking for me. Although I had known Nabil only for about a month, my intense longing for him was a feeling that I never experienced with my second husband, a decent man who died of pancreatic cancer more than twenty years ago.

When I arrived in New York City in 1912, Nabil's brother was there to greet me at Pier 54. He was a beefier version of his younger brother; the moment I saw him I rushed into his arms and wept. We had lunch in lower Manhattan and then went to Grand Central Station and boarded the train for Michigan. As we journeyed west through woods, I looked out the window, imagining myself on the train to Cherbourg sitting next to my love, holding his sweaty palm.

I Have Reason to Believe My Neighbor Is a Terrorist

B adria Sadek was peering through the open blinds of her front window on the day Lulu arrived from Lebanon and settled into the house next door to begin her new life in America. Earlier that afternoon, Lulu's husband had driven to the Detroit Metropolitan Airport to collect her and bring her back to his home in East Dearborn. As soon as she had heard her neighbor's pickup pull into his driveway, Badria had sprung from her couch and rushed to the window. The pickup's doors opened, and out stepped Lulu and Adel. Badria focused on the bride, who wore a hijab, a long-sleeved blouse, and tight blue jeans and sneakers. She was petite with wide hips. Adel ushered her inside, leaving the suitcases in the truck.

Badria hurried to the dining room to observe the west side of her neighbor's house, her hijab, draped loosely over her shoulders, nearly slipping off. There was barely any space between the houses in East Dearborn, allowing a person to see into the interior of their neighbor's house and glimpse the glare of the TV or someone peeling potatoes at the kitchen counter. Today Adel's blinds were closed. Badria cracked her window open in the hope of hearing their muffled voices, but all she caught was the September wind stirring the leaves of the plane trees lining the street. She returned to her couch. The dish of stuffed squash, Adel's favorite, sat in a pot on her stove. She had cooked the meal that morning, after her husband left for work. She'd give Adel and Lulu at least an hour before she rang their bell, the pot of koosa in her hands. Surely Lulu would be hungry and exhausted after a long flight; she'd feel more at home eating her native food.

Badria had often cooked Adel his favorite dishes, for he had been a bachelor who lived alone. But she had never ventured beyond his front porch. For a woman to enter a single man's house would have been sacrilegious, and she knew there were eyes peeking between blinds up and down the street, like those of sleepless cats in the night. This time would be different, given that Adel was now a married man.

Adel's screen door opened and slammed shut. Badria returned to her front window and watched Adel lift two suitcases from the truck bed and haul them inside his house. She needed to kill time. She would have called her son and daughter, who both lived in Ann Arbor, but at this time of day they were at work. She was too restless to visit her other neighbors.

Last spring, when she had dropped off a dish at his house, Adel had said he was traveling to Lebanon for a few weeks to visit his family and hopefully get married. Badria had felt a slight pang in her chest. Many years ago, she told Adel, her husband had also gone to Lebanon to find a bride, which was how she came to America. When Adel returned to Dearborn with the news that he had married Lulu, which was a nickname for Lilian, and that she would follow him once her visa application was approved, Badria rose on her tiptoes, reached for his face, and kissed his cheek, pressing her lips against his stubble and tasting his scent, a blend of aftershave and stale cigarettes. It was the first time she had ever touched him. She asked for more information about his new wife. Lulu came from his ancestral village near the Israeli border, he said, and was in her final year of high school. Badria had also been in her final year of high school when her husband had arrived at her doorstep, holding a bouquet of roses and a box of Belgian chocolates, eager to impress her family. He'd even had a silk handkerchief poking out of the breast pocket of his blazer.

Badria used to visit Adel's house back when Madame Ayda lived there; it was a three-bedroom bungalow with an old roof. However, she had no clue how Adel had furnished it or decorated the walls. He had moved into the house two years ago, following Madame Ayda's death in 1998, on a summer day as hot as the scorching summers in Badria's hometown of Tyre. She had watched from the front window as Adel and three men around his age moved furniture from a big truck into the house. Later, Adel sat in a folding chair in his backyard, smoking a cigarette. He wore a sleeveless white undershirt and shorts. His drooping neckline revealed a semicircle of matted chest hair. His arms were tanned and muscular, his legs pale and hairy. He had black hair and a mustache. Badria had taken lemons from the fridge to make a pitcher of lemonade, which she mixed with orange blossom water. She plopped in ice cubes, set the pitcher and a glass on a tray, and went outside to greet her new neighbor, crossing into his backyard and thankfully managing not to tip over the pitcher in her excitement.

"I thought you could use a cold refreshment," she had said in Arabic.

"Bless your hands, Khalto," Adel said, standing up from his chair and taking the tray, which he then set on the ground. As he introduced himself in Arabic, Badria could tell English was his first language. He flicked his cigarette into the grass and squashed the butt with the heel of his sneaker.

"Are you new to Dearborn?" she asked him.

"I grew up in the Southend. My father used to work at the Levy plant."

Before moving to East Dearborn in the early eighties, Badria said, she and her husband had lived in the Southend too. Her husband had worked at a gas station on Dix Avenue. He now owned a convenience store on Michigan Avenue. She wanted to linger and learn more about Adel, but she knew it wasn't appropriate, and besides, he was tired.

Over the next two years, Badria learned as much as she could about her new neighbor. After high school, he'd joined the staff of his older cousin's Lebanese sweetshop on Warren Avenue, which he now managed. His family must have helped him purchase his house, considering his modest salary. Every so often, he'd leave a plate of baklava or knafeh on her front doorstep.

At one point she wondered if Adel would be a good match for her daughter, but she suspected her daughter wouldn't fall for a man without a college education. Her daughter also wouldn't fall for a man with a temper like her father's. But Badria had seen Adel lose his temper only once, when a contractor had come to replace loose roof shingles. The two men had stood in Adel's yard, a metal ladder propped against the back of the house.

"You're charging me more than the estimate!" Adel said, towering over the contractor, a short Arab man in overalls. His hands were curled into fists, just like her husband's when he was overcome with rage.

"Your roof is in worse shape than I thought," the contractor said, cowering as if he were afraid he was about to be struck. But Adel wasn't that kind of man. He relaxed his hands and the contractor climbed up the ladder.

Badria checked the time—an hour had passed. She wrapped her hijab around her head, covering her silver-black hair, put on a cardigan over her long-sleeved dress, took the pot off the stove, and walked over to Adel's house and rang the doorbell. When no one answered, she rang again and again. Adel finally opened the door. He smiled.

"Your wife must be hungry after her travels," she said.

"Please, come in," he said.

He took the pot from her hands and led her into the living room and then continued into the kitchen to set the pot down on a table. The furniture was bulky, the walls bare except for a framed sura from the Qur'an. The coffee table was probably from Goodwill. He was still young and struggling to make a decent living. Badria sat down on the couch and felt the springs against her thighs.

"Lulu, come down for a minute," Adel said, calling up the stairs. "She's still unpacking," he told Badria.

"I should leave," she said, knowing Adel would insist she stay.

"No, Khalto, you must meet Lulu!"

Badria had never seen him this happy. He was often serious and quiet, as if troubled by his thoughts. The young man was in love.

Badria heard footsteps on the stairs, and soon Lulu appeared without her hijab. She had curly black hair. Badria rose from the couch and the two embraced, kissing each other thrice on the cheeks. Lulu smelled of fresh strawberries.

"I've heard so much about you!" Lulu said in Arabic. "Adouli tells me you're the finest cook in Dearborn."

"Adouli is exaggerating," Badria said, using Adel's pet name for the first time. It felt good to call him Adouli, as if they had known each other for years. The fact that he had mentioned her to Lulu told her she must mean something to him, however small.

They sat down. Badria took in Lulu's features. She had a round face, big hazel eyes, and thick lips. A charming little potbelly protruded from her blouse. Badria had imagined that Adel would marry a tall, slim woman in heels. How well did she really know him?

She asked Lulu about her flight.

"It's the first time I fly!" she said. "At takeoff I was scared out of my mind, but once the plane stopped climbing, I started to calm down. I can't wait to fly again."

"We'll do plenty of flying," Adel said.

"Can we fly to Las Vegas?" she asked.

He chuckled. "Sure."

"Why Las Vegas?" Badria asked Lulu.

"I've heard so much about the city—something made out of nothing, kind of like what they're trying to do in Dubai. I don't care to gamble. That's haram. I just want to see the singing and dancing, and the magic shows. Have you been to Las Vegas, Khalto?"

Badria shook her head. She was fifty-two, had been in America for over thirty years, and had yet to visit other states. She wouldn't have minded touring Las Vegas, or Los Angeles, New York City, or Chicago, for that matter, but money had always been tight. Her husband prohibited her from working, not wanting to send the message to the Arab community that he couldn't provide for his family.

Badria stood up to take her leave. "Consider me your mother in Dearborn," she told Lulu. "I'm right there," she said, pointing through the window at her house.

◆

BADRIA AND HER HUSBAND, Maarouf, dined in front of the TV. Ever since Iraq's invasion of Kuwait in the summer of 1990, Maarouf had become addicted to watching CNN. He sat in his recliner, bending over his dinner laid out on the coffee table. The top of his head was bald and shiny, the sides thick with black curls. Badria wished he'd shave off his bushy mustache because it reminded her of Saddam Hussein's, but she didn't dare suggest this.

"The koosa is delicious," he said, bringing a chunk of squash to his mouth, his eyes on Wolf Blitzer.

"Sahtein," she said. She wondered if Lulu had liked her koosa. She figured Lulu was fast asleep and would wake up in the early hours from jet lag. It had taken her a week to recover from jet lag when she came to America. She'd been just eighteen years old. Her first night in Dearborn, in Maarouf's top-floor apartment in a duplex in the Southend, she had woken up at 4:00 a.m. and left their bedroom. She poured herself a glass of water and sat by the window in the living room, and over the tops of bare trees, she spotted the smokestacks of the Ford Rouge plant in the distance. Although her body was now in America, her heart and soul were still in Tyre, at her limestone house a mile inland from the sea. With eight children to feed, her father had been eager to marry her off. Badria had been perfectly content to marry a local boy— she had no interest in leaving for a foreign land—but her mother insisted she marry Maarouf because he was coming from America, which meant he had money—money she could send back home.

Badria cried herself to sleep that first night in Dearborn. A month later, she called her family long-distance, but because the call was expensive and the reception was bad, she was only able to say a few words to her parents and siblings, nothing more than platitudes, and yet hearing the echoes of their voices thousands of miles away made her feel loved. Maarouf hadn't known what to do with her homesickness except to tell her that she would get over it just like he had. She cooked every day for him, washed and ironed his clothes and polished his shoes, kept the house spotless, grew basil and parsley in the backyard. She missed walking along the shores of the Mediterranean, exploring the souks in the heart of Tyre, braiding her younger sisters' hair, but she now had to chart a new life for herself in another continent, with a husband who was a stranger to her.

It helped that there were several Lebanese families in the Southend. Badria soon made friends with other young mothers and began visiting them in the afternoons for a cup of Turkish coffee, or accompanying them to talks and communal dinners in the basement of the Dix mosque. Maarouf played cards with other Lebanese men at the local coffeehouses.

Badria had returned to Lebanon twenty-five years later with her husband and children. The Lebanese civil war had prevented her from traveling earlier. Her parents and siblings had become strangers to her, their conversations as shallow as the long-distance telephone calls they had exchanged for nearly three decades. As she navigated the winding streets and alleyways of Tyre, she felt like an outsider, the same way she felt back in America. By that point, she had lived more years in America than she had in Lebanon. Did that make her more American than Lebanese?

In the living room, Maarouf looked at her, noticing her untouched plate. "What's the matter?" he asked.

"Nothing," she said, and picked up her spoon.

◆

THE NEXT DAY, a Sunday, Badria kept her eye on Adel's house. Although her windows were open, she was unable to overhear the newlyweds' voices.

"What do you keep staring at?" Maarouf asked, turning around in his recliner to look at her. She was standing at the window.

"Nothing."

"It's always nothing. Nothing, nothing, nothing."

"Adel's wife arrived yesterday."

"Is she pretty?"

"She's cute."

"That means she's ugly. When is Hisham going to marry? The boy's old enough."

Hisham was their son and eldest child. He was thirty-three and worked in the IT Department at the University of Michigan. After graduating from college in Dearborn, he'd moved to Ann Arbor and now rarely came home for visits, even though he was only about thirty miles away. The same thing had happened with Badria's daughter, Samira, only she worked as a paralegal.

"When he meets the right person," Badria said.

"We should send him to Lebanon to meet someone and marry. These Dearborn girls are nothing but trouble, just like Samira."

"Samira is doing well for herself."

"She moved out of the house as an unmarried woman. Allah only knows if she's behaving herself in Ann Arbor."

"She's a righteous Muslim."

"She doesn't wear the hijab. She's too Americanized."

Badria's greatest fear about her daughter was that she'd end up marrying an American. "Not wearing the hijab doesn't make her any less Muslim."

"What's gotten into you? America has changed you for the worse."

"I'm just being reasonable."

"Am I not reasonable?"

"That's not what I meant." She had pushed it too far.

"You believe I'm an old, dumb, backward-thinking man," he said, his mustache covering his upper lip.

"You misunderstood me, Maarouf."

"I kill myself at work for you, and this is what I get?"

"Maarouf, I'm sorry. I'm very grateful for—"

"Khalas skiti!" He turned up the volume on the TV.

Badria's heart was pounding.

◆

AS BADRIA WAS CHANGING the bedsheets, she heard the sound of water running in Adel's shower. She darted to her window and looked out. The bathroom curtains were closed. She opened the window and heard laughter, and moments later, a squeal of joy. "Shh," Adel said. "The neighbors will hear us."

Badria assumed Lulu had lost her virginity to Adel on their wedding night in Lebanon. On her wedding night, Maarouf had taken her to a three-star hotel in the port of Tyre. After making love, which had pained her, Maarouf said, "It'll get better with time." His thinning hair stood up like stray wires. How many American women had he slept with back in Dearborn? she wondered. He soon fell asleep and began snoring. She stepped out onto the balcony and looked at the sea, the docked boats bathed in moonlight, the smell of fish in the air. This was her favorite place in the world.

"Ya habibi," Lulu moaned.

A pair of hands parted the curtains and pressed against the steamy glass. They were small hands.

"Ya habibi," Lulu repeated.

Badria watched until the pair of hands withdrew from the window like birds taking flight.

◆

DAYS LATER, LULU CAME knocking at Badria's door, tears streaming down her face.

"I can't cook, ya Khalto!" she said. She had burned the kibbe balls she'd spent hours preparing in the morning, she told Badria, and yesterday, she'd overcooked the chicken and burned the bread for the fattoush, setting off the smoke alarm. If she continued to fail in the kitchen, what would Adouli think? Bless him, he had laughed off her culinary disasters thus far, but sooner or later he'd get upset and the last thing she wanted was for him to regret marrying her, because she loved him, had fallen in love with him the moment she saw him speaking to her mother in the formal living room of their village house, when he had come to express his interest in her.

"Come in, habibti," Badria said.

Badria had a pot of majadara boiling on the stove, scenting the air with lentils. She stirred the pot while Lulu stood next to her.

"I made enough to feed a family of six, so you can take some home," Badria said. "Tell Adouli that you and I made it together. He'll like that."

Lulu rose on her tiptoes and kissed Badria on the cheek.

"Listen carefully now," Badria said. "I'm going to teach you how to make this dish."

Over the following weeks, Badria taught Lulu how to cook. She started with the basics, from slicing and dicing vegetables and frying onions to boiling rice. As they cooked, Badria learned that Lulu's father had been killed during the final years of the Lebanese civil war when he went out to till a field and had stepped on an Israeli landmine. Her mother had struggled to raise the family after his death, and now they all depended on Lulu's uncle to help them survive.

Lulu's eyes moistened. "I miss my younger sisters—Jana, Rasha, and Souhayla," she said. "We all shared a room together. In the evening, I'd sing for them. They'd sit on their bunk beds and I'd stand in the middle of the room and sing Arabic pop songs, imagining myself on stage in Las Vegas.

"Adouli gave me a calling card, so I'm able to speak to them every day for a few minutes. My goal is to bring them to America— once I gain my citizenship."

Badria wondered if Lulu's eagerness to marry Adel had been less about love and more about her desire to grant her sisters access to America. Was she just after the passport?

The next time Lulu came over, she was beaming. "Adouli loved my moghrabieh," she told Badria. "He said I'm going to make him fat." She squealed with laughter, the same laugh Badria had heard coming from Adel's shower. How often did they have sex? Badria wondered.

One day, they walked together to Greenland, a Lebanese grocery store on Warren Avenue that sold imported goods. As they scooped up olives and pickled turnips from the olive counter, Badria told Lulu that when she first arrived in Dearborn, there were very few Arab-owned stores and restaurants. But when more Lebanese started moving into East Dearborn, they quickly turned half the city Arab, driving out the whites.

"Dearborn isn't Lebanon," Badria said, "but it has shades of home."

After cooking in the morning and cleaning the house in the afternoon, Badria had the rest of the day to herself before Maarouf arrived from work. She often used this time to watch soap operas or visit her neighbors, but now that Lulu was next door, she preferred to spend her time with the young woman. She wasn't sure if Lulu cared to spend as much time with her, but when she suggested they visit a neighbor together, Lulu readily agreed.

On their walk back home after a visit, Lulu locked arms with Badria. Badria's own daughter had never locked arms with her, and for the few blocks that they walked arm in arm down the sidewalk, the leaves shivering in the wind, Badria savored every step.

◆

IN EARLY OCTOBER, Badria began decorating her house for Halloween, her favorite day of the year. She hung cloth ghosts and plastic bats with red eyes from the branches of the tree in her front yard, stretched faux spiderwebs over the bushes, placed carved pumpkins on the steps leading up to her front porch, and on the porch itself, she installed a hijabi mannequin on a rocking chair, with red paint for blood dripping down from her plastic chin. She had purchased the mannequin from a clothing store that was going out of business for this very purpose. "Halloween is for kids, not grown Muslim women," Maarouf had once told her, but she ignored him. In years past she had dressed up as a witch, a female pirate, a firefighter, and a modest Scheherazade with Dracula fangs. As she dished out candy to the trick-or-treaters, she never broke from her character.

"I wish you could always be this defiant when it comes to Baba," her son had told her.

It was the magic of Halloween that gave her courage, the act of transforming into someone else and living in that person's shoes until November came calling.

That year, Badria taught Lulu how to carve a pumpkin and helped her decorate her front porch with spiderwebs. This would be Lulu's first Halloween.

"We need to figure out a costume for you," Badria said.

"A Las Vegas singer. What will you be?"

"Still thinking on it."

In the late afternoon on Halloween, Badria donned her costume. She could hardly wait for the trick-or-treaters. Once Maarouf returned home, she planned to take Lulu out for a stroll to admire the haunted houses.

The wizards, princesses, monsters, vampires, and fairies arrived at sunset. They were stunned by Badria's outfit.

"You're sparkling, Khalto," one girl said.

"Are you a famous singer?" a boy asked her.

She made eye contact with Lulu, who stood on her own porch.

"You look incredible!" Lulu said.

Badria made a three-hundred-and-sixty-degree turn. She was dressed in a gold-colored hijab, a gold-sequined, long-sleeved dress, and red heels. Her face was plastered with makeup. She held a microphone in one hand and a plastic pumpkin filled with candy in the other.

"We're the Vegas sisters!" she said and blew Lulu a kiss.

Darkness fell, and Adel's pickup appeared. Badria watched him as he slowly got out of his truck and walked up to the porch and opened the door. Lulu had gone inside earlier. Moments later, she heard Adel shouting.

"Trick or treat?!" a pair of girls asked Badria, as a parent waited patiently on the sidewalk. Badria's gaze was on her neighbor's house. "Trick or treat!" the girls repeated. Badria looked at them and dropped a handful of candy inside their bags. Maarouf wouldn't return for another couple of hours. She couldn't wait that long. She left the candy on the porch, went back inside to put on her coat, and walked out into the frigid night and up to her neighbor's front porch. She rang the doorbell. When no one answered, she knocked repeatedly on the door. Still no response. She returned to her house and dialed Lulu's number; no one picked up. She changed out of her outfit and cleaned the makeup off her face. She sat in the living room in silence, ignoring the trick-or-treaters. When Maarouf arrived, he was surprised not to see her in costume.

"I'm not feeling well," she said, and trudged upstairs to her bedroom.

♦

THE FOLLOWING MORNING, Badria went over to Lulu's to check on her. There were no bruises or swelling on her face. Before they sat down, Badria gripped Lulu's wrists and slid her hands up and down her arms.

"What are you doing, Khalto?" Lulu asked, pulling her arms free.

Badria heard the irritation in Lulu's voice. "I'm sorry," she said. It was something her son had done when he was younger to check her for bruises, bruises she'd concealed beneath her long-sleeved dresses but revealed through flinches when Hisham touched her.

Lulu apologized for not accompanying Badria on her stroll the night before. "Adel was exhausted after work," she explained.

Not Adouli, Badria thought. "You can trust me, my daughter."

"Khalto, please sit down."

♦

A WEEK LATER, Lulu lay in bed with the flu. While Adel was at work, Badria fed her chicken noodle soup and brought her tea and water. As Lulu was asleep one afternoon, Badria went inside the master bathroom to inspect the tub. Adel used Head & Shoulders shampoo. She stepped into the tub and pressed her palms against the window, spreading her fingers, and stuck out her ass. She closed her eyes and felt Adel's strong hands squeezing her waist. He pressed his face against her nape, his stubble scratching her skin, his hot breath smelling of cigarettes.

"Adouli," she whispered. She snapped back when she heard Lulu turn in bed. She returned to the bedroom. Lulu said she hated the gray, melancholic weather.

"You'll get used to it," Badria said.

Lulu burst into tears. Badria embraced her, cradling her head and stroking her hair.

"I miss my sisters," Lulu said. "I miss them so much."

"You can visit them."

"Adouli says we need to save our money." She blew her nose into a wad of crumpled tissues.

"You'll bring your sisters to America," Badria said, "and you'll all live in the same city. Doesn't that sound wonderful?"

Lulu nodded.

♦

THAT NOVEMBER, BADRIA INVITED Adel and Lulu over to her house for Thanksgiving. As she did every year, Badria insisted on making a purely American holiday dinner, replete with roast turkey, stuffing, mashed potatoes, gravy, cranberry sauce, green beans, and buttered rolls, and for dessert, pecan and pumpkin pies. Both Hisham and Samira drove down from Ann Arbor to spend the night. On Thanksgiving morning, the neighborhood yards were blanketed with snow, iced-over tree branches glimmering in the sunlight.

Adel and Lulu came with a tray of semolina cake and a dish of yams that Lulu had baked herself. Lulu's nose and cheeks were flushed red from the cold.

"Come sit by the fire," Badria told her, and led her to the fireplace, where logs of pinewood were crackling in the flames.

Lulu was shy around Badria's children, who were both over a decade older than she was. Badria was annoyed that neither Hisham nor Samira made any effort to converse with Lulu. Samira was flipping through a magazine while Hisham watched, alongside Maarouf and Adel, the Detroit Lions pound the New England Patriots in the first matchup of Thanksgiving Day football games. Hisham wore a baseball cap to hide his thinning hair. He was mortified by his hair loss, Badria knew, not only because he thought it would hurt his chances with the ladies but also because he had started to look like his father.

"Adouli has tried to explain the NFL to me, but I still don't understand the rules," Lulu told Badria, putting her hands up to the flames. They spoke in low voices, as if exchanging classified information.

"Neither do I. But the important thing is to root for the Lions. They're our team."

"Your daughter looks like you, but more American. Maybe because she's not wearing a hijab. Do your children speak Arabic?"

"They understand Arabic but prefer to respond in English."

"They must think I'm a simpleton."

"Why would you say that?!"

"They're college educated."

"Well, maybe one day you can attend university."

"I'd like that, but," and here she whispered, "I think Adouli would prefer that I stay home to help raise a family."

Badria had also wanted to attend university, thinking she'd major in biology or chemistry because she had excelled in science in high school, but Maarouf had seen no point in her obtaining a university degree when he was the breadwinner.

"You're still young," Badria said. "Kids can wait."

At the dinner table, Lulu asked Hisham and Samira if they enjoyed living in Ann Arbor. They both said yes.

"How do you like Dearborn?" Samira asked her in English.

Smiling, Lulu shook her head. "My English . . . very bad."

Badria repeated the question in Arabic.

"Oh, very much!" Lulu said. "Go Lions!"

Hisham laughed.

"What's so funny?" Adel asked Hisham in English, his fork and knife hovering over his plate.

"Nothing."

"Then why'd you laugh at my wife?"

"Chill out, man."

"Apologize, Hisham," Maarouf told his son.

"Apologize for what?" Hisham said.

"What's going on?" Lulu asked in Arabic.

"Nothing, habibti," Badria said.

"Hisham, apologize," Maarouf said, his voice louder.

"I'm not a kid, Dad," Hisham said.

"Just apologize and get it over with," Samira told her brother.

Hisham stood up from the table, pushed back his chair, and left the room.

"Khalto," Lulu said, looking desperately at Badria, "did I say something wrong?"

"Eat your food," Adel snapped at her.

Lulu looked down at her plate. Badria stared at her, desperate to make eye contact. Tomorrow, she wanted to tell Lulu through her eyes, it would be just the two of them together again, without the hassle of family. Lulu and Badria, that's all that mattered.

◆

BADRIA AND LULU TOOK walks in the neighborhood together, bundled in their wool coats and scarves, admiring the houses decorated with Christmas lights. Other times, they met for coffee at each other's houses or visited the neighbors.

"You're like each other's shadow," a neighborhood woman told them. Badria was pleased that she could evoke such envy.

On Christmas, Badria watched from her window as Adel and Lulu drove off with plastic sleds in the truck bed. Later, she learned they had gone sledding at Ford Field Park.

After the New Year, Lulu fell ill again, but this time she told Badria over the phone that she could take care of herself.

"Nonsense," Badria said. "I'm coming over."

"Don't! Khalto, please. It's nothing serious. I just need to be left alone."

The urgency in Lulu's voice worried Badria. But the next time they met for a walk, Badria didn't notice anything out of the ordinary.

In March, Lulu was missing a front tooth.

"What happened?" Badria asked.

"I tripped over the stairs and fell on my face!"

Badria wasn't convinced. Lulu visited the dentist and was fitted for a false tooth.

"Adouli isn't happy at work," Lulu told Badria over coffee. "His cousin can be really bossy. Adouli's dream is to open a chain of sweetshops all over Dearborn and the suburbs. Guess what he plans to call his stores? 'Lulu's'! Isn't that sweet?"

Badria didn't respond.

"He's still figuring out the finances. It might take a few more years before he can make this move. He wants to avoid taking out a big loan from the bank because of the high interest rates. If his dream comes true—and I know it will; I have confidence in him—maybe I can help him run the business. I'd get to leave the house more often, though I'd miss our time together."

"May Allah grant you everything you desire," Badria said.

On the morning of September 11, almost a year since Lulu had arrived in America, Badria was rolling grape leaves in front of the TV when she saw the breaking news.

"Allah have mercy on us," she prayed, hoping that the hijackers weren't Arab, because if they were, then she and her fellow Arabs were about to pay a heavy price for the actions of a few.

♦

IN A MATTER OF days Badria saw American flags go up on most porches along her street. Maarouf hung up their flag and also purchased one for Lulu and Adel, and he put a bumper sticker on his car that read, "God Bless America and God Bless Our Troops."

Badria heard stories of white men assaulting and killing turbaned and brown-skinned men across the country in revenge for the attacks, in some cases mistaking Sikhs for Arabs. The problem with living in Dearborn was that everyone knew where the Arabs lived. It didn't matter if Badria had American citizenship or that her children were born and raised in the US and spoke with American accents. They weren't white.

As Badria and Lulu were walking home from Greenland one afternoon, grocery bags in hand, a Ford Taurus pulled up to the curb right next to them. The driver rolled down his window and yelled, "Go back to Arabia, you fucking sand niggers."

Badria immediately dropped her bags on the ground and bear-hugged Lulu, squeezing her tight. "I can't breathe," Lulu wheezed. Badria didn't release her until the car drove off.

"Khalto," Lulu said. "Did you think that man had a gun?"

"Yes."

Lulu began to weep.

"Why are you crying?"

"Because you were willing to sacrifice your life for me."

◆

IN THE EVENINGS, Badria and Maarouf watched CNN. Badria despised listening to all the so-called Middle East experts, none of whom were Arab, discuss America's strategy moving forward. She loathed how self-righteous they sounded, be they conservative or liberal. War was coming; she knew it. America needed to exact retribution, flex its muscles to the world.

One night, Badria noticed that Maarouf was watching the news distractedly. He had barely touched his dinner.

"Would you like some coffee?" she asked him.

He looked at her, his eyes downcast.

"Is something on your mind?"

He shook his head. But a moment later, he said, "The cigarettes I sell . . ."

Badria sat up. Maarouf picked up the remote and switched off the TV. She had never seen him look so worried.

"My suppliers have been driving down to North Carolina to buy large quantities of cigarettes. They bring the cartons back for me and others. The tax on cigarettes in the South is lower than Michigan's, so I'm able to pocket the difference."

"Is this legal?"

"Not exactly. But I've put all the extra money I've made into our savings. It's for you and our children. I haven't touched a penny."

"What would happen if you got caught?"

"I don't know," he said in a pained voice. "With the police and FBI keeping a closer eye on us these days, this cigarette business has gotten riskier."

"I couldn't bear to see you in prison, Maarouf." Badria was surprised at the emotion in her voice.

"I'll stop, I promise you," he said. "Can I have some coffee?"

She made a pot of coffee, which they drank at the kitchen table. Maarouf sat with slouched shoulders, his hands cupped around his mug. His vulnerability gave her confidence.

"You should shave off your mustache," she said, "to look less Arab. I don't want some ignorant fool to hurt you."

She hadn't mentioned her and Lulu's encounter with the Ford driver, fearing Maarouf would restrict her movements if he thought her safety was at risk. He slurped the remainder of his coffee and went upstairs, returning twenty minutes later clean-shaven, his lip bare for the first time in all the years they had been married. He looked younger.

"Better?" he asked.

"You look handsome either way," she said, knowing that was what he needed to hear.

◆

STORIES OF FBI AGENTS kicking in doors and whisking away Arab men from the comfort of their homes spread across Dearborn. The agents came at all hours. Husbands, fathers, sons, and brothers were thrown into black holes, their loved ones unable to contact them.

Maarouf came home one evening demoralized. His good friend Naguib, he told Badria, had been arrested.

"They say he was donating money to Hezbollah," he explained.

"That's not a crime."

"To the FBI it is."

"Maarouf," Badria said, "have you ever—"

"I've only donated to Muslim charities."

◆

LULU WAS AFRAID THE government would revoke her green card.

"They can't," Badria said. "Your husband is American."

"I need the American citizenship, Khalto. I can't bring my sisters here without it."

"Do you think your sisters would be happy in America?"

As she asked the question, Badria thought to herself that she wished she had never left Tyre. She was ashamed of the implications of this thought: without Maarouf, neither Hisham nor Samira would exist. What kind of mother was she?

"They're not happy where they are," Lulu said. "My uncle's the problem. Bless him, he's helped support my mother and sisters, but he can be very cruel. And there's little money to spare. Allah forbid my sisters get sick, because my uncle won't be able to afford the medical bills."

"Can you send money home?"

Lulu's lips quivered. "That's not possible."

Badria understood. Adel wouldn't allow it. But it would take years before Lulu would be able to sponsor her sisters, assuming America would let them in.

◆

THE WEATHER TURNED COLD and gray. Fallen leaves scuttled down the pavement in gusts of wind. One morning, Badria answered a knock on her door to find a white man in a trench coat, his brown hair swept to the side. He had a dimpled chin.

"Mrs. *Baa*dria S*aa*dik?" he asked. Her name sounded awful in his mouth. But how did he even know it? He flashed his FBI badge and introduced himself as Agent Brandon Stork. It was about Maarouf. It must be about Maarouf and his cigarette supply.

"May I speak to you for a few minutes?" he asked.

Badria showed him into the living room.

"I hear that you've been living in Dearborn since the sixties," he said.

She nodded, still too nervous to speak.

"You must know a lot of Dearbornites, huh?"

"That's correct," she mumbled.

"Well, the reason I'm asking is because I need your help. I can tell you're a patriotic American. I saw the flag out front."

"God bless this country," she said. "And God bless our troops," she quickly added.

"Our troops are the finest. I need your help, Mrs. Saadik. There are a few bad apples in Dearborn. My job is to pick them out to protect peaceful Americans such as yourself. Do you know of any bad apples? Can you give me names of people who want to inflict harm on you and other Americans?"

So this had nothing to do with Maarouf. "I only know good Americans."

"I'm sure you do. But have you heard anything suspicious recently? Any folks sending a lot of money back to the Middle East? I really need your help to keep our country safe."

"I have nothing to report, Mr. Stork."

He removed his wallet and pulled out his card. "Will you call me if you hear anything?"

"Certainly."

As soon as the agent left, Lulu came over to ask about him. Badria told her.

"May Allah protect us!" Lulu said.

Badria's telephone rang. It was her neighbor across the street asking about the white man. The telephone continued to ring.

◆

TWO DAYS LATER, Lulu was ill.

"Your voice, it sounds muffled," Badria said over the phone.

Lulu began to sob. Badria hung up the phone and left her house without a coat, nearly slipping on the icy pavement in her rush to get over to Lulu's. She pounded on the door, forcing Lulu to crack it open.

"Khalto, this isn't a good time."

Shivering, Badria barged her way in. She looked at Lulu and gasped. Lulu's left eye was swollen shut and blackish purple, her lower lip plump as a slug.

"Where else did he hit you?" Badria asked.

Lulu shook her head. Badria gripped her wrists and then slid her hands upward. Lulu screeched.

"What's the matter with you?!" she said. Lulu was about to cry again.

"Let's take care of your eye."

Badria removed a bag of frozen peas from the freezer and pressed it against Lulu's face.

"It's my fault," Lulu said. "I kept asking him to give me money to send to my sisters."

"This isn't the first time he's hit you."

"He's stressed. After 9/11, we're all frightened and anxious."

"Don't make excuses for him."

Lulu checked the time on the oven clock. "I need to prepare dinner."

"I'll do it. Just rest."

Badria cooked a quick meal as Lulu slept on the couch, and then returned to her house. She called for a taxi and gave the address of Adel's sweetshop. At the shop, she stood outside the storefront window, watching Adel talk to a customer at the counter. If she confronted him, she'd make matters worse between Lulu and him. He might beat her again. Badria hated how she still found him attractive. Furious, she walked down the street and kept walking until she came across an Arabic café. She went inside, sat at a table, and ordered a Turkish coffee. The first time Maarouf had struck her she had been pregnant with Hisham. A backhand slap to her face. She'd tasted blood. The shock of it had reminded her of the time her sister had thrown a soccer ball at her face and it hit her square in the nose, stinging her eyes. When her kids were older, they'd howl with terror when he hit her. What horrified Badria most wasn't the rage inside Maarouf, but her children's fear of him. More than once, Hisham and Samira had begged her to leave him.

"We don't need him in our lives," Hisham said.

"We can support you," Samira said.

But Badria refused to leave her husband. A divorced woman was a disgraced woman. And despite his violence, Maarouf had taken care of them. He had paid for Hisham's and Samira's educations.

Badria finished her coffee, went up to the register, and asked to use their phone to call a taxi to take her back home. She still had to prepare dinner for Maarouf. As she was leaving the café, she noticed Agent Stork sitting at a corner table, typing on his laptop. She had been so lost in thought that she hadn't noticed him sitting there. She left before he spotted her.

That week, Badria spent most afternoons at Lulu's. Lulu refused to step outside until the swelling in her face had lessened. One day, Badria followed Lulu down to the basement so that Lulu could show her something on the desktop computer. As they sat next to each other, Lulu typed *Bellagio Hotel and Casino* into her search engine. A picture of the hotel at dusk came up, the majestic water fountain lit up by spotlights.

"This is the most famous casino and hotel in Las Vegas," Lulu said.

She typed in the names of other casinos. "The Colosseum at Caesars Palace puts on the best musical shows."

They saw pictures of the Strip, Madame Tussaud's, the Luxor Hotel, the Stratosphere Tower, and Vegas's Eiffel Tower.

"You can also take a helicopter ride over the Grand Canyon," Lulu said.

Badria knew Adel was never going to take Lulu to Las Vegas.

"Oh, and there's the Cirque du Soleil!" Lulu said.

The poor girl's black eye had changed color to yellowish green.

♦

ADEL WAS TAKING LULU to Port Huron over Thanksgiving. Lulu flashed Badria a silver bracelet dangling from her wrist.

"Adouli bought it for me," she said, smiling.

"It's lovely," Badria forced herself to say.

Lulu gave Badria a spare key to her house in case of an emergency. She returned from her vacation glowing.

"Lake Huron reminds me of the Mediterranean," she said. "And guess what? Adouli wants to visit Las Vegas! His cousin gave him a raise, so he thinks we can afford the trip."

Badria didn't want to ruin her mood. "What's the first thing you'll do in Vegas?"

"Walk on the Strip. And then ride on a gondola. I just can't wait!"

Weeks later, Lulu visited Badria to give her the good news. She was pregnant.

"I'm going to be a mother!" Lulu said.

"Mabrouk," Badria said out of instinct. She couldn't bring herself to congratulate Lulu further. "How do you know for certain? Have you gone to the doctor's?"

"I did the test. Twice."

"Are you sure you're ready to have a baby?"

"Do you doubt me, Khalto?"

"Of course not. But this can wait. You're still young."

"I'm having a baby. There's no turning back."

"It's still not a child," Badria said. "It doesn't even have a soul yet."

"What are you suggesting, Khalto?"

"Nothing. I'm so happy for you."

♦

BY SPRING, THE FBI had arrested hundreds of Dearborn men. The local field office had received countless tips from Arabs informing on one another. All it took was a call to the FBI for the agents to swarm a house.

"I hear Khaloud reported on Tala's husband," one neighbor told Badria over the phone.

"Tala's husband, Bahaa? Who owns the travel agency on Michigan Avenue?"

"That's the one."

"What did she accuse him of?"

"Said she overheard Bahaa at a charity event boasting that he donated money to Al-Qaeda."

"That's ridiculous. Even if Bahaa was guilty, he wouldn't be stupid enough to mention such a thing at a charity event."

"You don't have to convince me, ya ikhti. I hear Bahaa was threatening to sue Khaloud over a dispute concerning land back home in Lebanon, and she wanted to get him off her back."

"Khaloud's a cow. She once criticized me for not forcing Samira to wear the hijab. I told her to mind her own business."

"Let's report her to the FBI."

They laughed.

◆

ON A CHILLY NIGHT in April, Badria and Maarouf were watching the news when they heard pounding on their front door. Badria immediately exchanged glances with Maarouf. Had someone reported him to the FBI?

"Stay here," he said, and stood up to answer the door.

"Allah have mercy!" Badria heard him cry out. She rushed to the foyer and saw Lulu shivering outside, naked, her arms crossed over her breasts.

"Quick, come in," Maarouf said, his eyes cast to the floor to avoid looking at her.

Badria pulled her winter coat from the closet to cover Lulu. Lulu's eyes were pink and puffy. Her left cheek burned red. Badria sat her down on the couch.

"Maarouf, bring me a blanket," Badria said.

Maarouf left the women alone and returned with a wool blanket, which Badria laid over Lulu's legs.

There was pounding on the door.

"Don't let him in!" Lulu said.

"Ya Istaz Maarouf?" Adel said from behind the door. "Khalto Badria? Let me inside. I want to see my wife."

"Tell him to go away!" Badria told Maarouf.

Maarouf walked to the door. "Go back to your home, my son. We'll take care of Lulu."

"She's my wife! I want to see her. This is a family matter."

Maarouf turned to Badria and Lulu. "What do you want to do, Lulu?"

"We should call the police," Badria said.

"No," Lulu said. "I don't trust them."

"Let me talk to Adel and calm him down," Maarouf said. "I'll take him out for a drive."

When Lulu didn't respond, Maarouf put on his coat and left the house.

"What exactly did he do to you?" Badria asked Lulu.

She shook her head.

"Tell me," Badria said. "I'm your mother."

"I don't want to talk about it, ya Khalto."

"Whatever he did to you, he's going to do it again. What then?"

Lulu looked down at her hands.

"What then, Lulu?"

"I don't know."

By the time Maarouf returned, Lulu was asleep in their guest room.

"He'd been drinking," Maarouf told Badria.

Lulu had never mentioned his drinking. Was he a casual drinker or an alcoholic? Badria tried to think back—she would have remembered seeing alcohol in their kitchen. "He beat up a pregnant woman," she said. "Shame on him."

"He promised it won't ever happen again," Maarouf said.

Badria looked at her husband with a lifetime of spite. "And you believe him, Maarouf?"

"Don't use that tone with me."

"You're just like him!"

Maarouf slapped her. She reached up to her face, feeling the sting. Her eyes watered. Maarouf looked down at his open palm, confused, as if his hand had acted on its own. He turned around and walked upstairs.

Badria remained downstairs for the remainder of the night. In the morning, Lulu returned to her house.

♦

IF BADRIA DIDN'T TAKE matters into her own hands, sooner or later Adel would beat Lulu to death. She preferred to see Lulu as a single mother. As she sipped coffee at the kitchen table, she devised a plan, one with many careful steps to ensure that Adel would be gone for a long time. The first step was to contact Hisham. She called him at work.

"Is anything wrong?" he immediately asked.

"Promise me you'll keep this between us."

"You're worrying me."

"I need to borrow money," she said. "In cash. I can't withdraw from my account or else your father will find out. I'll explain everything later."

Once Hisham delivered the cash to her, Badria took a taxi to Naguib's gas station, the same Naguib who had been arrested by the FBI for funneling money to Hezbollah. No one had heard from him or seen him since his arrest. She entered the convenience mart and saw a young Arab man behind the register.

"Salam wa alaykum," she said.

"Wa alaykum salam."

"My son, my name is Badria Sadek. I've been living in Dearborn for longer than you've been alive."

"I recognize you, Khalto. I went to high school with Samira." Badria studied his face. "Remind me of your name."

"Jamil Ghamlouche."

"Jamil?! Roula's son? Is that really you?"

"I've been on the Atkins diet," he explained.

A customer came in to pay for his gas, and Badria stepped aside from the register. As soon as the customer left, Badria returned to her spot.

"Jamil, habibi," she said. "I have a strange favor to ask you."

"How can I help you, Khalto?"

"I need information on Naguib's cigarette supplier."

Jamil's face crimsoned.

"There's nothing to worry about," she said. "I'm not working for anyone but myself."

"Khalto, the FBI already interrogated me. I don't want any trouble."

Badria removed an envelope from her purse and placed it on the counter. "Open it," she said. Jamil opened the envelope, his eyes widening at the bills inside.

"I just need a name and telephone number," Badria said.

◆

IT TOOK SEVERAL TELEPHONE calls and a fair amount of coordination, but Badria was able to procure two thousand dollars' worth of cigarette cartons from North Carolina and have them delivered to her house while Maarouf was at work. She kept the cartons concealed in storage boxes in the basement.

Over dinner one evening, she suggested that Maarouf encourage Adel to take Lulu out for a weekend trip to Port Huron.

"Lulu loves that place," Badria said, "and I think it would be healthy for her and Adel to leave town and repair things between them, especially before Lulu gives birth."

"I'll talk to him," Maarouf said.

In late June, before Lulu and Adel left for Port Huron for the weekend, Lulu was about to give Badria her spare key when Badria reminded her that she still had it.

"Have fun on the lake," Badria said. "Soon all will be better."

Lulu was having a baby girl.

That night, Badria anxiously waited for Maarouf to fall asleep. In the early hours of the morning, she tiptoed out of her bedroom and put on her shoes. Still in her nightgown, her hair loose and reaching down her back, she went downstairs to the basement, picked up a box of cigarette cartons, and went back up and exited the house from the backdoor, making sure the screen door didn't slam shut behind her. Moonlight silvered the branches of the fir tree in her backyard. A firefly flickered in the air like a sputtering candle. All was calm and quiet. She quickly crossed into Adel's backyard and went to his side door. She placed the box on the ground, opened the screen door, fit the key into the lock, and turned the knob. Keeping the screen door propped open with her body, she reached down and picked up the box. Without turning on any lights, she made her way to the kitchen, found the door to the basement, switched on the light in the stairwell, and descended. She placed the box on the floor and then switched on the main light. The basement was unfinished, just as she'd remembered it, with the wooden beams of the ceiling exposed. She walked around, searching for a spot where the boxes could rest unnoticed. There were stacks of old boxes in a dank corner. She'd hide the cigarettes there. All she had to do now was bring the remaining boxes from her basement.

When Badria was finally done, she stood in Adel's basement with her hands on her hips, sweating. Up to this point, she had executed everything perfectly. She was proud of herself.

♦

ON SATURDAY MORNING OF the following week, after Lulu and Adel had returned from Port Huron, Maarouf left for the convenience store to work a half day. Badria pulled out Agent Stork's card from her purse and called him. His ringtone went to voice mail. "I have important information to share," she said, and left him her house number. He called an hour later.

"Thanks for getting back to me, Mrs. *Baa*dria S*aa*dik."

He'd always butcher her name, but no matter. "I have reason to believe my neighbor is a terrorist," she said.

"What makes you say that, Mrs. S*aa*dik?"

"He's been selling cigarettes from North Carolina," she explained, trying to keep her voice measured and composed. "He sends the extra money he makes to Hezbollah. His wife is too afraid to report him because . . . because he beats her. But she's told me where her husband hides the cigarettes."

There was a long pause. Had she not sold the story well?

"What's your neighbor's address?" Agent Stork asked.

♦

THE NEXT DAY, BADRIA saw from her front window two sedans and a white van pull up at Lulu's house. Agents in blue windbreakers stepped out of the cars. Agent Stork knocked on Lulu's front door. A moment later, he flashed his badge and entered the house.

Badria's telephone rang and continued to ring as if it were possessed. It was the neighbors calling. Badria ignored them.

Agents started coming out of Lulu's house carrying boxes, which they loaded into the van. The van drove off. Agent Stork's car and the sedans remained at the house for a while. When the agents finally left, Lulu rushed over to Badria's.

"You won't believe what's happening," she said in tears. Her stomach was the size of a cantaloupe. "The FBI went to Adouli's shop earlier this morning and arrested him!"

The next step in Badria's plan was to calm Lulu down. They sat in the parlor.

"He has nothing to do with what they're accusing him of!" Lulu said.

"You need to cooperate with the FBI."

"I told them everything I know."

"Maybe Adel isn't the man you thought you knew."

"How's that possible?"

"You've known him for less than two years."

"He's my husband and the father of my child! I have to protect him and hire a lawyer."

"He might be a terrorist."

"He's not a terrorist!"

"You don't know that," Badria said. "Let me make you tea. It'll relax you."

"I don't want tea. I need him, Khalto."

"You have me."

Lulu stared at Badria. "Did you have something to do with this?"

"With what?" she stammered.

"With Adel getting arrested?"

"How dare you accuse me of such a thing?!"

"Tell me the truth."

"I took care of Adel before you even knew him. Why would I harm him?"

"Swear to Allah."

"I swear. I swear on my children."

Lulu shook her head.

"You need to control yourself," Badria said. "All this tension isn't good for the baby. Are you hungry? I'm making roast and potatoes for lunch. We can sit in the kitchen, and you can watch me cook."

"I can't think of food right now!"

"But you need to eat or else you'll start to feel faint."

Lulu took big, deep breaths, and then stood up. "My key," she said, extending her hand.

"Excuse me?"

"My spare key. I want it back."

"Sit down, Lulu. You're not thinking straight."

"Give me back my key. Now."

"What have I done to deserve this? I love you like my own daughter."

"You're not my mother!" Lulu yelled. "You're my *neighbor*."

Badria retrieved the key from the foyer table and gave it to her. Lulu left without another word. Badria sat down on the couch, her hands trembling. There remained one final step in her plan to execute: give Lulu an envelope of money.

"Buy yourself a ticket to Las Vegas," she wanted to tell Lulu. "See a show at Caesars Palace, ride a gondola, dine at Bellagio's. Go gambling; don't worry, Allah won't punish you. He loves you. Just go! Walk on the Strip, feel the desert sun on your face. If you like the city, you might even decide to stay there. Give it a chance. Live it up, as the Americans like to say. Because if you stay here, you'll end up like me."

Zizou's Voice

Zizou never thought he'd make a living off his voice or return to reading the Qur'an, but both things happened after he was fired from his job in the winter of 2003. He had been a night watchman at an assisted living facility on Ford Road in Dearborn. The night hours had attracted him to the position; during his shift most residents were asleep, giving him the quiet and peace of mind to write his fantasy novel, THE LANDS OF SARA-BIA, at the front desk. Aside from his rounds of the hallways of each floor and the occasional glance at the CCTV monitors to make sure a resident hadn't left their room, he wrote his story on a legal pad, his inky scrawl wide across the page, to the distant whoosh of cars and trucks on the freeway. Once he finished a chapter, he would type it up at home on his desktop computer.

The novel was set in an Arab fantasy world. There were no dragons or bearded wizards, no elves or slobbering goblins. Instead of Arthurian swords there were scimitars inscribed with Arabic calligraphy; instead of blond maidens there were raven-haired princesses. And there were plenty of jinns, perhaps too many. Ten years after starting the book during his senior year of university, he wasn't anywhere near the end. The novel kept growing and spiraling in labyrinthine directions, leaving Zizou distressed and anguished. The more he worked on it the more he believed he had wasted his time, that he was a failed writer, a failed human. Even his breath, he thought, stank of defeat.

One night, frustrated by his writing, Zizou put on his coat and left the front desk and stepped outside into the frigid cold to clear his mind. He walked down the gravel driveway to Ford Road, where he stood on the curb of the sidewalk, dangerously close to leaning into the freeway. When a pickup came speeding down the road, he was tempted to step in front of it. *Stop being dramatic*, he chastised himself. Or was drama the natural inclination of an artist? But was he an artist? He was thirty-two years old with one publication to his name: a fantastical story that had appeared in his university's student literary journal about the misadventures of Abdelrahman Abu Fawaz, a melancholic Phoenician sailor who suffered from incurable insomnia.

Zizou was stuck at a pivotal moment in his novel where the main characters, who hailed from distant lands in his imagined world of Sarabia, were about to cross paths. Only Zizou didn't know how to pull this all off. He stood back from the curb and paced up and down the sidewalk, his head bent, hands deep in his coat pockets. The icy wind lashed at him; his eyes watered. Not for the first time did he contemplate whether he should give up the pen. He couldn't rely anymore on the excuse of being young and exploring different career paths. According to his parents, at his age he was supposed to be married with children, own a decent-sized house with a finished basement, and drive a good car. Zizou was single, lived in a studio that overlooked Mahmoud and Son, a car wash, and drove a 1992 Chevrolet Corsica with a dented bumper. Zizou's younger brother, Fareed, was a real estate agent—one of the big sharks, Fareed often boasted— whose smiling face adorned a billboard on Ford Road. Every evening on his way to work, Zizou saw Fareed's slicked-back black hair and bright white teeth, lit up by spotlights.

"When will I get to see your face on a billboard?" his mother often asked him.

In Dearborn, the successful Arabs advertised their businesses on billboards all around town. Zizou imagined seeing his portrait on the back flap of his book. He didn't have Fareed's good looks or physique—Fareed wore tight-fitting suits to show off his muscles—and his hairline had started to recede. But what Zizou did have was an arresting, sonorous voice—a movie preview voice, his high school classmates used to say. When meeting people for the first time, he caught the confusion on their faces, their surprise that a man as unassuming as he was could possess such a voice. Yet Zizou never knew what to do with it. He was a terrible singer and wasn't that much of a talker. He believed his true voice existed on the page. That's where he spoke his mind and opened his heart.

"Listen, Zaher," his father once told him. "I didn't kill myself at the steel mill to send you to university to become a security guard!" His father called him by his real name when disappointed in him. It had been years since his father had uttered "Zizou."

"I'm a writer," Zizou told his parents.

"Writing is like bowling," his father said. "A hobby."

"Don't misunderstand us, habibi," his mother said. "We loved your story about the Phoenician sailor, but you've got to think about your future."

When Zizou finally returned to the facility, he heard someone screaming from the stairwell. He ran to the stairs, where he found Mr. McRoberts, an eighty-four-year-old, splayed on the second-floor landing with his leg sticking out like a bent straw. Zizou was dismissed that morning for negligence.

"You better hope we don't get sued," his supervisor said. "What the fuck were you thinking, Z? Mr. McRoberts will probably walk with a limp for the rest of his life thanks to you."

Zizou apologized profusely and returned to his studio in East Dearborn. He made a pot of coffee and a bowl of cereal and sat at the dinner table, but he couldn't stomach a bite. All he could think about was the sight of Mr. McRoberts on the landing, writhing in pain. And the fact that he was now unemployed.

Later that night, feeling drowsy but unable to sleep, Zizou kept his window blinds closed. He was afraid a relative would see the light on and wonder why he wasn't at work. At times Zizou hated Dearborn, how small and provincial it felt; a city half filled with Arabs who shared his parents' notion of success. Zizou had traveled outside Michigan only once, the summer before university, when his family visited their village of Tebnine in southern Lebanon. As he'd walked down the main road lined with limestone houses and orchards, inhaling the scent of wildflowers and shrubbery, a spectacular world inspired by his surroundings had begun to take shape in his mind. He stayed up that night drawing a detailed map of Tebnine, and had burned the edges with a matchstick to make it look more authentic and ancient.

Now, an entire wall in Zizou's studio was covered with a large map of Sarabia, a tapestry of thick, cream-colored paper he had Scotch-taped together. The edges of this map were burned too. He had marked the seven kingdoms and colored in forests, mountains, deserts, a volcano, rivers, and seas. Not a day passed when he wouldn't stand before his map and lose himself in his creation. But now Zizou thought of ripping it all down.

◆

ZIZOU PERUSED JOB OPENINGS in the local paper. At university he had studied business because that's what his parents had insisted he major in. He'd graduated with average marks, knowing he wasn't a businessman. He was a writer, damn it!

Zizou knew he could find a menial job that would pay the bills and give him time to work on his novel, but was his novel worth continuing? Was his suffering worth it? He only felt purpose in his life when he was writing, not that he ever thought his writing could change the world. When his writing was going well, when he was in a hallucinatory trance and the words kept coming, he saw himself giving readings at bookstores before packed audiences, taking TV and radio interviews, and accepting a slew of literary awards. And even when his writing was going poorly, souring his mood, he understood this was part of the process and that he'd have to write his way through crushing self-doubt. If he eliminated writing from his life, he feared he'd lose his soul.

Zizou had enough savings to last him a few months without work, and as time passed, that money became his lifeline. He stayed home, in a sweat suit, unable to write, barely eating, watching TV. He stopped bothering to shave and showered only occasionally. He didn't leave except to buy groceries, and at night he kept the window blinds closed. His mother called one afternoon.

"How's the book going?" she asked.

Zizou felt a stab to his heart. He was filled with shame. "It's going."

"Ya Allah, when will you give me a different answer? When will I see your gorgeous face on a billboard?"

"I have to sleep before my shift. Bye."

If his parents discovered that he'd been fired, he knew they'd lose what little faith left they had in him. Fareed would call him a fuckup.

Weeks later, in the early hours of the morning and with only the glare of the TV for light, Zizou was about to fall asleep on his futon couch when a commercial came on advertising an audio version of the King James Bible read by James Earl Jones. "Do not be anxious about anything, but in every situation, by prayer and petition, with thanksgiving, present your requests to God," James Earl Jones said in his deep and resonant voice. Zizou sat up, his eyes focused on the screen. He associated the actor's voice with Darth Vader from *Star Wars*, but now, listening to him perform the Bible, he thought James Earl Jones was speaking directly to him, trying to ease his worries. Not since being forced to attend Qur'an classes every Saturday morning at the mosque as a boy had Zizou prayed. Islam had been a part of his parents' and brother's lives, not his own. His religion was fantasy literature, his prophet J. R. R. Tolkien. But a magnetic aura was in the air. Something important, he believed, was about to happen to him.

Zizou ordered the digitally remastered Bible read by James Earl Jones. Once it arrived in the mail, he spent the next nineteen hours and fifteen minutes listening to it on his CD player, barely moving from his couch, mesmerized by the voice speaking to him, soothing him, as inspiring soundtrack music played in the background. Once the fourteenth and final CD ended, Zizou looked up at the ceiling. He didn't see God but rather the glimmer of an idea: What if he performed the Qur'an in English? He had only heard Arabic recitations of the holy book and thought there might be a market for an audio version in English. It would be an easy way to make money and would provide more time to contemplate his next move. He could finally put his voice to good use. All he needed was a music producer, and that's when he thought of Hussein Jaber.

Zizou would bump into Hussein once or twice a year at a grocery store, a hookah café, or a restaurant. They had been in the same class at Fordson High, where Hussein had been a pothead with dreadlocks. From the rumors Zizou had heard around town, Hussein had later turned to heroin. Apparently, Islam had saved him, and he now managed his parents' laundromat and had a record label on the side.

In the morning, Zizou showered and shaved and then drove to Jaber's Epic Laundromat on Schaefer Road to see Hussein. There was nothing epic about the laundromat. A row of dryers on one side and a row of washing machines on the other, a few carts, and some tables to fold clothes on. A man with a potbelly was stuffing bedsheets into a washing machine. The front desk was off to the side, in an area for dry cleaning. That's where Zizou found Hussein, reading the Qur'an. Hussein was so absorbed in the book that he hadn't noticed Zizou. Zizou rang the call bell. Hussein flinched, dropping the book on the counter. He wore a white skullcap over a shaved head and a matching white thobe. His Abraham Lincoln beard was reddish black.

"Salams, cuz!" Hussein said. He stood up from his chair and hugged Zizou. "How you been?"

"I'm good. How about you? You look different."

"I ain't no druggie no more, that for sure. And I've got a new name. Haj Huss. That's right, cuz. I got hajjed. Went to Mecca and walked around the Kaaba seven times like I was on repeat. Best thing I ever done do, that for sure."

Even in high school, Hussein, or Haj Huss, had talked this way. Zizou wasn't quite sure why.

"Got clothes to drop off?" Haj Huss asked.

"Actually, I wanted to see if you're still producing albums."

Haj Huss sat back down, deflated. "You just pierced my happy bubble, cuz. Halal Records is as dead as my grandparents, Allah yerhamon."

"What happened?"

"What happened is that America ain't ready for Muslim hip-hop. I sent demos of a boy band I created called the Muhammadans to Sony and a bunch of other labels, but they ignored me like I was the devil coming after their kids. Maybe they hate Muslims and want nothing to do with us after what happened."

Zizou had never experienced any discrimination or racism for being Arab or Muslim, but perhaps that was because he had lived his entire life in Dearborn. He feared what lay beyond the city's borders. "So, you're not producing anymore?"

"I'm just running this place, cuz. But I still got my sound booth in the basement of my parents' crib."

Zizou perked up. "You can still record music?"

"You interested in reviving the Muhammadans? I mean, you do have a powerful voice—I always done tell you that. But I don't remember you singing."

"I don't want to sing. I want to recite the entire Qur'an in English."

"Say what now?"

"Listen."

◆

THAT NIGHT, ZIZOU MET Haj Huss at his parents' house, where they went down to the finished basement. A sound booth dominated half the area. After Zizou had explained his plan to Haj Huss at the laundromat, Haj Huss had praised Allah for sending Zizou to him.

"You're onto something, cuz!" Haj Huss had said. "Our audience will be Arab American and Muslim American. We about to make a motherfudging tsunami splash." Having given up cursing, he'd explained to Zizou, Haj Huss now filled his former potty mouth with entirely halal vocabulary.

Zizou hadn't mentioned his dismissal from the assisted living facility or his failed novel. He was interested in pursuing a new career, he'd said.

They stepped inside the booth. A stool stood by a microphone with a pop filter on a shock mount. In the back was a music synthesizer.

"How about you recite a sura," Haj Huss suggested.

Zizou took a deep breath and recited the Al-Fatiha in English, enunciating every word with purpose.

"Dang, cuz, you sound like a prophet preaching from a mountaintop. But get rid of your American accent. Pretend you an immigrant who's been here for years."

Zizou did as instructed.

"Holy fudge!" Haj Huss said. "You're a star!"

"I'm a failure."

"If anyone's a failure it's me. I was high off my buttocks all throughout high school and ended up failing out of community college. My parents kicked me out of the house. I was on the streets for a while and got into some shady-buttocks stuff. I finally went into rehab, and when I got out I started attending the mosque. My parents let me back in, Allah bless them. And then I launched Halal Records and failed at it. But I've got the laundromat to keep me going. I guess my mug won't ever be on a billboard, but I'm okay with that. Feel me?"

Zizou felt him. But he didn't want to keep failing. "When can we start recording?"

They held their first recording session the following night, after Haj Huss's shift at the laundromat. Zizou sat on the stool in the booth, a copy of the Qur'an in English propped open on a music stand in front of him. Haj Huss sat at a desk outside the booth with his laptop. After recording the opening suras, Zizou switched off the mic and stepped out of the booth with an idea.

"In the recording of the Bible I listened to," he said, "music was played in the background. What if we did the same?"

"That would be sacrilegious, cuz. It should only be the purity of Allah's words. Feel me?"

"Trust me, Hussein. Background music will enhance the recording."

"I got hajjed, cuz."

"Haj Huss, we need to attract folks in a variety of ways. Think of the Qur'an as a book of stories. We're acting out these stories. We can even have sound effects!"

It didn't take long to convince Haj Huss. When they performed the verse about the stoning of Lot's wife, Haj Huss played dramatic music on the synthesizer and howled like he was being stoned to death.

Between recordings, they went upstairs to the kitchen to eat late-night snacks. Haj Huss advised Zizou not to eat any food that would cause him gas or heartburn, and he made Zizou tea with honey to soothe his vocal cords. They spoke in low voices so as not to wake up Haj Huss's parents.

"One day I plan to move out of here," Haj Huss said.

"There's no shame in living with your parents. You're not married yet."

"You ever think about getting married, cuz?"

"I haven't met the right person."

Zizou had been so preoccupied with his novel during the past few years that he hadn't found the time to meet women. But he'd never had any luck with the ladies, not in high school or in university. He'd once had a fling with a white nurse at the assisted living facility that lasted a few months. When she visited his apartment and saw the map of Sarabia on the wall, she said, "What the hell's that?"

Zizou explained.

"You're a writer?" she asked.

"An aspiring one."

"Why didn't you ever mention this before?"

Zizou shrugged.

"Stop being a clam, Z. Show me your pearl!"

Zizou remained a clam.

When Zizou asked Haj Huss about his love life, Haj Huss said he was doomed.

"My past is like a stain that no dry cleaning can remove," he said.

"But you got hajjed."

"Don't matter. You know how Dearborn is. You fudge up, folks won't forget it."

A part of Zizou didn't want their recording nights to ever end, because every time he sat before the mic, he saw himself as a creator of words, even though they weren't his own. He spent his days aching for the night to come.

"Want to pray together?" Haj Huss once asked. "I got an extra rug for you."

Zizou shook his head.

"You atheist?"

"I don't know what I am."

When they finally completed their recording, Haj Huss began editing their work, adding new sound effects and background music where he deemed appropriate. It took him a number of weeks, during which he insisted on working alone, and Zizou found he could hardly stand the anticipation. When they finally listened to the entire album, a total of eight CDs, Zizou was surprised at how good it sounded.

"We about to turn Motown into Muhammedtown," Haj Huss said. "That's for dang sure."

♦

HAJ HUSS SUGGESTED THEY market their album to Sheikh Mahmoud Jaffar, the imam of the mosque he attended. Haj Huss thought Sheikh Jaffar might encourage his flock to listen.

"We got to dominate the local before we hit up the labels," Haj Huss said. "Build ourselves a following."

Zizou met Haj Huss at the laundromat on a Friday afternoon and the two walked a few blocks down to the mosque, salt crunching beneath their winter boots, the sky wool gray. Haj Huss carried the demo. Wind rattled the icy limbs of leafless trees. Snow flurries swirled in the air like maddened flies. In THE LANDS OF SARABIA, one of the kingdoms was located on a mountaintop thick with pine trees. In winter it snowed so hard that the kingdom hibernated until spring. The sultan and his sultana remained in their bedchambers, snacking on salted meats and dried fruit and smoking pipes of purple daisies, Zizou's substitute for opium.

"We got to pray with the congregants before we ask Sheikh Jaffar for any favors," Haj Huss said. "You okay with that?"

"Sure," Zizou said, lost in wintry Sarabia.

At the mosque, Zizou hung up his coat on a rack in the foyer and then slipped off his boots and placed them in the shoe cubby. He followed Haj Huss to the wudu room to wash his face, hands, and feet. It had been years since he'd performed wudu, but the routine came back to him as if he had never stopped praying. They continued to the prayer room and sat down on the rug among the men at the front. Hijabi women sat in the back. Propped in the corner was a TV camera.

"What's the camera for?" Zizou asked.

"Shoot, with FBI informants crawling around and suspecting we be spewing terrorist speech in the mosques, Sheikh Jaffar records all his sermons. You know, to protect his back." Haj Huss's face suddenly paled. "Oh no. Oh heck nah."

"What is it?"

Haj Huss looked directly into Zizou's eyes. "You undercover? Cause if you is, you'll send me into some serious heartbreaker pain."

Zizou shook his head. "I'm a failed novelist."

"Say what now?"

Sheikh Jaffar walked into the room to begin the service. He was a tall, thin man with a gray beard. A young man turned on the TV camera and returned to the front of the room. Everyone stood up, shoulder to shoulder. Zizou performed the steps, reciting suras mindlessly as he knelt and put his head on the floor, smelling the body odor of the man in front of him.

After the service, Haj Huss and Zizou approached Sheikh Jaffer, who sat with his back against the wall. Haj Huss introduced Zizou and then described their album. Intrigued, Sheikh Jaffer invited them to his office so that he could listen to the demo on his CD player. At first, the sheikh was noticeably impressed by Zizou's voice—"Mashallah, mashallah," he repeated—but as soon as the background music came on, he became horrified.

"Astaghfirullah!" he said. "The music is blasphemy! What's wrong with you, Hussein?"

"The soundtrack is necessary," Zizou answered. "It's what sells."

"Sells? That's all you're thinking about?"

"We spreading the word of Allah, cuz," Haj Huss said. "I mean Sheikh Jaffar."

Sheikh Jaffar took out the CD and returned it to Haj Huss. "Shame on you both!"

Outside the mosque, the cold hit Zizou and Haj Huss. The wind had settled down, but it was now snowing steadily. Zizou thought he wouldn't mind hibernating during the winter months like his fictional characters.

"We gonna have to hustle the streets with our demos," Haj Huss said. "You got time for that?"

"I've got nothing but time. Fuck the sheikh."

"Astaghfirullah! That's haram, cuz."

"I left the mosque because I got sick of the imams. I got tired of them saying Islam is the best religion in the world and that if we only pray five times a day, we'll get everything we want. I never believed any of it."

"I hear you, cuz. All religions think they the best."

"Then what makes you believe?"

"I'm trying to believe I'll never be the man I once was. Feel me?"

◆

IN THE WEEKS THAT followed, Zizou and Haj Huss put their money together to produce a first run of a hundred copies of their album, which they packaged in a box set titled *Zizou Reads the Qur'an in English*. On the cover of the green box was a picture of the Qur'an radiating light. They registered as a vendor at the Annual Muslim American Conference held over two days at the Marriot Hotel in Dearborn, where they'd get their own table to sell their album.

A month before the conference, Haj Huss encouraged Zizou to grow out his beard. "You wanna look more Muslim to attract more customers."

Zizou stopped shaving. A month later, his beard was thick.

"What's that mess on your face?" his mother asked him when he went over for dinner. His mother had made a pot of okra stew. Fareed sat across the table from him, wearing a suit with a silk handkerchief poking from his breast pocket.

"Change is good," Zizou said.

"You need a change of careers," Baba said.

"You can work with me, bro," Fareed said. "I'll teach you the ropes. Sold two houses this week and have an offer on a third. And I've got a new billboard going up on Southfield."

"Praise be to Allah!" Mama said, beaming at Fareed.

"I enjoy what I do," Zizou said.

"It's not a good time to have a beard," Mama said. "The FBI is hunting down men who look like you."

"Listen to your mother, Zaher," Baba said. "If you end up in a black hole, I won't know where to find you. You're already lost as it is."

Zizou kept his head down.

In playing the role of a devout Muslim, Zizou bought a white skullcap and a white thobe to wear at the conference. On the morning of the event, he wrapped prayer beads around his wrist and drove to Haj Huss's house to load boxes of their album into their cars. When Haj Huss saw Zizou in costume, he said: "Fudge yeah! That's what I'm talkin' about." They were dressed exactly alike.

They packed the boxes into the trunks and back seats of their run-down cars and drove to the hotel. Their table was at a prime spot outside the double doors to the main auditorium. They set up stacks of their box sets on the table, as well as a pile of Halal Records business cards. Haj Huss put the music stand and a stool at the side; he took out his Qur'an and placed it open on the stand. Zizou would read suras aloud throughout the day to attract customers.

The attendees had yet to arrive for the morning session, but the vendors were all set up. There were tables selling hijabs, long-sleeved dresses, religious books and children's books in Arabic, Islamic paintings, Islamic ornaments and talismans, Islamic greeting cards, prayer beads, homemade henna kits, boxed chocolate, baklava, dates from Saudi Arabia, and halal beef jerky. The female vendors all wore hijabs; most of the men were bearded.

Seated at the table, Zizou could hardly believe he was there, at the Annual Muslim American Conference, bearded and dressed in traditional clothing. He wondered when, or if, he'd ever return to his novel.

As soon as the attendees shuffled into the area, lanyards hanging from their necks and folders in their hands, the vendors tried to lure them to their tables.

"Recite like you the Prophet, cuz," Haj Huss told Zizou. "Peace and blessings be upon Him."

Zizou sat on the stool before the music stand, extended his hands, and began to recite.

"Allah! Allah!" a hijabi attendee said.

"What a voice," a man said. "A true revelation."

A bottleneck soon formed at the entrance to the auditorium. Although Zizou didn't look up from the Qur'an, fearing he'd lose his place, he knew he was being observed, being listened to, being adored. This had never happened to him before.

"There's a special discount on our box set," Haj Huss said. "Only $39.99 for a limited time! Come and get them while they're hot. Praise be to Allah!"

Several attendees swarmed the table, pulling out cash and checkbooks.

Once the vendor area quieted down, Zizou sat behind the table and gulped down a bottle of water. He was sweating, his heart pounding.

"We've already sold fifteen box sets!" Haj Huss said.

All Zizou could think about was performing again. Throughout the day, when he went to grab a cup of tea or strolled down the hallway, people came over to congratulate him on his recitation. If they had asked for his autograph he would have pulled out his pen immediately.

By evening, Zizou and Haj Huss had sold all their box sets and taken advance purchase orders for several dozen more. To celebrate their success, they went to Halal Burgers on Michigan Avenue for dinner; the diner made burgers the Lebanese way: packed with coleslaw and french fries slathered with ketchup. Zizou and Haj Huss sat in a booth and washed their burgers down with fountain sodas.

"I been meaning to ask you a question, cuz," Haj Huss said. "A while back, you said you was a failed novelist. Whatcha mean?"

Zizou put down his burger. "I tried writing a novel, but I couldn't finish it."

"Ain't no thang. I done start many albums I ain't finished."

"I spent ten years writing it."

"Shux. What the thing about?"

"It's a fantasy novel."

"Like *Harry Potter*?"

"More like *Lord of the Rings* but set in an Arab fantasy world."

Zizou told Haj Huss all about Sarabia and the seven kingdoms; the more he spoke the more he became animated. His fictional characters came to life, as if they were all at the diner too. He loved them like a proud father.

"The detail about the purple daisies is mad dope," Haj Huss said, "and that's not because I'm a recovering druggie. I ain't no reader—except for the Qur'an—but I would read your novel, that for sure."

"I have to finish it first."

At the conference the next day, Zizou recited suras in front of big crowds as Haj Huss took orders. Representatives from smaller Arab and Muslim associations invited Zizou and Haj Huss to participate in their upcoming conferences as a vendor.

Over the next several months, Zizou and Haj Huss invested their profits from the conference into producing more copies of the album and creating a website to promote and sell it. They went to more conferences and advertised their album in the newspapers and on the local Arabic radio station. They attended open mic readings and Islamic community events, where they sold their product on the sly, and passed out flyers advertising the box set at various mosques following Friday prayer.

When Zizou's parents found out about the album, his mother asked him, hopeful, if he had returned to the teachings of Islam.

"No," Zizou said. "It was just a gig."

"Don't be a heathen, Zaher," Baba said.

While Haj Huss worked at the laundromat, Zizou processed the online orders and mailed out the box sets to addresses across America. Occasionally, Zizou and Haj Huss received online death threats from white supremacists and from other Muslims for incorporating music into the recitation of the Qur'an. "I declare jihad on you sisterfuckers," one anonymous Muslim wrote.

"Fudge them ditches," Haj Huss said.

Zizou sent free samples of their album to Islamic centers and contacted NGOs, student clubs and organizations, and university departments. "We'd be happy to perform live for you," he wrote in all his communications.

They received several invitations. He and Haj Huss rented a U-Haul van and drove to venues in Chicago, Toledo, Cleveland, Windsor, New York City, and DC. They flew out to LA and down to Miami. They spent nights in motels and ate at cheap diners. Haj Huss maintained a strictly vegetarian diet since halal meat was mostly unavailable outside of Dearborn.

One night, at a motel in Silver Spring, Maryland, as Zizou and Haj Huss were lying on separate single beds in their shared room, surfing TV channels, they heard sounds from next door—a bed squeaking and a woman screaming, "Fuck me, Al, you filthy bastard!"

Zizou and Haj Huss exchanged glances. Zizou wasn't sure whether to laugh or cringe in embarrassment. Haj Huss looked sad and desperate.

"Is that all you got, Al? Pump it like you mean it."

Haj Huss started to pray in Arabic.

"There you go, Al. You better unload a big one on me, you bastard."

Zizou thought of the white nurse he had dated from work. She also liked to talk dirty in bed, which had turned him on. It had been three years since they'd dated, three years since he'd last had sex. Thinking of her made him hard. He covered his erection with the blanket.

"There is no Allah but Allah, there is no Allah but Allah," Haj Huss repeated.

The woman screamed as she came. Al grunted.

"I need to use the restroom," Haj Huss said, and got out of bed. He was inside for several minutes. Zizou turned on his stomach and humped the mattress.

◆

BY LATE SPRING, they had sold thousands of copies of their album. They invested most of their profit into advertising and production expenses and split the remainder evenly. Zizou needed a job or soon all his savings would be wiped out. When one of Haj Huss's employees quit, Zizou stepped in. He learned how to inspect dirty garments for stains, holes, and missing buttons, and afterward sort them into separate bins. He dumped the garments into a mammoth green washing machine and poured in chemical solvent, and once the washing cycle was completed, he used the same machine to dry them. Zizou then pulled out the warm garments, dropped them in a bin, and headed over to the pressers. There was another quality check before scanning the items, bagging them, and hanging them on the conveyor.

"Treat cashmere like a baby's bum, cuz," Haj Huss said.

Zizou soon fell into a work routine. He arrived in the early morning and stayed until dusk. When there was downtime, he and Haj Huss read at the counter, Haj Huss his Qur'an and Zizou a fantasy novel. Zizou read to the sound of Haj Huss thumbing prayer beads in his palm: *tick, tick, tick*. It was in such moments, especially when he enjoyed the book he was reading, that he thought he could be happy. That life had its small pleasures to savor. But as soon as he recalled his failed novel, he turned grim. He returned home smelling of fresh laundry and spent his evenings in front of the TV or reading. He had let his beard grow long and enjoyed stroking it.

Some nights after work, he and Haj Huss dined at Halal Burgers. Because of his former nighttime work schedule, Zizou had missed spending time with friends. Over the years his friends had either drifted away or gotten married and started their own families; they didn't have time for him anymore. As he and Haj Huss chowed down on greasy burgers, coleslaw and fries falling from the buns, he made up for lost friend time.

One afternoon, as Zizou and Haj Huss were reading at the counter, a muscular man in a three-piece suit entered the laundromat carrying a garbage bag swollen with clothes. When Zizou looked up, his heart dropped. It was Fareed.

"What the fuck?!" Fareed said. "You work here?"

"Please say fudge," Haj Huss said.

Ignoring Haj Huss, Fareed asked, "What's going on, bro?"

"New job," Zizou said.

Fareed looked beyond the counter and then off to the left, at the other room filled with washing machines and dryers. "Come work with me, bro. You're better than this."

Zizou bristled at Fareed's air of a wiser, more successful, superior brother. He wanted to remind Fareed that he was older and more experienced. "I'm happy here."

Fareed placed the garbage bag on the counter. After he left, Zizou took his brother's clothes to the back room to sort through them. He found a ketchup stain on a vest. A shirt was missing a middle button. He remained in the back for the rest of the day, grateful that Haj Huss was giving him his space.

That night, Mama called.

"A laundromat?" she said. "You work at a laundromat?!"

Fucking Fareed, the bigmouth. "It's got great benefits," Zizou said, itching for a fight.

"Your baba sacrificed his best years so that you can work at a laundromat?! What's gotten into you? Here, speak to your baba."

"Zaher, a laundromat?!" Baba said.

Zizou hung up the phone. He looked across the room at his map of Sarabia. Like a tiger, he leapt from his couch and ripped it down, tearing it to shreds.

◆

THE GOOD NEWS WAS that the sales for *Zizou Reads the Qur'an in English* were steadily rising. Haj Huss and Zizou bought billboard space on Ford Road and Michigan Avenue to advertise their album. On the morning the first poster on Ford Road was to be unveiled, Haj Huss closed the laundromat and he and Zizou drove to the spot. Standing on the side of the freeway, they watched as the installer, high up in the cabin of his crane, removed an old ad attached to the billboard, cleaned over the space, and pasted in their poster sections. Once he was done,

Zizou saw an enlarged version of himself in prayer. Against a black backdrop, Zizou's open palms were extended, his head bent and his eyes closed. He wore a skullcap and thobe. Between his palms a green-colored Qur'an radiated light.

"That's mad dope!" Haj Huss said, gripping Zizou's forearm. "We finally did it, cuz! We got our own motherfudging billboard! Who dares doubt us now? We the A-Team."

The person up there wasn't him, Zizou thought. It was an impersonation. No family member called him about the billboard; they hadn't recognized him.

The A-Team continued to perform at various venues. A full year passed, and then another.

"It's time we contact the major labels," Zizou said. They had established a strong following. Sales continued to grow.

"But them labels ain't ready for us yet," Haj Huss said. "They see what's going on in Iraq, and they think all Arabs do is blow themselves up."

Zizou understood his friend's hesitation. He was afraid of rejection. "It won't ever be a good time for us. We might as well try."

They submitted demos of their album to all the major record labels and were categorically rejected.

"We don't produce this Moslem stuff," one assistant producer wrote back.

Zizou and Haj Huss were demoralized. But still they sent their demos to dozens of independent labels. In the summer of 2006, as war raged in Lebanon between Israel and Hezbollah, they heard back from a label in Minneapolis called Ethnic Records.

"We'd love to produce and distribute your album," they said.

Zizou and Haj Huss jumped and screeched like schoolboys at recess. "We did it!" they cried.

Their album sold well with the label, but not enough to make a national splash. Riding on momentum, Haj Huss decided to recruit young religious rappers and hip-hop artists to Halal

Records. He put the word out on the streets; Zizou advertised through local and national outlets. One day, during the recession of 2008, they received a demo from a Muslim boy band in Windsor called the Islams. The band consisted of five men in their late teens who sounded like the Backstreet Boys and mixed Arabic into their English lyrics. Haj Huss was so blown away by the demo that he got in his car and drove across the border to Canada to meet them.

Zizou stayed behind in Dearborn, where he now lived in a two-bedroom apartment overlooking a small park and drove a new car. He hadn't written a word since abandoning his novel but still had the file on his laptop. He had grown a belly, which he attributed to weekly visits to Halal Burgers. His beard was thick and well maintained. He tried online dating, but nothing serious ever came of it.

Haj Huss returned from Windsor, having signed the Islams. Later that month, the band members came down to record their album in Haj Huss's sound booth. Meanwhile, Zizou managed the laundromat. He hardly heard from Haj Huss, and dined alone.

The Islams' debut album, *Preachin' to the Masses*, sold decently in America but was a surprise hit in Canada. As this was Haj Huss's project, Zizou didn't profit from it, not that he minded. He only missed hanging out with his friend.

Haj Huss put up billboards all over Dearborn advertising the Islams and Halal Records. To kick off their road tour, the Islams performed songs from their album at the Ford Performing Arts Center. Zizou was given backstage access, and watched the show from behind the curtain alongside Haj Huss, the manager of the Islams, and the band's family members. All five singers wore black leather jackets, white T-shirts, baggy jeans, and high-top sneakers. Zizou couldn't stand the corny lyrics or the religiosity of the songs, and wished he could head home. He stayed out of respect for Haj Huss, who didn't seem to care that Zizou was even there, the way he was texting obsessively on his Blackberry and conversing with the manager.

With his new earnings, Haj Huss moved out of his parents' house and into a five-bedroom brick mansion in Dearborn Heights with a backyard lined with arborvitae trees. He converted his basement into a high-tech recording studio. Now hip religious artists from all over the world flocked to him. Halal Records was finally on the map.

"This is the life, cuz," Haj Huss said, standing in the foyer of his mansion. "Praise be to Allah!"

"I'm happy for you," Zizou managed to say. He felt small standing in a place so big. He also understood this was the beginning of the end of their friendship. Haj Huss was onto greater things that didn't include him. Perhaps they hadn't been so close after all, their need for each other having been fulfilled.

Haj Huss offered to sell the laundromat to Zizou at an affordable price. Zizou accepted and changed the name of the place to "Zizou's."

"You've got your own company!" Mama said when she visited the store with Baba.

"Our son is a damn cleaner," Baba said.

Zizou clenched the counter, holding in his rage.

During lulls at work, Zizou would read at the counter, but one day he decided to bring his laptop to pass the time. He opened THE LANDS OF SARABIA, and before he lost his resolve, he began reading the manuscript. He only stopped to attend to customers. At closing time, he lowered the blinds and continued to read. He read through the night, not wanting to go home for fear he'd lose something—what it was he didn't quite know. As he read, he experienced a feeling of discovery, or rather rediscovery, because with all these years spent apart from his novel, he now saw the glaring lack of character arcs and the convoluted subplots, and realized that the narrative would be better served with five kingdoms instead of seven. Electricity coursed through him, a charge he hadn't felt in years. Next step? Rewrite the motherfucker.

Two years later, at thirty-eight years old, Zizou completed THE LANDS OF SARABIA. He grew anxious, because now he had to market the novel. Otherwise, his book would remain on his computer for only him to read. He wanted to share what he'd written with the world.

Zizou submitted query letters to ten agents and heard back from four who were interested. He sent those four his manuscript and was told to wait at least six weeks for a response. Those six weeks were excruciating; he checked his email every five minutes. In the end, the agents all passed on his book, sucking the life out of him. He contacted more agents and got more rejections. After receiving over thirty agent rejections, he was about to give up when a new literary agency in Brooklyn offered him representation.

"Let me start by saying that I love THE LANDS OF SARABIA," the agent wrote.

Zizou could hardly believe what he was reading; he was expecting a massacre of his work. He read the email half a dozen times until he could reconcile himself to the good news. He had an agent. He had an agent! "I'm a writer, I'm a writer," he repeated like a mantra.

As Zizou revised his novel according to the agent's suggestions, he pictured himself giving readings at bookstores. When he drank a bottle of water, he drank it the way he imagined a writer would, standing at the podium, the bottle in one hand and the cap in the other, hesitating before taking a sip. He conjured different writerly scenarios: this was how a writer faked laughter during an interview, this was how a writer rolled up his sleeves before answering a challenging question at a reading, this was how a writer made small talk during book signings. He purchased a Montblanc fountain pen and practiced signing a new autograph: Z like *Zorro*.

The agent approved Zizou's revisions and submitted his manuscript to the big-name publishers of fantasy books. A month later, the first handful of rejections trickled in. In the second round of submissions, an editor said she was "super close" to offering a contract, but held back at the last moment. "If you ever write something else, please send it my way," she wrote. Before the third round of submissions, Zizou's agent suggested he revise his novel based on some of the editors' notes.

"Get rid of the kingdom on the snowy mountaintop," his agent said. "You'll be able to cut at least two hundred pages."

If Zizou didn't make ruthless cuts, there was a good chance his novel would be passed on again. Against his will, Zizou followed his agent's suggestion.

The publishers rejected him. His agent stopped answering his calls and emails. He sold his Montblanc pen on eBay, not wanting anything to do with it.

◆

ONE SUMMER DAY WHEN he was in his early forties, Zizou was sitting at the laundromat counter, reading a novel, when a life-sized black cat entered the front door, carrying a plastic-covered garment. Zizou put down his book and stared at the cat. She had big brown eyes, a black nose, and whiskers. Her pointy ears were pink on the inside.

"Are you an actor?" he asked.

"I perform for kids," she said. She placed the garment on the counter. It was a penguin costume. Zizou had dry cleaned his fair share of Halloween costumes. He made a ticket for her, noting her Arab name: Rana Siblani.

"Break a leg," he said.

When she returned for her costume days later, Rana was dressed in a T-shirt and jeans. Her thick curly brown hair was pulled back in a loose ponytail. A small ringlet hung coyly at the side of her face. She appeared to be in her midthirties.

"How was the performance?" Zizou asked.

"The kids dug it." She looked at the book open facedown on the counter. On the cover was a bearded horseman in sheepskin clothing against a backdrop of snowy mountains. "Looks interesting," she said, pointing. Zizou caught a tattoo of comedy and tragedy theater masks on the inside of her left wrist. They got to talking. She had attended Edsel Ford High and had left town to study theater at Michigan State.

The next time Rana came to drop off a costume, Zizou asked her out on a date. To his delight, she accepted. They met at Osaka Sushi on Michigan Avenue for dinner. When Rana wasn't performing for kids, Zizou learned, she worked as a part-time receptionist at an accountant's office, a soul-crushing job that paid the bills.

"I was a night watchman for ten years," Zizou said, and went on to tell her about the night Mr. McRoberts fell down the stairs at the assisted living facility and broke his leg. He talked about his reading of the Qur'an, his failed novel.

"I'm a failed actress," she said.

Following university, she told him, she'd moved to Chicago to act in local theater. Her ultimate dream was to act on Broadway, but New York was too intimidating. She thought she'd first establish herself in the Midwest before venturing to the Big Apple. "I recently met a young man from Dearborn at a theater production of *Hamlet*—his name is Youssef Bazzi—and he told me that he'd tried to make it as a stage actor in New York. He looked so broken; said the city had spat him out. I guess I was scared of that happening to me."

In Chicago, she continued, she shared a one-bedroom apartment in Ukrainian Village and waited tables at a busy diner in Greektown. She only ever landed minor roles in minor theaters. After several years, having grown tired of waitressing, the icy wind, and patronizing directors, she returned to Dearborn.

"I've lost count of the number of times my parents have disowned me," she said. "First for leaving town for college and then for wanting to pursue acting as a career, which they labeled a shameful profession. Then they disowned me for moving to Chicago and now for living alone in Dearborn as an unmarried woman."

They continued their conversation over banana splits at Dairy Queen, over beer at an Irish bar on Telegraph Road, over coffee and hot dogs at an all-night Coney Island diner in Detroit. They returned to Dearborn and sat on the crest of the hill at Ford Field Park to watch the sunrise. They had both sledded down the hill in the winters of their youth.

"Do you mind reciting the Qur'an to me?" she said.

"I didn't think you were religious."

"I'm not. I just want to hear your storytelling voice."

Zizou recited one sura after the other. Rana leaned against him, resting her head on his shoulder. "I love your voice," she said, and fell asleep.

After they started dating, word got around to Zizou's parents that they were an item.

"That girl is nothing but trouble!" Mama said over the phone.

"I hear she was a prostitute in Chicago!" Baba said on the other line.

"She's an actor, and a great one!" Zizou yelled.

"Is she a practicing Muslim?" Mama asked.

"I'm not. So why should it matter?"

"Astaghfirullah!" his parents said.

Zizou and Rana married later that year and moved into a ranch house on Outer Drive in West Dearborn, a good distance from their parents' houses. A birch tree shaded the backyard. Rana resigned from her part-time job to help Zizou at the laundromat. She still performed acting gigs and, encouraged by Zizou, began taking roles in the community theater.

Three years later, they had a daughter and named her Mira. Zizou read to Mira every night before bed, and when she was old enough to understand the words, he transitioned to chapter books, impersonating the characters' voices. With Mira in his lap, her big eyes trained on him instead of the book, he felt his heart expand. She had given him a new identity, one that exhausted him and filled him with anxiety, but above all nourished him.

One day at the laundromat, Rana wondered aloud if Zizou would ever consider pursuing a career as a voice actor. She had recently finished listening to an actor's memoir in audio format. "You already have a title to your name," she said.

Considering Rana's suggestion, Zizou listened to several audio books and thought he could be a decent voice actor. Invigorated, he rehearsed novel excerpts with Rana and Mira as his audience.

"You're overacting," Rana would sometimes say, or "You've got to be angrier," or "Let your voice tremble," or "A pause can be incredibly powerful." Zizou practiced and practiced, assuming different accents, adjusting his voice and pitch, once impersonating a deep-throated woman. It was essential, he realized, to capture the narrative tone of a book through his voice. When he was ready to record a demo, he paid a visit to Haj Huss, whom he hadn't seen in years.

Haj Huss answered the door of his mansion in a cheetah-patterned robe and pink bunny slippers. He still wore a white skullcap.

"Salams, cuz!"

They embraced. Haj Huss's noticeable belly pressed against Zizou's. Haj Huss had diamond studs in his ears and a gold chain around his neck. He wore a Rolex and a ruby ring on his pinkie.

They sat in the living room. A Persian rug covered the floor. A stuffed tiger stood in the corner, baring its fangs.

"It's been too long, cuz," Haj Huss said. "I miss our nights at Halal Burgers."

So did Zizou, but he suspected Haj Huss was reminiscing out of sympathy. Haj Huss was now big-time. Halal Records was the premier Islamic hip-hop and R&B label in North America. Through the label he had launched several other Muslim boy bands, including the Real Osamas, New Muslims on the Block, and the Bearded Bards. He'd also had success with a girl group called the Hijabi Hipsters. Zizou had heard he was in and out of relationships.

"What can I do you for, cuz?" Haj Huss asked. Zizou explained.

Over the course of three days, Zizou recorded his reading of an obscure novel by an Iraqi American writer in Haj Huss's sound booth. Haj Huss didn't charge for his services.

"We still the A-Team, cuz," he said.

Zizou submitted his demo to several publishers. An independent press in Chapel Hill offered him a contract.

"Are you interested in doing more books?" an assistant editor at the press asked Zizou. "Because we've got some upcoming titles that we think you'd be perfect for."

Zizou agreed. He had nothing to lose.

◆

YEARS LATER, ON A cold, wintry November night, Zizou waited in the upstairs reading room of a bookstore on the Upper West Side of Manhattan. Two standing microphones were placed in front of two stools. The room was packed with three hundred audience members sitting on folding chairs. The young, famous writer was going to arrive at any moment. The audience kept turning around to see if she had appeared.

Zizou stood at the front of the room, dressed in a wool blazer over a turtleneck. He had given readings in New York before, standing alongside the author as he read excerpts from the writer's work. He was now one of the most sought-after voice actors in the business, having won three male solo awards from the Audio Publishers Association. His most celebrated performance was a reading of the novel *The Sailors of Thessaloniki* by the Greek writer Kleopatra Kakoulidi, in which he captured the voice of the first-person narrator, Maria, the chain-smoking madame of a brothel. Although Zizou had been criticized for his performances of women's voices over the years, he had nailed Maria's.

Zizou had built a sound booth in his basement and worked from home. When recording, he lived with the fictional characters over several days. He'd first read the manuscript, highlighting key scenes, and then rehearse. The sound booth became his special place, a portal to an imagined world that he created through the power of his voice. Whenever he wished the author had expressed an emotion or described a landscape differently, or when he thought he could have crafted a better scene, he had to remind himself that he wasn't the writer; he was the voice actor. In any case, he didn't have time to write, what with raising a family and his day job, a great day job. *Be grateful*, he told himself. *You were destined for the mic, not the pen.*

His success as a voice actor allowed his family to move into a spacious colonial house in Dearborn Hills, the most exclusive area of Dearborn, with a backyard view of a golf course. He and Rana had hired a manager to look after the laundromat. Rana now managed the community theater and continued to act in plays. Mira was nine years old, and her younger brother, Jad, was six. The family dog, a goldendoodle, was named Fifer.

As soon as the writer entered the room, accompanied by a bookseller, and began to walk toward the mics, the audience whispered in excitement. The writer was barely five feet tall and wore a black, long-sleeved dress and red Converse sneakers. Her dark hair was in a chignon. Zizou still couldn't believe she was only twenty-four. Her debut novel, *The Cedars of the Mountains*, was the first volume in a planned trilogy. The *New York Times* had named her the most exciting new voice in fantasy literature, and the *New Yorker* had featured her in a profile. The book was already a bestseller and was being translated into fifteen languages. A Hollywood film production company had bought the rights to her series.

The writer's name was Alma Al-Awar, born to Lebanese parents and raised in Washington, DC. Zizou had read the *New Yorker* profile with anguish, learning that a summer trip to Lebanon had inspired Alma's series. Zizou had performed the role of the heroine's father, a blacksmith who lived in a mountaintop village. When he'd first been given a PDF of the novel, he'd refused to read a single word once he learned what the book was about and who the author was: a fellow Arab American, and worse, a kid! He was more than double Alma's age, old enough to be her father. As he'd sat in his sound booth, he'd thought he was too famous a voice actor to read a novice's work and decided to decline the publisher's offer. But when Mira came down to the basement to record an adventure story she'd written, and Zizou had given her his stool and watched as she read her piece into the mic, fully inhabiting her characters, mumbling words in her excitement, his envy had lessened. Fatherhood, he'd reminded himself, was his greatest blessing.

The bookseller introduced Zizou to Alma.

"It's so nice to finally meet you!" Alma said, shaking his hand.

"Likewise," Zizou said.

Zizou and Alma read a scene together involving the heroine and her father. The audience applauded, demanding more. Zizou and Alma obliged them. During the Q & A, Zizou sat silent, sipping from his water bottle.

The bookseller then informed the audience that the book signing would take place at the table to the side. Zizou and Alma stood up from their stools.

"I'm meeting my agent for a drink right after this," Alma said. "Care to join us? Please say yes."

"I'm afraid I already have plans."

Alma was ushered to the book signing table, where Zizou lost sight of her among her readers. He picked up his overcoat and scarf from the staff room and left the bookstore, heading south along Broadway, walking aimlessly, icy rain stinging his face. The wind lashed at him. A taxicab blared its horn.

One summer many years ago, before Mira was born, Zizou and Rana had visited New York together, the first time for them both. They had stayed in a low-budget hotel in Morningside Heights and spent their days walking the streets, visiting museums, exploring Central Park, and seeing Broadway plays. Once, in the dark of a theater, Zizou had glanced at Rana to catch the look on her face. She had finally made it to Broadway, but not as an actress—as an audience member. How did this affect her? He'd expected her expression would break his heart, but instead he saw that her eyes were shining with enchantment.

Afterward, over coffee and cheescake, he said, "You should be up on that stage. You would kill it every time."

"I'm over it, Zizou. But thank you."

Now, as Zizou approached Times Square, he realized that he had walked nearly forty blocks. His ears were frozen and about to fall off. He stepped inside a pub off Broadway, sat at the bar, and ordered a straight whiskey. A Knicks game was playing on the TV suspended above the bar. As Zizou sipped his drink, warming up, he wondered if Mira, who loved writing adventure stories, would eventually become a writer. Would he see, years from now, his family name printed not on the spine of his own novel but his daughter's? Would that be enough for him? Was he selfish to think this? He ordered another whiskey.

In Memoriam

I grew up in East Dearborn. In summer, my parents hosted gatherings in our detached two-car garage, which was built of wood and had a high, peaked ceiling. Folks sat in folding chairs arranged in a wide semicircle facing the open double doors, the smell of rusty tools and mildew in the air. In the dim yellow light, the men and women would chat and share news and stories about the old country as they sipped Turkish coffee and puffed on hookahs, the thick smoke curling above their heads. At some point, after hours of chatting and laughing, someone would tell a terribly sad story about a tragic death, which would inevitably lead to more stories about tragic deaths. Most were set in Lebanon, a land thousands of miles away that I had never visited. The Lebanese civil war had taken the lives of a hundred thousand civilians, so my parents and their friends had plenty of material to draw from. Like the story about a mother and her infant son who were stopped at a roadblock in Beirut and forced out of their car. A militiaman dragged them down an alley and threw them to the ground, then pulled back their chins and slit their throats. For some reason, I pictured the boy in a sailor outfit. I had nightmares of him choking on his own blood.

Mama once spoke of her childhood neighbor Wasila, a young woman from Baalbek, my parents' hometown in the Bekaa Valley. When Wasila was betrothed, against her will, to her second cousin, she begged her parents to break off the engagement, as she was deeply in love with a barber. Her parents refused. One night, they were all seated together in the winter room, warmed by the stove filled with crackling pinewood. Wasila stood and picked up the can of kerosene stored in the corner and poured the liquid over herself. "If you don't allow me to marry my love, I'll burn myself," she threatened. Her parents began panicking, praying for Allah's mercy. "We'll honor your wish," they said. "You promise?" Wasila asked. "We promise," her parents said. Just as Wasila was about to leave the room to bathe, a glowing ember popped out of the stove and landed a few inches from her feet. A drop of kerosene on the floor caught fire. The fire leapt from drop to drop, following a trail to Wasila's feet. She howled as the flames consumed her.

"I remember her howls to this day," Mama said. "Allah rest her soul."

Occasionally, local tragic death stories surfaced. Baba spoke of his six Yemeni coworkers, all of whom were killed when a boiler at the auto plant exploded. There were stories about the young Arab men who drag raced in the early hours of the morning on Warren Avenue, wrecking their cars and bodies. I imagined the horror of parents identifying their sons' smashed faces at the morgue.

When I first started attending my parents' gatherings, they made me go inside the house when the stories turned dark. But then I'd creep back out into the garage, finding a place to sit unnoticed among Baba's gardening tools. Eventually, my parents allowed me to stay.

The gatherings would last till well past midnight. As soon as our guests left, Mama and I would remove our hijabs and clean up while Baba went to bed. My two older brothers had no interest in spending time with my parents' friends and instead hung out with their own friends from Fordson—because they were male, they had no curfew and stayed out late. I envied their freedom. As we cleaned I'd pester Mama, who was still mired in the melancholy of the evening, for more information about the sad stories she had shared.

"Wasila burped like a man," she said.

Mama had experienced her own tragedy. When she was nine her beloved father was driving a tractor down into a valley when he lost control of the wheel and the machine rolled, crushing him inside. Destitute, Mama's mother was unable to care for her children and put them in a Muslim orphanage in a southern suburb of Beirut. Mama hated the orphanage and wet her bed for the next three years.

I once invited a friend for a sleepover on the same night as a gathering. We sat behind the semicircle, snacking on popcorn and gummy bears.

"This is boring," my friend Tamara said. "Let's play Nintendo."

"Shh," I said. "The best part's coming."

When the best part came, Tamara began crying. "I don't like these kinds of stories. What's wrong with you, Farah?"

Nothing was wrong with me. What was wrong with her?

"Grow up," I told her.

"Fuck you."

Our friendship ended that night.

♦

I HAD FEW FRIENDS in high school. The goth crowd tried to recruit me, being that I only wore black—black hijab, black overcoat, black long-sleeved blouse, black jeans, black Converse sneakers, hell, even black lipstick—but I wasn't interested. I was only interested in tragic death stories, which I wrote for my English class, putting the tales I had listened to in the garage down on paper.

"Life is also beautiful, you know," Mr. Bursk, my English teacher, said. "Consider writing about happier subjects."

Mr. Bursk was fresh out of college and still naïve about the world. He wore bow ties.

As an English major at the local university, I continued writing my stories. I wrote obsessively. Could I consider myself a writer, an artist? I wondered. Or was I too much of an amateur to claim such an identity? I wasn't sure. But one day, as I was working on an assignment in the library, a classmate from a fiction writing class came up to me. Andrew had shaggy brown hair and a pale face chewed red by acne. He wore an extra-large Metallica T-shirt, which hung loose on his skinny frame. "I like your writing," he said, and sat down across from me. His lips were flaked with dead skin. "The story about the woman dying by accidental self-immolation, is it true?"

"All my stories are true."

"My story is also true."

He had submitted a story about a teenage girl killed by a drunk driver. A middle-aged man had swerved his pickup from the opposite lane and crashed head-on into her car at over a hundred miles per hour. Both were pronounced dead at the scene. The girl had gone out to buy a gallon of milk.

"Was the girl related to you?" I asked him.

He nodded. "My sister. She died two years ago."

"Allah rest her soul—I mean God."

"I know what Allah means. I grew up in West Dearborn."

"Would you like to grab a coffee at the cafeteria?" I was keen on learning more about his sister. He agreed. He bought us coffees and we sat at a window table. He licked his dry lips.

"Was your sister's name Carol?" I asked.

"No. It was too painful to use her real name. Her name is—was—Samantha. We called her Sam."

"What was Sam like?"

"She was a rock climber. When we were younger, she'd climb up everything—trees, fences, the garage. She once climbed up our school's flagpole." He sipped his coffee.

"Tell me more."

Sam had had a boyfriend on the wrestling team, he continued, who once passed out in the bathroom from trying to cut weight for a match. The wrestler's name was Jack, and he had loved Sam.

The sun started to set. Blood-orange rays slanted through the window, casting Andrew's face in fiery light. I heard Wasila howling, smelled her flesh burning. I could hardly breathe.

"What's wrong?" Andrew asked me.

"Nothing. Let's go out for ice cream. My treat."

We ate sundaes at Dairy Queen. We sat in a booth with red plush seats.

"Did Sam like ice cream?" I asked.

"More than anything, but for Jack's sake, she didn't eat any during the wrestling season."

We couldn't stop talking; this, I thought, was what it meant to fall in love. Like most Arab parents, mine didn't allow me to date. I was expected to marry a Muslim man, preferably Arab, and until that time came, I was to remain at home. Fuck that.

Over the next couple of months Andrew and I spent most of our days together, at the student union, at the library, at Dairy Queen, at Ford Field Park, at Fairlane Mall. When Mama questioned my whereabouts, I said I was out with friends. If I ever came home past my curfew, which was set at 9:00 p.m., I'd find Mama stressed out, clenching her Qur'an. "You're late!" she'd say, her voice hoarse from having recited countless prayers, begging Allah to return me safely to her. Baba never cared as much, tired as he was from his long days at the factory.

One afternoon, Andrew invited me over to his house. His parents were out of town. We sat on the bed in his room. He leaned over and kissed me. His peeling skin prickled my lips. Almost magically, as if my mouth was used to such a rhythm, I kissed him back, my tongue as aggressive as his. I realized we were French kissing and was baffled at how automatic it was, how seemingly natural. My eyes were closed. I didn't remember closing them. I opened them and saw Andrew with his eyes closed, lost in the rapture of our kiss.

"Can I see your hair?" he asked.

I removed my hijab and loosened my black hair. It fell down to my shoulders.

"Allah have mercy," Andrew said. "What lovely hair."

We had dry sex with all our clothes on. It would have been sacrilegious to lose my virginity before marriage. As we lay on the sheets, I wondered if Sam had died a virgin.

On another afternoon, after dry sex, I left Andrew asleep in bed and went to explore Sam's room down the hall. Andrew's parents had changed nothing. The closet and drawers were filled with her clothes. Her perfume bottles and makeup still rested on her vanity table. Strands of blond hair were tangled in the bristles of a brush. A film poster of *Titanic* hung on the wall, with Leonardo DiCaprio and Kate Winslet embracing on the deck of the ship. I lay down on the bed and fell asleep. Andrew jerked me awake.

"You're not supposed to be in here!" he wailed. "No one is. You've ruined it."

"Ruined what?"

"Everything. Leave. Now."

When I returned home later that day, Mama asked me who had died.

"No one," I said. "How come?"

"You look devastated."

Andrew stopped speaking to me; I kept my broken heart to myself. We remained Facebook friends, but with time I lost sight of his news. Neither of us posted often.

♦

AFTER UNIVERSITY, I LANDED a job as the copy editor and obituary writer at the *Dearborn Post*. The weekly paper reported on the Arab American community and was located on the second floor of a three-story building on Michigan Avenue. On the ground floor was an Irish bar called the Green Clover. The editor in chief had the only office, and except for a conference room and a claustrophobic kitchen, the space was a maze of cubicles. I sat in the back near a window that looked out onto the street below. In the late afternoon, I'd occasionally hear the patrons of the Green Clover chatting and smoking on the pavement in front of the bar.

It didn't take long before the journalists started calling me "the reaper," not only because I wrote obituaries but also because I slashed their articles, my editorial scythe dripping words. They were mostly in their twenties, Arab men and women who had grown up in the area and aspired to move to one of the big papers in Detroit or, even better, to a national one. They stayed a few years at the *Dearborn Post*, gaining whatever experience they could, and then left. When they went out to lunch down the street—Halal Burgers was their favorite joint—they never invited me along. I brought food from home and ate alone at my desk.

After work, I went home and had dinner with my parents and then I'd head upstairs to my room to read or watch movies on my laptop. My brothers had both married and moved out. On the weekends, I'd go for long drives—I once drove to Grand Rapids, bought a coffee in town, and then returned home. Occasionally I'd socialize with cousins, whose parents felt sorry for me and insisted that their adult children hang out with me. These were miserable occasions spent mostly at a restaurant. My cousins found me strange and I found them boring. Thankfully, our outings ceased when they got married and started their own families.

In winter my parents hosted their gatherings in the basement. I never missed a night. Although the tellers often repeated the same stories, they added new details with each retelling, painting an even more vivid image.

One December night, as I was puffing on a hookah packed with apple-scented tobacco, I began telling my own tragic death stories to my parents' guests—stories I'd learned through my obituary writing and from what I'd overheard around town. I spoke of Wessam, who had died from a heroin overdose; Layal, who had swallowed a bottle of pills; Rifaat, who had hanged himself in his room after coming out to his parents. All three had grown up in Dearborn and were around my age.

"Astaghfirullah!" Uncle Jihad said. "You're telling lies. I heard Wessam died of a heart attack."

"He was a drug addict," I said.

"Layal died of pneumonia," Auntie Ghada said.

"She was battling depression," I said.

"Rifaat was madly in love with his fiancée," Mama said, desperate.

"He was gay, Mama," I said.

My parents and their friends didn't want me around them anymore. At later gatherings, I remained upstairs in my room, smoking my hookah and listening to the sound of the water bubbling in the urn on each inhalation.

One day, I approached the newspaper's editor in chief with the idea of expanding the obit section. I wanted to give readers an intimate glimpse into the lives of the deceased. To do this, I was willing to interview the families to obtain more information about them; and, if we attracted more readers with a revamped section, I explained, the paper would benefit financially.

The editor in chief, a man named Ibrahim, leaned back in his chair, brushing his bangs from his forehead. He'd been a journalist at the paper for many years before being promoted to his current position. He'd never shown any interest in moving to another paper because he'd only wanted to report about Dearborn Arabs. The journalists thought he was simply a big fish in a small pond, which was probably true, but I understood him. I hoped he understood me. I didn't see myself working at a non-Arab or non-Dearborn paper, either. I was loyal to the city. Ibrahim tugged at his blazer. "Why don't you try your hand at an article about the living?"

"Not my thing."

"Then just do your job, sister," he said, and took a massive bite of the falafel sandwich that was lying on his desk.

That evening, I entered the garage. My parents and their friends were seated in a semicircle, hookah smoke clouding the air. Side tables were cluttered with demitasse cups and plates littered with the sodden shells of pumpkin seeds. When they noticed me, they grew quiet. No one cracked a seed or took a puff from a hookah. I heard only whisperings of prayers, as if I were the shaitan come to take their souls.

"Is something wrong, ya binti?" Mama asked. She was perched on the edge of her chair.

"May I join you?"

Mama and Baba exchanged worried glances.

"Oh, it's getting really late," Auntie Ghada said, grabbing her purse from the floor.

The friends all stood up to leave.

"Wait a sec!" I said. "Please, sit down and listen to what I have to say. I'm begging you."

In a rush of emotion, I explained my plan, making eye contact with each of them. When I was done, an excruciating silence fell upon the garage.

"When would you like to start?" Auntie Ghada finally said.

I nearly wept in gratitude. "How about tonight?"

"Tonight?! I need to prepare."

The following night, I met Auntie Ghada at her house. She was in a long-sleeved black dress and matching black hijab. As soon as I stepped into the foyer, she said, "You're too skinny! And you've got dark circles under your eyes. How are you ever going to get married if you look like shit?"

I was used to such criticism. It ran in the Arab community: honesty without subtlety.

I set up my digital camera on a tripod in the living room and shot the scene with Auntie Ghada seated by the fireplace. She told the story, slowly and with care, of her cousin Hamida, who had drowned in the Litani River in southern Lebanon in the winter of 1981. Hamida had been collecting rocks when she'd gotten too close to the rapids and slipped in. Days later, her bloated body washed ashore in a town miles away. She was only nine years old.

Auntie Ghada handed me pictures of Hamida (Hamida's mother had given Auntie Ghada her blessing), and days later I posted the video.

◆

MY PHONE PINGED WITH notifications: likes, loves, cares, and heartfelt comments. Never before had I received such praise or acknowledgment of my work. I felt that I had done something extraordinary. This was all strange to me; I was used to minding my own business. I was both nervous and giddy with excitement.

When the rest of my parents' friends saw my video about Hamida, they became more eager to tell me their stories. Since these deaths had mostly occurred in Lebanon, I included landscape shots and clips of the old country I had obtained online, as well as the mellifluous voice of Fairuz in the background. In talking about the dead, my parents' friends reminisced about a country they longed for but was irretrievably lost to them. The Lebanon they knew and loved was the one of their childhoods.

Grieving families soon discovered my work and asked me to memorialize their dead. I began charging a modest fee. I consulted with them over Skype, at their homes, or at a hookah café in town. I spent nights in my room editing the pieces, sipping strong cups of Turkish coffee and puffing on my hookah to stay awake. But the more videos I made, the more I yearned for companionship. When people spoke of their lost loves, I hungered for someone to be devoted to me.

I hadn't kissed a man since Andrew and craved the brush of lips and tongue against my own. I set up a Tinder account and began dating. Mama had ended my curfew now that I was an adult, but she still waited up at night for me, unable to go to bed until I entered the front door. I made sure to date outside of Dearborn so that no community member would spot me and report back to my parents. To disguise myself, I removed my hijab, though I still wore all black. I dated men of all races and ethnicities. I dated women, too, thinking they might understand my interests better; they didn't. No one did. But I had lots of dry sex.

I went to Facebook to view Andrew's page. According to his personal information, he worked at an advertising agency in Detroit. I wondered if he still lived in Dearborn. In his profile picture, he sat on a park bench next to his wife, a toddler in a pink frilly dress squeezed between them. All were smiling. I had seen this family portrait before, when Andrew first changed his profile picture a year or two ago. He looked happy, not Facebook happy but genuinely happy. I was glad for him. He deserved it. Looking at the picture, I didn't feel heartache—my heart had healed since Andrew had broken it—but bottomless sorrow. What if it had worked out between us? What if I had been the one on that park bench with a child between us? Instead, I still lived at home and continued to tell death stories.

I messaged Andrew on Facebook to ask if he'd be interested in meeting for a coffee to catch up for old time's sake. He replied that he'd be happy to see me, which brought me tremendous joy. We met a week later at Qahwah House in East Dearborn, a Yemeni café whose walls were covered in murals of the country's traditional stone buildings. When I saw Andrew enter the café, I got up from my table and waved to him, fearing he'd forgotten what I looked like. But he hadn't. He came over and we embraced. The other patrons eyed me suspiciously—I was a hijabi making physical contact with a man who clearly wasn't my husband or brother. Fuck them. Andrew and I sat down. He wore a button-down shirt and slacks. His hair was cut short. His neatly trimmed beard covered his acne scars. His lips were moist and plump. As we shared a pot of Adeni tea, he told me that he lived in Royal Oak and that his wife was pregnant with their second child. His parents had sold their house and moved down to Tampa.

"I've seen your videos," he said. "Pretty morbid stuff."

"You know me. I mean . . ." I didn't know what I meant. I just wanted to be back in college, when the two of us were dating and I was in love for the first and only time in my life. Although our conversation was fluid, I'd been expecting more intimacy, more electricity, like the way we had once talked with each other when we were younger. He was married and had a child, I reminded myself. He hadn't even asked if I was seeing someone. What was I hoping for? We began to discuss the ways Dearborn had evolved since we'd been in college, and then we ran out of words. We both sipped our tea. In the ensuing silence, I found the courage to ask him if everything was truly all right in his life.

"What do you mean?" he asked.

"Sam."

"Oh. Well, I'll never get over her loss, but I've learned how to live with my grief. I have therapy to thank for that."

"I still remember Sam's bedroom. The *Titanic* poster on her wall. Her belongings."

Andrew stared at me.

"I remember that story you wrote about her for class. I remember how she loved climbing up things and how much she cared for her boyfriend, the wrestler—what was his name again? John, no Jack. Yes, Jack. I remember—"

"Do you mind if we change the subject?"

"Forgive me. . . Would you like a pastry?"

"I'm good." He checked the time on his watch.

"It's just that," I said, "if you'd like, I can make a video about her?"

"A video?"

"Like the ones I've made for my page. I can interview you for it. It'll be a tribute to her. I wouldn't charge you because . . . because you're my friend."

Andrew's face turned red. "Now I understand why you contacted me." He wiped his mouth with a napkin, looked out the window, and then stood up. "You just want me for my sister's story. Shame on you."

"I promise you that's not it!" The patrons all looked at us. "I missed you. I wanted to see you."

"We only dated for a few months, Farah. *Years* ago. It was nothing serious."

"It was everything to me."

He remained standing, me seated. "It's so sad," he said, peering down at me. He didn't have to complete his thought. Andrew left the café without saying goodbye. The patrons were eyeing me, wondering what I was going to do next. I got up in tears.

Later that night, I tried to Facebook message Andrew to apologize, but he had already defriended me. In fact, he had blocked me. I was a horrible person.

♦

AND NOW HERE I am; an owl hoots outside my bedroom window. It's past midnight. My parents are asleep. The house is quiet. I've got a video to edit, but since seeing Andrew, I haven't been able to work on my page. I stare at my laptop without moving my fingers on the keyboard. I'm stuck. Life stuck. I don't know how to proceed. If I delete my page, what will I do next? I'm tired of being alone.

Hiyam, LLC

Hiyam straddles her American husband in bed, her arm stretched behind her back, fingers stroking his moist balls. In the dim lamplight, she looks down at his pink face, his walrus mustache covering his upper lip. He's squinting like she's the brightest thing he's ever seen. When she feels he's about to come, she slows down, and when she's ready, she quickens her pace until both are howling like jackals under the moon. As they lie on their backs, catching their breath, Hiyam realizes she hasn't seen a jackal in five years, not since the last time she was in Lebanon and made love to her ex-husband. Sex with her ex had been sublime. Sex with Bobbie is like mayonnaise, something she doesn't mind in her sandwiches but can do without.

Hiyam reaches for her vape pen on the night table and inhales. Bobbie rests his hands on his belly, beads of sweat glimmering on his bald head. He turns toward her.

"Did I tell you about the time my buddies and I went up to the Upper Peninsula to hunt grouse and I got lost in the woods?"

Hiyam shakes her head. "Tell me, Bobbie."

As Bobbie tells his story, Hiyam plans her day for tomorrow.

◆

IN THE MORNING, as Bobbie sleeps, Hiyam puts on a long-sleeved dress, covers her hair with a hijab, unrolls her prayer rug in the living room, faces in the direction of Mecca, and prays, whispering suras from the Qur'an, touching her forehead on the floor. She prays for her divorced son, her youngest child, who lives on the east side of town; for her middle daughter in Kuwait, an optometrist with a baby girl; for her eldest daughter in Dubai, an elementary school teacher. She prays for her ex even though she's heard he's taken up with a new lover half his age and rides up and down the coast of Lebanon with her on his Harley, her arms wrapped around his waist. She prays for Bobbie because he's a good man and cares for her, though she knows his two daughters from his previous marriage, both in their forties, despise her. The bitches. *Aayb, shame, you're praying. This is Allah time.* But those bitches think she married Bobbie for his money and to obtain her American citizenship. They're wrong on both counts; she came with money *and* a green card, having been sponsored by her son. Since she's been in America, she's built herself a nice real estate business called Hiyam, LLC. *I'm a CEO, bitches. Think of Allah, think of Allah.*

"Praise be to Allah!" she says.

She changes out of her prayer clothes and puts on a blazer over a blouse and slim jeans. She loosens her dyed black hair and lets it fall down to her shoulders. In the kitchen, she makes a rakweh of Turkish coffee, which she sips by the window, looking out at the deck and the trees in the backyard. A red canary lands on the deck railing. She can now identify several breeds of birds thanks to Bobbie, who likes to spend the early evenings bird-watching out on the deck with his binoculars. She puts her demitasse cup and the rakweh in the sink, picks up her purse and laptop bag, slides on her Ray-Ban sunglasses, and heads out to begin her day, her vape pen hanging from her neck like a talisman.

◆

HIYAM DRIVES A BLACK Escalade with tinted windows. She makes a right on Telegraph Road, takes the exit ramp for Michigan Avenue, and crosses into East Dearborn. On the east side the driving turns suicidal, with drivers cutting in front of each other without signaling, or making illegal U-turns, or reversing in the wrong direction down one-way streets. Hiyam drives like she once did in the maddening traffic of Beirut: hyperalert, firmly gripping the steering wheel, finding order in the chaos. When a pickup truck swerves in front of her, she honks at the driver, only to see him give her the finger. She merges into the other lane, drives side by side with him, and lowers her window.

"May Allah castrate you, you son-of-a-whore-sisterfucker," she yells in Arabic.

She makes a left on Schaefer Road and another left on Warren Avenue and then a right down a side street and into Detroit. She parks in front of a wood-frame house with a screened front porch and a leaning, detached garage. Inside lives a Syrian refugee family. They're late to pay the rent and haven't been answering her calls. Hiyam steps out of her Escalade, looking from side to side. Most of the wood-frame houses on the street sag, their concrete front stoops cracked. Three other Syrian refugee families live on the block. A Black boy rides his bicycle in circles in the small intersection at the end of the street. An elderly woman sits on her front porch, listening to her portable radio as she rocks in her chair. Hiyam drives here only in the morning, when it's quiet and few people are out. She doesn't dare come at night. In fact, she prefers not to leave the house after sunset, though she will when Bobbie wants to dine out. During the civil war in Beirut, militiamen and hoodlums roamed the streets at night, high on testosterone, thirsty for blood and money. She'd venture out of her apartment only during the day, when the bombings and gun battles had subsided for a few hours, allowing Beirutis to shop for groceries and buy medicine from the local pharmacists.

Hiyam walks up to the house, opens the screen door, and knocks. She hears the high-pitched sound of cartoons coming from inside. She knocks repeatedly until a woman in a hijab answers.

"Madame Hiyam," the woman says in Arabic. "Ahlan wa sahlan."

Hiyam enters. "How are the kids?"

"Good, thanks be to Allah."

Hiyam peers inside the living room, where four children, from ages six to eleven, are splayed out on the couches, watching cartoons on TV.

"Why don't they play outside?" Hiyam asks their mother. "It's summer."

"You know why, Madame."

"There hasn't been a shooting here in weeks."

"Doesn't mean there won't be one today."

Hiyam owns two other houses in the area and rents them out to Syrian refugees. Her tenants all complain about the crime. If you're not happy here, move to Dearborn, Hiyam tells them. But she knows they can't afford Dearborn rent, at least not yet.

Hiyam follows the mother into the kitchen. The mother takes out a kettle to make tea.

"I don't have time," Hiyam says. "I'm here for the rent. You're three months late."

"Madame, as Allah is my witness, Tarek is trying his best to pay you."

"Where is he?"

"He's out looking for work. Construction."

"Don't lie to me, Samia. Is he in the bedroom?" Last time Hiyam had come to collect the rent, Tarek had lain motionless in bed.

"This week he worked a few hours at the auto repair shop."

"Is he in the bedroom?" Hiyam asks again.

When Samia doesn't answer, Hiyam goes to the bedroom and knocks on the door, announcing that it's her. She steps inside. Tarek is lying in bed on his side, a blanket pulled up to his neck. The room is warm and smells of body odor. Hiyam walks around to the edge of the bed and kneels down to face Tarek. His black eyes are open but vacant, his cheeks sunken, his hair oily. He looks starved.

"Tarek, you need to get out of bed and find work to support your family and pay the rent," Hiyam says. Her other tenants haven't missed a single payment, the men finding steady work, the women looking after the children. But she knows the other men haven't experienced Tarek's horrors. A former taxi driver, Tarek was pulled from his car in downtown Aleppo by an undercover agent working for the regime. He was accused of supporting Daesh and thrown into an underground cell that stunk of shit and piss. Guards punched his face, breaking his jaw and teeth. They sliced off his nipples with a razor, demanding names from him. They smashed his toes with a hammer. Hiyam suspects he was also raped. He didn't have any names to give because he wasn't a Daesh supporter; they had mistaken him for someone else. When he was released, he and his family fled to Damascus, and then to a refugee camp across the border in the Bekaa Valley. Years later, they were offered asylum in Michigan.

Hiyam tells Tarek that she survived fifteen years of bloodshed, fifteen years of terror, and yet she still gets up every day to make the best out of it. Life goes on because it must; there's no other option. She knows she's no motivational speaker, but if Tarek doesn't work, she'll have to evict the family. His stare is blank, his breath sour.

Hiyam follows Samia out of the room to the kitchen.

"Be patient with us, Madame," Samia says. "Perhaps the mosque can help Tarek find work, inshallah."

As soon as Hiyam is back in her car, she reaches for her vape pen and sucks in the nicotine. She lets out a massive sigh, as if the pain of the world were lodged in her lungs. She has to be tough on her tenants, she reminds herself, or else they'll take advantage of her. Business is business. *I'm a CEO, bitches.*

♦

HIYAM STOPS AT YASSER'S Meats in East Dearborn to buy kafta, her son's favorite brunch meal, and heads over to his place. Fadi is in a sleeveless undershirt, gym shorts, and flip-flops when he answers the door. His double chin hangs from his jaw like a rooster's wattle. A tattoo of a fire-breathing dragon covers his left bicep. His hair is messy, and he needs a shave. In the kitchen, Hiyam takes charge as Fadi sits at the table, drinking a mug of Nescafé. She preheats the oven and then opens two loaves of pita bread, unwraps the butcher paper, and with her bare fingers scrapes off a chunk of kafta, the velvety meat a beautiful pink with flecks of parsley and onions, and spreads it over one loaf and then the other. She places the kafta sandwiches on a tray, washes her hands, and then sticks the tray inside the oven. She joins Fadi at the table as the kafta bakes.

Fadi recently resigned from GM, where he worked as a data analyst, because he was tired of working for the "boss" and wanted to start his own business. Only he'd had no plan in mind before resigning, let alone an idea for his own company. Hiyam worries that he doesn't have what it takes to be a CEO. He's been out of work for two months, and she fears his meager savings will carry him only to the end of summer; he also pays child support. But she's careful not to ask him about his job status; he's got his father's, her ex's, volatile temper. Instead she asks if Karim, his nine-year-old son, is enjoying summer camp.

"He likes it enough," Fadi says. "But his mother isn't doing anything about his cursing. The other day he called an Arab kid at camp a 'cock-sucking sisterfucker' in Arabic."

"Are you doing anything about it?"

"About what?"

"Karim's cursing. Maybe he hears you cursing. You curse a lot."

"So does his mother," Fadi says, his voice rising. "So do you." Although he cusses out his ex-wife, Hiyam knows Fadi is still in love with her. She left him for a plastic surgeon whose billboards are all over town. To Hiyam's knowledge, Fadi hasn't been seeing anyone. He's not a looker like his father, and he's gained too much weight. (She should have grilled kafta fingers instead and served them without bread.) His current unemployment, his temper, the fact that he has a son—all these things make him unattractive to single Arab women. Is it her fault he's ended up where he is? Could she have been a more supportive mother? A better guide? But why does it matter whether Fadi makes himself attractive to Arab women in particular? His ex-wife is Lebanese American and it didn't work out between them. Perhaps he'd be happier with an American-American like Bobbie.

Hiyam gets up and pulls the tray from the oven. Fadi removes plates from the cupboard and bottles of ketchup and hot sauce from the fridge.

"You're going to ruin the taste of the kafta with the ketchup," Hiyam says as they take their seats.

"You say that every time I eat meat with ketchup."

They devour the sandwiches, the toasted bread crunching with each bite. The meat is juicy and flavorful, Hiyam thinks, the best in town.

"Thanks for bringing the kafta," Fadi says, a drop of ketchup on his chin.

Hiyam reaches across the table and wipes his chin with a napkin. She knows his tough-man demeanor, the tattoo on his arm, is for show. He was born in 1988, thirteen years into the war, and was picked on in middle school for being pudgy. Instead of fighting back, he came home in tears, sometimes with a bloody nose.

"I've got a third daughter for a son," Hiyam's ex had often said of Fadi.

But Fadi found the courage to come to America to pursue an MBA, where he met his ex-wife at university. If it weren't for Fadi, Hiyam would never have met Bobbie, let alone launched Hiyam, LLC. It was on a summer trip to Dearborn to see her son and grandson that she'd connected with Bobbie through an online dating app. This was after her divorce, when she was already a permanent resident. She'd wanted to test herself in the American dating scene, to see if she could dine with a man who wasn't her ex-husband. She hadn't ever kissed another man. After several unsuccessful dates (the men had bored her), she'd met Bobbie at the Dearborn Country Club for lunch. She'd worn a low-cut dress and heels for the occasion—she didn't know the meaning of casual when she went out. He'd been dressed in a polo shirt and slacks. He was bald, she'd realized when he walked in, which hadn't been apparent in his pictures online, where he wore a Michigan State baseball cap. She'd caught the look in his eyes the moment he saw her: one of rapture. He couldn't believe his luck. They'd both had poached salmon and roasted potatoes and had split a bottle of sauvignon blanc. After his second glass of wine, Bobbie had said he had a confession to make.

"We're already at that stage?" Hiyam had teasingly asked. She was a natural flirt.

"You're the first Arabic woman I've ever gone on a date with."

Arabic was a language, but she hadn't bothered correcting him. "And how do you like it?"

"I hope it never ends."

"Is that the wine talking?"

"It's my old beating heart talking, sweet gal."

Gal? Hiyam had thought. Though her English was good, she didn't understand this word. She'd excused herself to the restroom, where she looked into the mirror to check if there was any food stuck between her teeth. She refreshed her lipstick and combed her fingers through her hair, giving it more volume. And then she googled "gal." One definition included "young woman." This made her happy. She was glad she had agreed to meet Bobbie, glad that Dearborn was a place she could always return to. She had been living in the city on and off, spending the majority of her time in Beirut. When in Dearborn, she stayed with her son, which wasn't to her liking. She preferred her privacy. But living in Beirut as a divorced woman was difficult; she was forced to live with her mother, an elderly woman who complained about the world from the moment she woke up until the moment she went to bed, and prayed to Allah to finally end her life. All the women in Hiyam's social circle were married, and although most of them were unhappy in their marriages, they didn't dare risk their reputation by leaving their spouses.

When Hiyam returned to the table, Bobbie asked if she golfed. His face had turned salmon pink.

"Never tried it," she said.

"Want to take a few swings tomorrow?"

The next day, at the Dearborn Hills Golf Course, Bobbie taught Hiyam how to swing a club. It had taken her several swings before she made contact with the ball.

"Great job!" Bobbie said. "Believe and you'll achieve! You've just got to keep grinding at it."

He was one of *those*, Hiyam thought with revulsion. A positive reinforcer. A fucking cheerleader.

They'd dined that night at an Italian restaurant. When Hiyam returned to her son's place past midnight, Fadi was up and seated on the couch.

"It's late," he said. "I don't like my mother running around with men at night."

"Mind your own business."

"You're at my house."

"Which I helped you purchase."

"Baba helped me."

"It's our money."

"You're divorced."

"And single. Like I said, mind your own business."

After a week of dating Bobbie, Hiyam had explained to him that she had to return to Beirut at the end of the month. Bobbie had pleaded with her to postpone her flight.

"And then what, Bobbie? For what?"

"To marry me, gal!"

"We've only spent a week together."

"That's more than enough time for me. I am what you see. Nothing complicated."

"We haven't even kissed yet."

Bobbie kissed her. She didn't mind the feel of his prickly mustache against her lips.

"If we marry," she said, "I want to start my own business and not be told what to do."

"You can do whatever you want, gal. There's only one request that I have ... that you support the Spartans," he said, and laughed.

She'd already known about his religious devotion to the Michigan State football team. He was an alum of the university and had told her over golf that he "bled green."

"I'll be a Spartan," she said, "under one condition. You convert to Islam. I'll only marry a Muslim."

Not too long afterward, they'd gone to the Islamic Center of America, the biggest mosque in the country, where Bobbie became a Muslim and was given a new name: Mohammed bin Abdullah Farouk. Later that afternoon, over burgers and beer at a diner, Bobbie had asked, "Do you expect me to pray in the mosque every Friday?"

"No, Bobbie. You don't have to do anything else."

They'd ordered a second round of beer.

Now, looking across at her son, Hiyam, unable to restrain herself, asks if he has any job interviews lined up.

"I already told you, I want to start my own company. I'll be the one who interviews people."

"What kind of company?"

"Still working out the details. But I've got a name for it: Dearborn Deluxe, LLC."

If her business continues to prosper, Hiyam figures she can hire him, if it comes to that, as an assistant. "May Allah grant you all the success in the world," she tells him.

When Fadi leaves the table to use the bathroom, Hiyam pulls out an envelope of money from her purse and sets it on the kitchen counter. She rinses the plates and Fadi's coffee mug and places them inside the dishwasher. At the front door, she suggests that Fadi shave, maybe join a gym.

"Do you think I'm fat, Mama?" he asks.

"You're as handsome as your father."

♦

HIYAM SITS AT AN outdoor table at Sky Lounge on Warren Avenue, her unofficial office space in summer, perusing house listings on her laptop as she polishes off a rakweh of Turkish coffee. Arabic and English words swirl in the air like hookah smoke. Fairuz's voice flows from the suspended speakers. Hiyam comes across affordable houses in Dearborn Heights and Canton. There's an open house in Canton today that she may check out. With the influx of Iraqis and Yemenis in East Dearborn, she knows that Lebanese, who prefer to live among their own, are moving out west. She looks away from her laptop to take in her surroundings. A young man and woman have just sat down at a table. A group of teenagers share a watermelon hookah. A middle-aged hijabi woman sits alone, smoking a pineapple hookah, as she discreetly turns the pages of a calendar featuring dark-haired men in Speedos—or is it the same male model for every month? Hiyam can't tell. She could sit here for hours, observing the city. In Beirut, she took her morning cup of coffee on the balcony, which she'd lined with potted plants and flowers, and watched the street below. At some point, a man pushing a wooden cart of kaak would appear, crying out in his nasal voice, "Kaak, kaak." The florist would sweep away the dust in front of his shop. A line would form outside the manakeesh bakery. The hairstylist would smoke cigarettes under her awning between clients, sometimes feeding scraps of meat to the stray cats.

Longing for Beirut, Hiyam pulls out her smartphone and goes to Facebook, where she's still friends with her ex. She doesn't have the heart to defriend him, and every time she visits his page, she feels like a lovesick teenager. In his profile picture, he sits alone on his Harley on a seaside street, probably in Byblos, their second favorite city after Beirut. She wonders who took the picture—his new girlfriend? He wears a black T-shirt and cowboy boots. He's smiling, revealing the gap between his front teeth. In his youth, he was often mistaken for Omar Sharif, and he played along with it. They were once treated to a free dinner at a fancy French restaurant in Achrafieh on the east side of Beirut when the manager mistook him for the actor.

Hiyam met Makram when she was seventeen and he nineteen. They lived in the same building on Hamra Street, a few streets up from the American University. Makram's family had recently moved in. Makram had skipped university to work at his father's construction company. When they'd come across each other for the first time in the elevator, Hiyam asked him if he was Omar Sharif's stunt double. She had seen all of

Sharif's films and was, like most women, infatuated with the actor. Makram grinned. When she glimpsed the gap between his teeth, she could hardly believe the resemblance.

"I do the most dangerous stunts," he said.

"Not as dangerous as mine."

"Like the one you're doing right now?"

The elevator stopped at the ground floor. Both stepped out. Hiyam responded to Makram's question a week later, in the stairwell, with a kiss on his lips.

Instead of attending university, Hiyam married Makram and had her first child two years later. Their marriage was one filled with incendiary shouting matches and reconciliatory lovemaking. They hated and loved each other, not knowing the difference between the two. Makram prohibited her from working, claiming he was the sole breadwinner. Some nights he returned home smelling of another woman's perfume. She considered leaving him, but thought to wait until her children were older. When she looked in the mirror, she wondered what she was lacking. She was still in good physical shape— she swam laps at the Sporting Club every afternoon and was careful about what she ate—and drank plenty of water and applied anti-wrinkle cream daily to her face and neck. She was happy with her body, and she had thought Makram was, too. When his infidelity persisted, she underwent nose surgery, which led to Botox injections in her forehead and, months later, filler injections under her eyes and in her cheeks and lips. She couldn't feel herself smiling anymore and had the face of a swollen cat. "Enough with the cosmetic shit," Makram told her. "You're naturally beautiful." But after he slept with his young secretary, Hiyam got a face-lift.

On her first trip to America to visit her son, she saw that she could reinvent herself in Dearborn, a place that resembled Lebanon but wasn't Lebanon. In order to leave Makram, she had to leave the country, otherwise she'd stay with him forever. She was fed up with rearranging her face.

When Makram had learned of her intention to marry Bobbie, he'd called her immediately, begging her to return to him all these years later.

"We'll remarry," he had said, "and this time I won't disappoint you."

It's been nine days since they last spoke over the phone. She goes to WhatsApp and scrolls down her contacts list until she reaches his name. *Don't dial, don't dial.* Heart pounding, she dials. She's desperate to see him on video chat, to hear his voice. He doesn't pick up. He's seven hours ahead of her and is probably at dinner. Or is he in bed with his girlfriend? She draws on her vape pen to ease the ache in her chest.

♦

HIYAM STANDS IN THE living room of a colonial house for sale in Canton. The kitchen cabinets are outdated and the roof needs to be replaced. The master bedroom is big but the other two bedrooms are small. Usually, when she visits potential houses, she prances from room to room like a predator. But today she's sluggish. The image of her ex sucking on his girlfriend's breasts haunts her. *I'm the one who left him. Don't forget that.* She smells strong cologne and turns around.

"Like the house?" a man asks her.

She recognizes him from his billboards. His name is Fareed. He's considered Mr. Real Estate of Dearborn. He's nowhere near as muscular as he appears in the ads—he's got a double chin and a belly. His three-piece suit is too tight on him. His black hair, which is slicked back with gel, is thinning.

"How's the vape working for you?" he asks in English, staring at the swell of her breasts.

"Better than my smoking."

"So how do you like the house?"

"Not bad."

He's not the listing agent, so she doesn't have to answer him.

"See yourself living here?" he asks.

"It's not for me."

"For a friend?"

She shakes her head.

"Oh, I see. Who do you work for?"

"Myself."

"Yourself?" he asks, incredulous.

She gives him her business card.

"Hiyam, LLC," he says, looking down at it. "So, Hayoumi, how's your company doing?"

"Hiyam. My name is Hiyam." She says this in barely a whisper. "It's going great, actually."

"How many houses do you manage?"

"A lot."

"Mm. You know who I am?"

She doesn't answer. She hates how small she feels.

"Folks call me 'the Shark,'" he says. "You know why? Because I eat up all the competition. You don't look like no shark to me. More like a dolphin. A baby dolphin."

She sucks hard on her vape.

"I own Canton," he says. "I own all of Southeast Michigan. Number one agent in the state. Allah has blessed me. He can bless you, too, if you'd like to work for me."

"I'm a CEO."

"That's cute."

"I'm older than you."

"And hot."

"Aayb. Respect yourself."

He takes out his business card.

"I don't want it," she says.

"What if you'd like to call me? For business or pleasure."

"I'm a married woman."

"You're talking to the Shark, Hayoumi."

She feels unsteady on her feet. They're all alone in the house. She's about to walk to the front door when he grabs her arm.

"Remove your hand," she says in Arabic.

"Chill, Hayoumi." His grip tightens.

"Let go of me!"

He releases his grip. She hurries to the door, gets in her Escalade, and steps on the gas. At a red light, she swallows a mouthful of tears.

♦

IT'S APPROACHING DUSK WHEN Hiyam returns home. She finds Bobbie on the deck, peering up at the trees through his binoculars. He's wearing a baseball cap and a green Michigan State T-shirt. She pours herself a glass of red wine and gulps it down. Still feeling unnerved, she pours a second glass and steps outside. She and Bobbie kiss. He asks about her day and she says, "The usual." He tells her about his rounds at the golf course. She pretends to understand this talk.

"I was thinking about grilling lamb chops for dinner," he says. "How does that sound?"

"Delicious. Guess what?"

"What, honey bunny?"

"I saw a red canary this morning."

"Lucky you. But not as lucky as me! I just spotted a yellow goldfinch."

Hiyam knows Bobbie will never cheat on her or degrade her. He's easy to please. During the week he plays golf. In the fall, on Saturdays, he spends the entire day down in the basement, which he calls the "Spartan Cave," watching college football. On Sundays, he watches the NFL. Every so often, they go out for dinner. The rest of the time, she enjoys cooking Lebanese food for him. He files her taxes. With time, she believes she'll begin to understand his golf talk and everything else he says and feels. Will he understand her better? She hopes so. Hiyam wishes he could have seen her before she worked on her face, back when she was her true self. She misses that Hiyam, the life she once had. *Be grateful! You're in America now. Lebanese would kill to have your passport.*

"Bobbie, tell me that story again, about the time you got lost in the woods."

"But I told it last night."

"I want to hear it again. From the beginning."

"It's a pretty darn good yarn, isn't it, gal?"

"It sure is, Mohammed bin Abdullah Farouk."

They sit down in the deck chairs. She sips her wine as he narrates his story. This time she listens. Bobbie is halfway through when she feels the vibrations in her blazer pocket. It buzzes and buzzes. Her heart pounds. She reaches inside for her phone, clenching it until it goes still.

Yusra

t's July and I'm walking down Caniff Street in Hamtramck, covered from head to toe in black. I wear a niqab, leaving only a slit for my eyes, and an abaya. My furry hands are gloved. Despite my getup, I worry that someone might recognize the way I walk, tilting from side to side like a juiced-up bodybuilder. Though I'm of average height, my massive chest and big biceps make me stand out. I remind myself that I'm miles away from my Lebanese neighborhood in East Dearborn. My wife and son would never trek this far into Detroit, nor would my buddies. Lebanese don't come here. I hear Polish folk once ran this city within a city, but now Yemenis and Bangladeshis have taken over with all their grocery stores, restaurants, and mosques. I spot a pack of niqabis across the street, and I almost wave to them like we're all friends and haven't seen one another in months.

There are no clouds and few trees to provide shade. Sunshine floods the street, reflecting off the hoods of parked cars and storefront windows. I'm sweating like a sisterfucker. My abaya sticks to my bulk; my underwear is soaked. I can't remember walking as much as I have in these past weeks; my feet are blistered and my knees are sore. My lower back is starting to give out. And with my face covered, I keep smelling my stale breath. But I'm walking free as Yusra.

I wear mascara, lipstick, and clip-on earrings, and beneath my abaya a sleeveless dress for plus-sized women. I'm walking in high heels, my second pair; I broke the first pair learning how to walk in the fuckers. But I love the sound of heels clicking against asphalt, a sound that I can finally make.

I pass a Yemeni grocery, a secondhand clothing store, a gift shop, a used record store, and a Polish deli before arriving at a bakery with outside seating at the end of the block. When I order an iced coffee and two red velvet cupcakes, I adjust my voice, aim for a higher pitch. I sound ridiculous, but who fucking cares? No one knows me here, and the young woman at the register, who has long pink bangs gelled back and the sides of her head shaved, looks about as bored as my son does when he's working the register at my butchery. I take my drink and cupcakes outside and sit at an aluminum table under a striped awning. Sweat trickles down my back like every drop can't wait to kiss my ass. I peel off my heels and sigh in relief, resting my bare feet on the sidewalk. I pull back my niqab without exposing my face, and in the small space between the cloth and my mouth, I squeeze in my drink and suck from the straw with the force of a vacuum. I smack my lips and feel drunk happy even though I've never tasted a lick of alcohol. I haven't felt this exhilarated in a long time, not since my son was born and I held him in my arms for the first time, which was twenty-three years ago. I scarf down the cupcakes, fitting each under the niqab. If I've got frosting on my mustache, no one can see it.

I pull out my smartphone to check the time. It's not even noon yet, so I can relax. I'm not expected back at the butchery until late afternoon, when the weekend rush begins. As of three weeks ago, I told my wife and son that I was going to start taking Friday mornings off.

"To do what?" my wife had asked in Arabic. This was after dinner.

"Work on myself."

"Geez, Baba," my son said in English. "That sounds really New Agey."

I almost smacked him across the back of his head but held back. Ignoring him, I explained to my wife that I planned to start walking the Dearborn streets.

"Are you having a midlife crisis?" my son asked me.

This time I smacked him.

I bought women's clothing from an outlet far from Dearborn and a niqab and abaya from a store in Hamtramck. This is my third time dressing up as Yusra, and each time I've ended my walk at the bakery.

Allah bless this country. In Bint Jbeil, the village where I was born and raised in southern Lebanon, I'd never be able to dress up as Yusra. I was only Yasser there, Yasser who worked at his father's butchery and slaughtered animals, Yasser who smoked hookah with his childhood friends in the evenings at the pool hall, Yasser who married his second cousin not to keep the land in the family but because he truly loved her. I'm Yasser here, too, but I would like to think I can also be Yusra, if only for a few hours a week. I must be careful; if I'm found out, I could be beaten up or killed. But who dares fuck with me? In Bint Jbeil I got into fistfights like they were daily prayers. I've broken more noses and cracked more jaws and smashed more ribs than I can remember. Even at sixty-two years old, I've got enough power left in my hands to knock out a horse.

I hear the call to prayer. The muezzin's voice floats in the sky like Allah herself is in the air. I feel like praying now, to give thanks for the chance to eat cupcakes as Yusra. I follow the muezzin's call to its source and enter the mosque. The atrium is filled with niqabis and hijabis and men with skullcaps and beards. I look from side to side; no one suspects anything, and why should they? I'm just a big-sized woman. But my palms are sweating. Before entering the prayer room, I remove my heels and put them in the shoe cubby for women. I should head to the women's wudu station to wash myself, but if I keep my niqab on while I try to splash water over my face and rinse my mouth, it'll only attract more attention.

"Excuse me, do you need help with something?" someone behind me asks in Arabic. The voice has a Yemeni accent.

I turn around. A young, short woman is looking up at me, her hijab wrapped tightly around her face. There's a bump at the bridge of her long nose. Her skin is chestnut brown.

I shake my head, too afraid to speak.

"Is this your first time here?" she asks.

I nod.

"Want me to show you the wudu station?"

I shake my head.

"Ah, you must have already performed wudu."

I nod.

"Then let's go pray."

I follow her into the back of the prayer room, where the women are seated on the rug. The men are seated up front. My heart is pounding like a sisterfucker on speed, not that I've ever taken speed. I sit next to the young woman against the back wall.

"My name is Petra," she says. She waits for me to give her my name.

"Yusra," I say in the same voice I used at the bakery.

"Are you Yemeni?"

"Lebanese."

"Welcome."

Thankfully, our conversation is cut short when the imam walks up to the microphone placed at the front of the room. We all stand up and form lines shoulder to shoulder and the imam begins reciting the Al-Fatiha. As I kneel and touch my forehead on the floor, I have to stop myself from laughing because I'm drunk happy again.

Following the service, I pick up my heels from the cubby and have a cup of tea with Petra in the foyer. We stand among dozens of women on one side of the room and the men on the other side.

"Do you live in Hamtramck?" Petra asks me above the buzz of chatter. She must be around my son's age. I notice a wedding band on her finger.

"Dearborn," I say.

"And you came all the way out here to pray?"

"This city is special to me . . . my husband, Allah yerhamo, used to work with Yemenis at the Ford Rouge plant. I wanted to come here and pray in his honor." Lying comes easy for me.

"I'm so sorry for your loss," Petra says. "I didn't mean to pry—"

I leave the mosque, get into my van, and drive to an abandoned warehouse and park on a dead-end street. Keeping the van running with the AC cranked up, I crawl into the rear and change into Yasser.

♦

MY SON, ABDULLAH, SITS behind the register, all three hundred pounds of him. He wears an extra-extra-large Detroit Pistons jersey over a T-shirt and cargo shorts that reach down to his shins. Years ago, he wore sports jerseys without a shirt underneath to show off his biceps, but these days he's got more flab than muscle. The poor boy used to be a star offensive lineman on the Fordson High football team; Division One programs were interested in him. But in a Friday night game his senior year against Dearborn High, the biggest game of the regular season, he snapped his leg in two and dislocated his knee in a single play. I could hear him screaming from the bleachers, the worst sound I've ever heard. I ran onto the field and held his hand.

His teammates were all on their knees. I begged Allah to spare my son and inflict the pain on me instead, but my prayers went unanswered. I was utterly helpless.

Abdu had a metal rod and pins installed in his leg and never played football again. After attending community college for a couple of years, he gave up on his education and joined me at the butcher shop. He still lives with us. I have no interest in him taking over the shop once I retire. I plan to sell it. My father, my grandfather, and my great-grandfather were all butchers; the cleaver runs in our family like a curse. I want Abdu to be a doctor or a lawyer. Shit, I know that's not going to happen. Abdu wasn't ever good at school. But he can go into real estate or some other business. I want him to wear a suit to work and one day see his face on a billboard. For now, my wife has encouraged me to pay for space on a billboard to advertise Yasser's Meats, home of my famous kafta, but I think my ugly mug would only scare drivers. If it was beautiful Yusra up there, maybe then it would be a different story.

Abdu looks at me like he can see right through me and my heart thumps again. Is there still mascara on my lashes or rouge on my lips? I cleaned myself silly in the van. After changing back into Yasser, I dropped off Yusra's clothes at a dry cleaner, where I also pay the clerk a little extra to keep my heels, bag of makeup, and jewelry in the back room. I reach for my ears and feel only lobes.

"What?" I ask in Arabic.

"How was walking?

"Good."

I roll up my sleeves and put on my apron, tying the straps across my lower back. My assistant, Sleiman, a Syrian from Homs, is in the back carving up a cow carcass. I slip on disposable gloves and begin cutting chunks of meat for shish kabob and stew, and as I cut, I taste a terrible bitterness. Being Yasser makes me feel immensely sad and lonely. It's not that I don't enjoy being Yasser, because as Yasser I'm a husband and a father, a successful butcher, a man with loyal friends. It's just that I don't want to be Yasser all the time.

A mother and her young daughter enter the shop and the mother orders my famous kafta. I take out another knife, the blade curled at the tip like a crescent moon, and over a wooden board I cut a batch of parsley in half and then I quarter onions so quick that the mother and her daughter gasp in fear I'll slice off my fingertips—*tap, tap, tap,* the blade sounds on the board, reminding me of heels on asphalt. For a moment, I see myself as Yusra, and I can taste the cupcakes again. I slide everything into the food processor with my blade. I remove a slab of meat from the counter, slice it up into big chunks, and slide it into the meat grinder. Clumps of ground meat ooze out onto a tray. I reach back into the counter for a piece of tail fat, cut it up, and throw that into the grinder. I carry the tray to the counter and slide its contents onto the wooden board, pour the mash of onions and parsley on top, and garnish the mound with my secret blend of dark spices. I replace my knife with a cleaver, and with blistering speed I fold all the meat and fat and greens into each other, my cleaver gliding the meat in one direction and my free hand sending it back until the meat turns into a light brown oval studded with parsley.

At closing time, Abdu tells me that I've been grumpy since I returned from my walk.

"Are you happy?" I ask him.

"I hate that question."

"Count the till."

◆

AFTER DINNER, MY WIFE and I sit in the living room to watch TV. Abdu has left the house to smoke hookah with his former teammates.

"You've been quiet all evening," Samar says. Her hair is long and silver.

"Just thinking about Abdu's future," I lie.

"At least he's working."

Samar and I grew up together in Bint Jbeil. In our youth I never paid much attention to her at family gatherings, but after what happened to her parents and siblings, I started to look after her. For years our village and other towns in southern Lebanon were bombed by Israeli fighter jets on the hunt for Palestinian militias. The militias would camp in our woods and launch attacks across the border. We supported their cause, but we paid for it with our lives. One day, Samar's mother sent her to the souk to buy lemons. As Samar was on her way to the main square, she heard the thunder of a fighter jet, and moments later, a bomb exploded. I was at my father's butchery when I heard the blast. Samar's house had been flattened. Her parents and four siblings were buried under the rubble.

At the funeral, Samar remained at her mother's sister's house to accept condolences. When I went inside to offer mine, I found her in the living room surrounded by women: her aunts, cousins, neighbors, schoolmates. They were all dressed in black. A Qur'an lay open on a side table. A middle-aged woman recited suras from the holy book. The aunt sitting next to Samar, Samar's mother's sister, began slapping her chest and howling. Soon all the women were wailing and crying for Allah's mercy, all except for Samar, who sat with a straight face. *She's an orphan now*, I thought. *She must be in shock.* I wanted to console her, but I had no words except for the ones I whispered in her ear: "If anyone bothers you, let me know." She moved in with her aunt, and when she turned eighteen, I married her. Villagers were surprised that such a soft-spoken woman would end up with a brute like me, but Samar felt protected by me. More than anyone else.

We immigrated to America following the Israeli invasion of Beirut in 1982. Samar's happy in Dearborn, where she can live without the fear of fighter jets and still speak Arabic on the streets. She thinks of her dead family every day, carrying that pain with her wherever she goes, though now she's accustomed to its weight. She's the strongest person I know, and I try my hardest not to think of the pain I'd cause her if she ever found out about Yusra.

She pulls up her pants leg and glides her hand over her hairy skin.

"Time for sukar," I say.

I'm the one who prepares her wax, always have. We go into the kitchen, and she watches as I pour a cup of sugar into a pan and squeeze half a lemon on top and wet with water the sugar that hasn't been juiced over. The water hardens the forming wax, and the lemon juice softens it; I find the right balance and turn off the stove, wet a slab of marble with cold water, and pour the melted sugar onto it. I nudge the sides to the center with my stubby fingers and keep doing this until the color turns from amber to golden yellow and the glob starts to cool and becomes pliable.

As a boy, I used to watch my mother make sukar. She'd tear off a small piece for me to eat, but I wasn't so much interested in its taste as how Mama used it, which was to wax her legs and underarms. I once flattened a piece of sukar on my shin and pulled it up, removing my hair. Mama snatched the sukar from my hand.

"If your Baba sees you waxing your leg he'll beat you," she said.

That day she allowed me to wax her legs on her bedroom floor to the sound of Umm Kulthum on the transistor radio. We kept our ears open in case Baba returned home from work early. When I was older I started to wax my younger sister's legs in secret. I'd also wax a spot on my upper thigh, which was hidden from view. At night I rubbed that smooth spot over and over.

Samar and I return to the living room. We sit on the floor and I watch her wax her legs. Once she's done and the sukar is covered in black specks of hair, I glide my hands up and down her soft legs, wishing that mine felt the same. We kiss and her saliva wets my mustache. We move to our bedroom and make love.

Once Samar falls asleep, I pull out my phone and visit my favorite online chatrooms, where I'm known as "Yusra_right-hooktothechin." I discovered everything I know about the LGBTQ community on the internet. Before my online research I had no fucking clue about what those letters represented, and I became pissed off at Americans' obsession with acronyms. I now understand the whole pronoun business, and although I don't mind being a "he" or a "she," I wonder if I should just be a "they." If the Dearborn community ever found out about Yusra, I'd shame my family not only here but also in Bint Jbeil, because word would reach them as quick as it takes to send a text message. I'd lose my customers and then my business. How would I support my family? That's assuming they wouldn't reject me. I understood all these risks I was taking when I first dressed up as Yusra, but I had to try it out—my anonymous friends in the chatrooms rallied for me to embrace my true self, whatever the fuck that means.

Yusra has always been a part of me. I first spoke her name when I was sixteen, and I met my friend Rami down in the valley to hunt birds. Only we didn't hunt. We went into the shade of an oak tree where no one could see us. I pulled a tube of red lipstick, which I had stolen from my sister's drawer, from my pocket and applied it over my lips. Rami slid his pants and underwear down to his ankles. "Call me Yusra," I told Rami. I got down on my knees and took his cock in my mouth and began sucking him off. "Yusra," he moaned again and again, pulling on the back of my hair. He ejaculated and I spat his cum in the dirt.

Rami got on his knees to suck me off. When I was done, I said I'd kill him if he ever mentioned what we'd done to anyone.

"Relax, Yusra," he said.

I punched him in the face, breaking his jaw. As he wept on the ground, blood pouring from his mouth, I said he could call me Yusra only when I said so. Otherwise, he was to call me Yasser. Rami's mouth was wired shut for the next six weeks. When he healed, we continued sucking each other off under the oak tree. And then I married Samar and he married a woman from the town across the valley. We lost touch after I left the country.

◆

IT'S FRIDAY AND I'M back at the mosque in Hamtramck. I've had my iced coffee and cupcakes and now I'm ready to pray as Yusra again. I look around for Petra but I don't see her anywhere. I enter the prayer room and head toward the back.

"Salam wa alaykum," the women tell me as I waddle past them.

"Wa alaykum wa salam," I respond. I see the suspicion in their eyes and I tell myself, "No one knows. No one will ever know."

Following prayer, I retrieve my heels from the cubby and slip them on and sip tea in the foyer. It's while I'm standing among the women that I notice Petra coming out of the prayer room. We make eye contact, and she darts over to me.

"I arrived late today," she explains. "My husband called, and when he calls, I have to answer because I don't know when he'll call again."

"I miss the sound of my husband's voice."

"Allah yerhamo," she says, and holds my free hand.

"Is your husband not in Hamtramck?"

"He's away at sea." Her eyes fill with tears. She removes a tissue from her purse and blows her nose. "I need to buy a few groceries from the store. Care to join me?"

"I'd love to."

We step outside and walk down the street. In heels I tower over Petra.

"I'm glad you came back," she says. "I was hoping to see you again."

"How come?"

"Because I don't know any other Lebanese. I only leave Hamtramck when my husband is in town. I don't drive."

I tell her that a few Yemeni restaurants and cafés have opened in East Dearborn. When Samar and I first arrived in Dearborn, the east side was dominated by Lebanese. Then the Iraqis entered the area, and the Yemenis soon followed.

"I'm still new to America," Petra says. "I don't have many friends."

At the grocery store, Petra buys milk, a carton of eggs, and some vegetables. I insist on carrying the plastic bag.

"My house is just around the corner," she says.

"I'll walk you there."

Petra lives on the upper floor of a duplex. At the stoop I hand her the bag.

"When does your husband return from sea?" I ask.

"He should be back by the fall. He works as a sailor on the Great Lakes, though sometimes they go out much wider. He's now on the eastern coast of Africa. He sends me the most beautiful pictures of the ports he's visited."

She invites me inside for tea. I say that I've got to get back to work.

"Where do you work?"

"Oh . . . At a butchery. I clean in the back."

Petra suggests that we exchange numbers. We do.

"Do you have any children?" she asks.

"I'm all alone."

That evening, as Samar and I are watching TV, I receive a text message from Petra. She's sent me a picture of her husband standing on the bow of his freighter. He must be in his early thirties and has buck teeth. He's squinting in the sun, his black hair blowing in the wind. In all the years I've lived in Dearborn, I've never had a Yemeni friend. I feel rotten that some of my buddies think that Yemenis are beneath Lebanese. It's because Yemenis are mostly darker-skinned than us, and thinking of dark skin reminds me of Jamon, who owns a gas station in Detroit near the border with Dearborn. One day, after stopping at an Arab butchery in the Eastern Market, where I buy my meat in bulk, I was on my way back to Dearborn when I stopped to fill my tank. I went inside the little mart to pay for my gas and saw a Black man reading behind the register. He was holding a book in one hand while biting the nails of his other hand. His fingers were long and slender. He put the book on the counter and nudged his glasses up his nose. After I paid, I asked if he was enjoying his book, and he said that he was and recommended the novels of Walter Mosley.

Two weeks later I returned to the gas station. The man handed me a copy of *Devil in a Blue Dress*.

"Thought I'd give this to you in case you returned," he said. "It's Mosley's first novel and my favorite."

I stayed for an hour, just talking in my halfway decent English. Jamon was around my age and had been born and raised in Detroit. He refused to cross the border into Dearborn, not even to eat the city's delicious Arabic food.

"Why not?" I asked.

"Don't you know about what happened in '67?"

"Of course. The Six-Day War."

"No. I'm talking about the Detroit Rebellion. We went into the streets to protest against police brutality. The mayor of Dearborn lined up police forces on the border and told his men to shoot any Black person who entered the city. Only he didn't refer to us as Black folk. The man was mayor for nearly forty years, and from what I hear, he didn't care for Arabs either."

I then understood why so few Black people lived in Dearborn. I didn't tell Jamon that some people in our community called Blacks "Abeed," the Arabic word for slaves. The next time I visited Jamon was after he'd closed for the day. We went into his back room, where he made a pot of coffee. We sat and talked about *Devil in a Blue Dress*. I had read the book in two days, I liked it that much.

When things got quiet between me and Jamon, he began biting his nails. He bit them until they bled.

"Don't do that!" I said. I got up from my chair, took his hand, and sucked on his fingers, swallowing his blood. He stood up and leaned in to kiss me. His breath smelled of Pet Milk. I shoved him back and he fell on his ass; his glasses flew across the room. I picked them up and handed them to him and then helped him up. He winced in pain. I left the gas station without another word.

These days, when I'm driving back from the Eastern Market, I take another route to Dearborn. If I drive by Jamon's gas station I fear that I'll stop to see if he's there.

What's your husband's name? I text Petra.

Mohammed. What was your husband's name? Allah yerhamo.

Yasser.

Samar looks at me.

"The guys," I tell her, shaking my head. "The guys" means my WhatsApp group made up of my Dearborn buddies. We mostly send each other filthy jokes.

◆

ON SUNDAY, SAMAR AND I attend my friend's barbeque. We're sitting in his backyard, where he's grilling kabobs and lamb chops. All my buddies are here. We sit in plastic chairs on one side of the yard with our wives on the other. There's a hookah for every two men just as there's a hookah for every two women, although Samar doesn't smoke and glances at me every now and then.

I watch the women chat and smoke as I sip a bottle of nonalcoholic beer; I wish I could sit with them. The men are dying to tell raunchy jokes, but with our wives nearby we can't. If I were drinking real alcohol maybe then I'd forget about what I'm thinking, and what I'm thinking is that I can't wait for Friday to come, that it's too far into the week. My phone pings with a text. I pull it out and see a message from Petra and instantly I'm giddy. She's asking if I'd like to come over for coffee. We're on the same wavelength!

I wish, but I'm busy with family, I write.

Another time . . . I haven't heard from Mohammed in days. Do you think he's safe?

Don't worry. Allah is watching over him.

"Who're you texting, dirty boy?" my friend Louay asks me.

Startled, I look up at him. A wide grin stretches across his greasy face. "Sleiman. He works at the shop."

"But you're closed on Sundays."

"We're working out his schedule for the week."

Louay leaves his chair to refill his plate and I put my phone on silent and return to texting.

There's something that's bothering me, Yusra, Petra writes.

I fear that she's found me out and I begin to panic. My hands are trembling as I text: *What is it, habibti?*

I hear that sailors spend so much time at sea that when they return to land they're hungry for women. Do you think Mohammed is cheating on me?

Relieved, I type: *But he loves you. I can see it in his eyes, from that picture you sent me.*

You're right. I'm just being paranoid. We've talked about having kids!

"Still texting Sleiman, dirty boy?" Louay asks me. I didn't even notice that he returned to his chair. Across the yard, Samar is staring at me.

Petra continues to text; I'll arouse more suspicion if I respond to her. Instead, I go inside my friend's house, step out the front door, walk onto the sidewalk, and call Petra.

"You'll make a wonderful mother," I tell her. My voice is high-pitched and squeaky.

"You're so comforting, Yusra. I thank Allah for bringing us together. The women in my neighborhood are nice to me, but I can't open up to them like I can with you."

"You're like my own daughter, habibti," I say, and I go on and on about how much I love Hamtramck and Yemeni people. I'm not sure what I'm saying but it all sounds good to me; I'm overcome with joy. And it's then that I notice an Arab teenage boy on the street, sitting on his bicycle with one foot on the asphalt. He's staring at me like I'm a zoo animal.

"What's wrong with your voice, uncle?" he asks in English.

I put my phone on mute and switch back to Yasser. "Fuck off," I tell him.

◆

THAT EVENING, WHILE SAMAR and Abdu are watching TV, I go upstairs to the master bathroom and look at my reflection in the mirror. I've had my mustache since I could grow facial hair and can't imagine myself without it. Still, I pull out my electric razor and put it to my face. As my black and gray bristles fall in the sink, I feel lighter, like I'm floating. I wash and dry my face and then lick my smooth upper lip. I go downstairs and sit in my recliner in the living room. When Samar looks at me, she screams. Abdu cups his mouth.

"How do I look?" I ask them.

"Strange," Abdu says.

"What's gotten into you, Yasser?" Samar asks.

"Nothing."

"Who were you texting at the barbeque?"

"What does that have to do with anything?"

"I saw you texting like your fingers were on fire."

"What's going on?" Abdu asks.

"I was texting Sleiman," I say, and I tell her the same lie that I told Louay. Samar does and doesn't believe me. Abdu is still confused.

"There's nothing to worry about, habibi," I tell him.

♦

THE URGE TO SEE Petra is unbearable. On Monday, I call the dry cleaner and tell him I need to pick up my belongings today. Until that time comes, I cut up meat and chicken and make more of my special blend of spices. Abdu sits at the register with his face buried in his phone and Sleiman is in the back carving up another cow. Later, Sleiman leaves for the day and I go out to buy lunch for Abdu and me. We eat our sandwiches and drink coffee in silence. I prefer it this way because all I can think about is driving to Hamtramck. About twenty minutes before I'm supposed to leave, I make kafta for Petra. I'm mixing the greens into the meat with my cleaver and free hand when Abdu asks me who the order is for.

I stop what I'm doing. "Why does it matter?"

Abdu fiddles with his thumbs, which he does when he's nervous. "I spoke to Sleiman. He said you never texted him over the weekend."

I raise the cleaver above my head and slam it into the cutting board, breaking the wood in half.

"What the fuck!" Abdu says.

"The kafta is for a poor widow. She's the one I was texting. I didn't mention her to your mother because it doesn't look good—me texting another woman. The widow is old enough to be your grandmother. She came in one day when you were off."

Abdu nods. He does and doesn't believe me. He returns to his phone.

I take out another cutting board.

◆

"I'VE BROUGHT YOU KAFTA," I tell Petra, standing on her stoop. I texted her that I was bringing early dinner. I'm in my black getup. In the van I changed into my dress and put on makeup in a hurry. "The meat is from my work."

"Bless your hands. Come in, ya ikhti." Ikhti, my sister. It sounds wonderful.

I follow her upstairs and enter her two-bedroom apartment. She removes her hijab and unpins her shiny black hair and lets it fall down to her shoulders.

"We can grill the meat out on the kitchen balcony," she says. "The balcony is private, so no one will see you if you'd like to remove your niqab."

"Oh, I'd prefer to keep it on."

I grill the meat with onions and tomatoes as Petra sets the table and makes a pitcher of fresh lemonade. I told her that I already ate and not to account for me, but she does. Once the meat and vegetables are cooked, I carry the food inside on a tray and we sit at the table.

"Wouldn't you rather remove your gloves and niqab?" Petra asks. "It's only you and me here."

I knew this moment would come and I'm prepared. "I have a skin rash. And I'm not hungry."

"I don't mind what you look like."

"It's a really bad rash, with puss and blisters. I often get these rashes in the summer. I've got allergies, and in this heat—"

"Yusra, I don't mind." She's looking straight into my eyes, into my soul.

"The rash . . ."

"I already know, Yusra. I knew from the moment I first saw you. It's okay, I won't tell anyone. Trust me."

I remember the terrifying thrill of sucking Rami off in the shade of the oak tree as Yusra. That was over forty years ago;

desire seared through me then. What I want now, more than anything, is to stop hiding. I pray that Petra doesn't betray me.

I remove my niqab.

Petra smiles and takes a bite of kafta. "Delicious," she says. As she continues to eat, I stand up and remove my gloves and abaya.

"Nice dress," Petra says with a full mouth.

I sit back down and join her in the meal. My feet are aching; I keep my heels on.

Rabbit Stew

I n the international arrivals area of the Detroit Metropolitan Airport, I waited with my parents for my uncle Ramzy to arrive from Beirut. This would be his first trip to America. It was March 1991, months after the end of the Lebanese civil war and the end of the first Gulf War. I was seventeen.

A handful of other Lebanese were waiting around for the same plane from Paris, a common stopover from Beirut. Unlike Mama, most of the women wore hijabs. Bundled in my thick winter coat, I kept monitoring the flight board to see if my uncle's plane had landed. I was nervous with anticipation. I hadn't seen him since 1980, when I was six years old, right before my parents and I left Lebanon to immigrate to America.

My most vivid childhood memory of Lebanon is of Uncle Ramzy. In the memory, we are sitting on the couch in the living room of my parents' apartment in Beirut, my uncle opening the silver lid of his Zippo, flicking the spark wheel with his thumb, and holding the blue flame to my face so I can blow it out like a birthday candle. My parents are out somewhere with my older sister and have left my uncle to look after me. He relights the flame again and again and then a bomb explodes, shattering the windows; glass shards fly across the room. I drop to the floor, covering my head as my parents have taught me to do, crying in terror. Uncle Ramzy scoops me up and carries me out of the apartment and down six flights of stairs to the basement, which has been converted into a shelter. We sit on thin mattresses with our backs against the wall, surrounded by other frightened tenants. It is hot and dusty. My uncle checks my body for cuts; I am unscathed. I lean into him, comforted by his warmth. A trickle of blood drips down from his forehead. I point it out to him. He wipes off his blood with the hem of his shirt and then pulls out his Zippo to light a cigarette. The bombing continues as my uncle smokes one cigarette after the other, keeping his arm draped around my shoulders. Although I am sweating, I don't want him to remove his arm. Our building shakes from the reverberations. When a woman sitting across from us begins wailing that it is only a matter of time before the enemy breaks through the front entrance and massacres us, the children start to cry. I bury my face in Uncle Ramzy's chest. His shirt is plastered to his skin; I can taste his sweat.

"Don't worry, Captain," he tells me, his hot, smoky breath in my ear. "No one fucks with me."

Some months later, my family and I left for America. We maintained communication with my uncle and other family members over long-distance telephone calls with spotty reception. I was always eager to speak with Uncle Ramzy. I saw him as a hero; he had saved my life. But when I was nine or ten, my uncle asked me, his voice blasting over the line, if I had started growing pubic hair. Standing in the foyer where we kept our phone, I was too shy to respond. My parents had heard the question and looked horrified.

"As soon as you start sprouting some curls down there," my uncle said, "watch out for the girls. They're going to chase after you."

Mama snatched the phone from my hand and quickly ended the call.

Over the years, I learned little about my uncle from conversations with him, but after prying information out of my parents, I found out that he had worked several jobs, including as a car mechanic and a personal driver. In the eighties, whenever reports about war-torn Beirut came on the evening news and scenes of mayhem were shown, my parents murmured prayers even though they weren't practicing Muslims, dreading the sight of a loved one on a gurney. Mama would then call her younger brother to make sure he was still alive.

Growing up, Mama and Uncle Ramzy had been terrified of their father, who had a bad temper and was known to squeeze my uncle's arm in a vicelike grip, sometimes bruising it, whenever my uncle misbehaved.

"Touch Ramzy like that again and I'll bite you till you bleed," Mama once told her father, pointing her trembling index finger at him. She was only twelve, Ramzy eight. Her father's face turned red. Mama braced herself to be struck. Instead, her father walked out of the room as if ashamed. He never laid a hand on Ramzy again.

Mama had urged Uncle Ramzy to follow her to America to escape the war, but he refused. "I can't live without Beirut," he had told her. But now that the civil war was over, he was willing to visit and planned to spend a month with us.

I looked up at the flight board. The plane had landed. Forty-five minutes later, Uncle Ramzy appeared, dragging a suitcase. He wore a black leather jacket and blue jeans.

"Habibi ya Captain!" he said, rising on his tiptoes to kiss my cheeks, as his intense underarm odor wafted to me.

His curly black hair was flecked with silver. His bushy mustache consumed his upper lip. When we embraced, I was stunned by how short and skinny he was; in my mind he was much bigger than me. But it had been eleven years since I'd last seen him, and I was now as tall as Baba.

"Look at that hair!" my uncle said. My black hair was down to my shoulders, my beard a mess of scruffy patches.

"I can't believe you're here," Mama said, beaming at her brother. "I've been waiting years for this moment."

"Welcome to America," Baba said.

"I already miss Beirut," Uncle Ramzy said.

"We miss it every day," Mama said. By "we" Mama meant Baba and she, because for me, my hometown was Dearborn, where I had grown up.

Uncle Ramzy took out a pack of Marlboros and a Zippo. I wondered if it was the same lighter he had used when I was six. He lit up and inhaled deeply. This was the first time that he had flown in an airplane, and in his anxiousness, he admitted, he had slept fitfully.

I pulled the suitcase on the way to the parking lot as Uncle Ramzy and my parents walked ahead of me. When we reached the exit doors, Baba zipped up his down coat and instructed us to remain inside while he went out to get the car. Uncle Ramzy clearly wasn't dressed for Michigan weather, and we didn't want him to catch a cold. Mama went to the restroom, leaving me and my uncle alone.

"You look like a hippie," Uncle Ramzy told me, sucking hard on his cigarette. "Do the ladies like it?"

"Not sure."

"You've got to read them better, Amer. Got a girlfriend?"

I shook my head.

"Still a virgin?"

I blushed.

"Shit," Uncle Ramzy said. "I lost my virginity when I was fifteen. To the baker's daughter. A wild thing, that one. Nearly broke the Arabian Peninsula."

"The Arabian Peninsula?"

"My scimitar. Don't tell your mother about the baker's daughter. The two of them were close."

I was relieved when Mama returned from the restroom.

◆

WE LIVED IN A three-bedroom brick house in East Dearborn. My sister was away studying law in Los Angeles, so Uncle Ramzy stayed in her room. Mama had prepared roast chicken, but before we all sat down at the table, Uncle Ramzy presented us with gifts. He had brought packages of thyme, sumac, fermented wheat, pine nuts, sugared almonds, nougat candies, and jars of pickled eggplant and homemade fig jam. He gave Baba a bottle of Bien-être cologne and Mama a wooden jewelry box with mother-of-pearl inlaid on the arabesque cover. I got a dented silver flask.

"It used to be mine," he told me. "Mostly filled it with vodka."

We sat down at the table. Uncle Ramzy shoveled the food into his mouth, grunting and licking his fingers as he chewed on a drumstick, his greasy chin flaked with parsley from the tabbouleh. He ate with his mouth open, smacking his lips. Instead of spooning hummus onto his plate, he scooped it directly from the bowl with pieces of pita bread and smeared the edges of his mustache when he brought them to his mouth. For a man so small, he ate like a heavyweight boxer.

After the meal, Uncle Ramzy sat back in his chair and lit a cigarette. Mama made a rakweh of Turkish coffee and brought it to the table.

"Amer's hair reminds me of yours back in the day, Fysal," Uncle Ramzy told Baba, slurping his coffee from the demitasse cup.

I had seen black-and-white photographs of Baba during his student days at the American University of Beirut, wearing button-down shirts with pointy collars and bell-bottomed pants. In one, he stood next to Mama in the shade of a banyan tree near West Hall. My parents met at the university, where they were both scholarship students. They had grown up in Dahieh, a Shiite suburb of Beirut. Baba's hair was now gray and cut short and brushed to the side. He was the manager of a local bank. Mama supervised the human resources department of an accounting firm.

Baba delicately sipped his coffee. "I miss those days before the war."

"Before the war" was a common refrain that I was accustomed to hearing whenever my parents waxed nostalgic about Beirut. When they had started dating—a few years before the war—they spent their free time roaming the city streets, walking down the Corniche to enjoy the sunset; eating chocolate éclairs and sipping cappuccino at Café Paris on Hamra Street, where intellectuals and artists gathered; watching movies at the Rivoli in Martyrs' Square; losing themselves in the labyrinthine souks downtown. When the war broke out in April 1975, it became impossible for them to cross into East Beirut, the Christian sector. An imaginary green line had divided the city across religious lines, confining them to the west side.

"Is Beirut all destroyed?" Mama asked Uncle Ramzy.

"Downtown is a wasteland," he said. "It'll take time for the city to rebuild itself."

My parents had discussed returning to Beirut for a visit now that the war had ended. They were waiting for June or July, when my sister and I could join them over the summer break. They wanted to return to their beloved city as a family, the way they had left it.

I recounted my memory of Lebanon, describing how Uncle Ramzy had carried me down to the shelter as the sky was raining bombs.

"Too bad that's all you remember of Beirut," he said. "It was once a beautiful city. But I never gave up on it."

"What're you trying to say?" Baba snapped. I was surprised at his tone. Mama gave him a look that said *not now*.

"Too many people abandoned the city."

"We didn't abandon the city. We left because we feared for our children's safety."

Uncle Ramzy finished his cup and refilled it.

♦

IN THE EARLY HOURS of the morning, I went to get a glass of water and found Uncle Ramzy sitting at the kitchen table, eating from a jar of peanut butter.

"I can't sleep," he said.

"It's jet lag. You'll need a few days to adjust."

He offered me his spoon to dig into the peanut butter.

"No thanks."

"I love this stuff. It was hard to get during the war."

He ate a chunky mouthful and then had trouble swallowing it. I poured him a glass of milk, which he guzzled down.

"We also never got fresh milk," he said. "Just Nido. Pour me another glass."

I poured him more milk.

He took a gulp. "Delicious," he said, giving himself a milk mustache. "I bet Americans are feeling really good about themselves these days. After their army crushed Saddam's forces."

"Did you follow the coverage?"

During the Gulf War, I had sat riveted in front of CNN: the tragedy of the world available to us twenty-four hours a day. I watched with awe as General Norman Schwarzkopf, known as "the Bear," walked into an army base near the front lines of the Saudi-Iraqi border and saluted his soldiers. General Schwarzkopf looked about as big as a bear in his camouflage and boots. When the camera zoomed in on his face, his gray hair blowing in the desert wind, I knew Saddam's army didn't stand a chance against our M1 Abrams tanks and Humvees topped with fifty-caliber machine guns, or our Black Hawk helicopters and F-15s and F-16s.

Whenever American casualties were reported and the names of fallen soldiers flashed across the screen, I felt sad for them and their families, as if I had known them. Some of the dead were just a year older than me.

"Think of the thousands of Iraqis who have been killed in this war," Baba had said. "Not just soldiers. Innocent civilians, too."

It had been hard for my parents to watch America and its coalition of allies bombard Iraq, no matter how much they despised Saddam. We were Arabs, after all.

"I was too busy brokering peace with the enemy to follow the news in Iraq," Uncle Ramzy said.

"What do you mean?"

"I mean putting down my gun."

I was confused.

"I see," Uncle Ramzy said. "Your parents never told you."

"Told me what?"

"About me and the militia. That I was a fighter."

"You? A fighter?"

"Why do you sound so surprised? Yes, a fighter."

"But I thought you worked as a driver. Or something like that."

"For a short time. But then I became a full-time fighter. A sniper, actually. And a damn good one."

I was sitting across from a killer and I wasn't quite sure what to make of it. I couldn't imagine Uncle Ramzy harming anyone. He seemed too small to cause damage. But it was more than this. He was family, and we were a peaceful bunch. Or at least I'd thought so.

"I never knew I was such a good shot," Uncle Ramzy said, "until me and the boys trained up in the mountains. This was back in '75, during the early months of the war. We took turns firing Kalashnikovs at bullseyes nailed to pine trees. I had never fired a gun before but I hit the target eight times out of ten. I was born to snipe." He yawned. "I've got plenty of stories. Just you wait."

◆

AFTER A BIG SUNDAY breakfast, I borrowed Mama's car to take Uncle Ramzy to Fairlane Mall to buy him a warm coat and other winter clothes. Uncle Ramzy had suggested to my parents that he and I go alone to catch up man-to-man, whatever that meant. Before we left the house, Mama slipped me several hundred-dollar bills. "Make sure you pay for everything."

As we drove, the heat cranked up high, Uncle Ramzy looked out the steamy window. The sky was overcast, the road wet with dirty slush. Icicles hung from the eaves of houses.

"I thought Dearborn was a city," Uncle Ramzy said. "I don't see any big buildings or people walking the streets."

"It's not Chicago or New York, if that's what you mean."

"Or Beirut. You know what Dearborn looks like to me?"

I kept my eyes focused on the road.

"A shithole," he said.

I gripped the steering wheel. "You haven't even been here for twenty-four hours."

"I can recognize a shithole when I see one."

At Macy's Uncle Ramzy gravitated toward a rack of down jackets with fake fur lining the hoods. He stroked the fur as if he were petting a cat.

"One of my comrades used to wear a black fur coat in battle," he said. "We all loved running our hands across it. Marwan had inherited the coat from his father, a Russian from Saint Petersburg. It was his most valuable possession. Following his shift, he'd sit on his mattress and clean the dirt and dust from the coat with a damp towel. He cared more about cleaning that coat than his gun. He was our most fashionable warrior."

"Wasn't there a dress code? Like a uniform?"

"We were in a militia, not an army."

"What did you wear?"

"A cowboy hat. The boys called me 'Cowboy.'"

"You like Westerns?"

"Not really. I just thought I looked good in a cowboy hat. Marwan once let me try on his coat. He was a big guy, so it swallowed me up. It was the warmest coat I've ever put on; it felt like a bear was hugging me." He smiled. "I have an idea. Follow my lead."

I followed him around the department store until he screeched like a child when we came across a display of fur coats in the women's section. The coats were arranged by fur—mink, beaver, red fox, otter, lynx, and rabbit. When I checked the price tag on one of them, I gasped: $10,000. Meanwhile, Uncle Ramzy had put on a full-length lynx coat and was standing in front of the mirror. The coat reached down to his ankles.

"How do I look?" he asked.

"It's a lady's coat, Uncle." I looked around the store, fearful of encountering anyone from school. I would be made fun of for weeks, if not months, for checking out women's coats.

"Doesn't matter. Does it look good on me?"

"The coat suits you, sir," a saleslady said. We both turned to her; she had crept up on us. She wore a business suit and heels, her brown hair puffed out in a perm. Her perfume was overpowering, enough to counter Uncle Ramzy's underarm odor.

"Real men wear fur coats," Uncle Ramzy said. "Don't you agree, Madame?"

"Fur is fur; I think anyone can wear it."

Uncle Ramzy checked the price. "Can't afford it. Unless," he said, grinning, "you give me a special discount. I'm sure you can do that," he said, lowering his voice and squinting. I assumed squinting was part of his seduction. "A discount for poor Ramzy."

I was desperate to leave. The saleslady sniffed the air. "Let me show you our faux-fur coats," she said.

Uncle Ramzy chose a faux-fur coat made to look like red fox. At the register, I pulled out the cash.

"What are you doing?" he whispered to me.

"I'll take care of it."

"That's your parents' money?"

I nodded. I also bought him a pair of black leather gloves and some clothes (from the men's department). When we left Macy's, Uncle Ramzy invited me to lunch at the food court. We sat in the smoker's section, where we ate cheeseburgers.

"Did you notice how the saleslady ate me up with her eyes?" he said.

"She was making professional eye contact."

"That's your problem, Captain. You don't know how to read the signs."

"Then why didn't you get her number?"

"She's not my type."

After finishing his meal, Uncle Ramzy reached for his cigarettes. I asked for one. At school I smoked with my friends in the parking lot during lunch break.

Enjoying the rush of nicotine in my blood, I asked, "Do you think Marwan still wears his fur coat?"

"We buried him with his coat on."

"He was killed?"

"A bullet went through his eye and out the back of his head. The enemy also had good snipers."

I had seen such violence only in movies, all fake blood and gore, guns shooting blanks. But to witness such scenes in real life, in real time, as Uncle Ramzy had, was something entirely different.

Before returning home, we stopped at a liquor store so that Uncle Ramzy could buy a bottle of vodka and more cigarettes.

"Vodka was all we drank in the militia," he said. "It's the drink of revolutionaries."

Even though I had never tasted vodka, I now craved a shot.

◆

THAT NIGHT, AFTER MY parents had gone to sleep, I saw that the light in Uncle Ramzy's room was still on. I knocked softly on his door.

"Come in," he said.

He was sitting back against my sister's headboard, smoking in bed. The vodka bottle and a shot glass were on the nightstand. I closed the door behind me and sat at the foot of the bed.

"Did you come to tuck me in?"

"How's the vodka?" I asked.

He poured a shot. "You tell me."

I drank the shot and grimaced. I preferred beer, which my friends and I drank at parties, but I told him it tasted good. Then I asked, "What was it like being a sniper?"

"Shit. Hand me back the glass."

He poured himself a shot and swung it back.

I asked for a cigarette and he passed over his pack and the Zippo. I lit up.

"Before joining the militia," he said, "I was sick of living at home and having to deal with my father. I never finished school; I wasn't smart like your mother. I always confused my letters and had trouble reading. After dropping out I worked from job to job. I trained as a car mechanic but hated coming home all filthy and greasy. And the pay was lousy. The militia offered me something different. Not just a salary and a place to live. It offered me a brotherhood. Me and the boys, we were willing to die for each other." He refreshed his glass and drank. "My post was along the green line. We'd camp behind barricades and fire at the enemy across the street. We battled over city blocks. I'd sit by a window in an upstairs room of an abandoned building and just wait for the enemy to make a move. When he did, I'd shoot him."

I stubbed my cigarette into the ashtray on the bed. "Weren't you scared to die?"

"All the time. But when fighting broke out, we just thought of defending ourselves. We lived for those moments when our adrenaline kicked in. I've never felt so alive as when I was fighting. My body was on fire; I could feel every particle of hair, every drop of sweat. The sound of bullets whizzing by, the clang of my shells on the floor, the smell of sulfur in the air, it was all, it was all—"

He paused, seeming lost in the image he was shaping from memory. I hadn't expected his poetic flare.

"It was majestic. But the fighting lasted for only a few minutes, and then we'd return to waiting. We did much more waiting than fighting. So much waiting that we got bored and fell asleep at our posts. That's how Marwan was killed. He was sleeping in his chair while on guard duty. We found him on his back on the ground, in a pool of blood."

I listened to Uncle Ramzy's war stories until three in the morning. He talked about the Battle of the Hotels, the time his Kalashnikov jammed and he started firing with an old revolver, night skies lit up by the arcing flares of RPGs, the horrid bombing of West Beirut during the Israeli invasion in '82, the winter morning a piece of shrapnel sliced his stomach open.

"Did it leave a scar?" I asked.

He lifted his shirt to reveal a purple starfish-shaped mark on his abdomen.

"It was during my militia days that I met Faten," he said, but before I could ask who that was, he told me it was time to go to bed. Like Scheherazade, he was skilled at spacing out his stories, knowing that I'd return to listen to each one.

◆

UNCLE RAMZY HAD THE house to himself while I was at school and my parents were at work. I was the first to return home and I often found him smoking in front of the TV, watching a soap opera or a talk show. Twinkies wrappers littered the coffee table—Uncle Ramzy had become addicted, calling Twinkies America's greatest invention. My parents had bought him several boxes from the grocery store, as well as an extra jar of peanut butter and a gallon of whole milk. I'd join him on the couch and we'd smoke together until my parents arrived home from work. Although they prohibited me from smoking, I was able to get away with it by blaming Uncle Ramzy for the smell of tobacco on my clothes.

At dinner one night, Mama asked if Café Paris was still open.

"Yes," Uncle Ramzy said.

"What about the Hamra Theater?" Baba asked.

"It closed down. Most of the movie theaters in Hamra closed during the war."

My parents loved talking about Hamra Street, which was only a few blocks up from the American University.

"Do you have any news about Sahar, the baker's daughter?" Mama asked.

Uncle Ramzy looked at me and winked. "After her father died, she moved down to her village in the south."

"Allah yerhamo. How'd he die?"

"He had joined the communist wing of our militia. He'd bake in the mornings and fight in the evenings. But one day he didn't return home; he went missing for weeks. His body was later found in a ditch off Damascus Road. He was missing his limbs."

Mama covered her mouth.

"The enemy had tied his wrists to the back of one car and his ankles to the back of another. Then both drivers stepped on the gas."

"Barbaric," Baba said.

I hoped Uncle Ramzy hadn't done anything so heinous.

"Those days are behind us now," Uncle Ramzy said. "You should return. I mean permanently."

"I wish, but—" Mama said.

"But what?"

"This is our home now," Baba said. "We have good jobs. Lara is in law school, Amer will be in college soon."

"I fear that the Beirut we remember and love is gone forever," Mama said. "Sometimes I'm not even sure I want to see what the city has turned into."

Mama took a sip of wine and wiped the edges of her mouth with a napkin. Although she was in her early forties, she looked two decades younger. She never left the house without putting on makeup, fixing her hair, and spraying herself with Chanel N°5 perfume. She once told me and my sister about Georgina Rizk, a Lebanese model who at the age of eighteen won the Miss Universe pageant in 1971. Georgina was the first Arab woman to ever win the award. She was fluent in Arabic and French and also spoke English. At the time, Mama was a student at the university, and like most women her age, she wanted to look like Georgina. One day she and her friends went to a salon to get their hair blow-dried and brushed to resemble Georgina's long, wavy locks.

"Georgina is a Beiruti," Mama had told us. "She let the world know what our city's women are made of."

Mama's life before the war always seemed too good to be true. With time I understood that she was trying to preserve the illusion of her past, an illusion that was richer and more meaningful than reality.

From across the dinner table, Uncle Ramzy looked at me. "You can study at the American University of Beirut."

"I plan to attend the University of Michigan."

He shook his head. "You've all become American."

"We're Lebanese and American," Mama said. "You could become one, too, you know. A Lebanese American. There are a lot of opportunities here to start a new life for yourself. I could sponsor your immigration."

"I'm a Beiruti."

"You can be a Beiruti and a Dearbonite," I said. I could imagine myself listening to his stories for years to come over shots of vodka.

"And what would I do here? I've got no skills except—"

Mama gave him a stern look.

"I already told Amer about my Cowboy days."

"That is in the past," Mama said.

Baba sipped his wine. He didn't appear too keen on the idea of Uncle Ramzy settling down in Dearborn.

"It's too cold here," Uncle Ramzy said.

"You've got your fur coat to keep you warm," I said.

"The sky's too gray and cloudy."

"Only in winter," Mama said. "You'll get used to it. We all did."

"Dearborn is filled with Arabs," I added. "You'll make friends in no time."

"My brothers are back in Beirut. They need me."

◆

I WAS SMOKING IN the school parking lot during lunch break with my friends when I saw Uncle Ramzy walking down the street. He didn't notice us.

"Who the fuck is that?" Khaled asked, pointing.

"He looks like a pimp in that fur coat," Mazin said.

That's my uncle, I wanted to say, *a sniper who battled in the streets of Beirut. He's not someone to fuck with.* But I remained quiet.

When I returned home from school, I plopped next to Uncle Ramzy on the couch and pulled a cigarette from his pack. *Oprah* was on TV. I asked him about his day, feeling guilty for ignoring him on the street.

"Did some push-ups and sit-ups in the morning," he said. "Went out for a walk, too. I've got to get back in shape after all the Twinkies I've been eating."

Skinny and not especially strong, I'd never cared about sports or calisthenics. I had lost the few fistfights I'd been in, coming home each time with a swollen eye and a busted lip. It struck me that Uncle Ramzy's diminutive size had never been an obstacle because he had been endowed with the power of a gun.

"What was it like to kill someone?" I asked.

The serious look on his face made me regret my question.

"It was the ugliest part of my job, but it was a job I had to do. I still remember some of their faces, those I killed. They keep me up."

"You mean nightmares?"

"Terrible nightmares."

We watched the rest of *Oprah* in silence. Then Uncle Ramzy went to his room and didn't come down until dinner.

♦

AS I WAS WALKING home from school on an unseasonably warm and sunny Friday afternoon, my coat tied around my waist, a red Mustang pulled right up to me at the curb. The tinted passenger window slid down. "Need a ride?"

I knelt to see the driver's face. I couldn't believe it.

"Get in, Captain," Uncle Ramzy said. He was wearing aviator sunglasses and eating a Twinkie. His hair was slicked back with gel. Despite the summery weather, he was in his fur coat.

The car's black leather interior gave off an opulent scent. The chrome dashboard glimmered. With one hand on the steering wheel, Uncle Ramzy looked like a gangster.

"It's a rental," he explained. "I've got it for the day."

It was my first time in a Mustang. "Where are we going?"

"Detroit. I want to see a real city."

He offered me his box of Twinkies. I pulled out a pack.

"You know how to get there?" he asked.

I told him to go up Schaefer Road and take a left onto Michigan Avenue, which led us into the heart of Motor City. Crossing the border into Detroit always thrilled me. My friends and I thought we were daredevils whenever we drove in. On the local news, most of the reported violence took place in Detroit, though occasionally it spilled over into East Dearborn. My parents had forbidden me from visiting, warning me of gang violence and muggers.

Uncle Ramzy tore down Michigan Avenue, the engine roaring like a beast. I gripped the side handle. "There's a speed limit!"

He slowed down. "We don't have speed limits in Lebanon. Another reason you all should return."

I switched on the radio to the rock station. R.E.M.'s "Losing My Religion," a song I was obsessed with, was playing. When the skyscrapers appeared around a bend, Uncle Ramzy said, "Now that's what I call a city!"

We parked on a side street up from the Detroit River and strolled down the River Walk. Across the water was Canada.

"This reminds me of the Corniche in Beirut," Uncle Ramzy said.

The wind coming off the river was cool. It felt good to be out in the sun after a long winter, and although I knew the warm weather wasn't going to last, it held with it the promise of Saturday barbeques and swimming in the neighborhood community pool, of late-night walks with my friends and passing 40s in the park. I had been distracted all day at school, looking out the window, itching to go outside.

Most of the passersby were Black, and Uncle Ramzy stared at them.

"Stop that," I hissed. "You're drawing too much attention."

"I've never seen so many Africans before."

"African Americans. Detroit is a Black city."

As a Black woman in a pink jumpsuit was approaching us, pumping her clenched fists, Uncle Ramzy pulled out a Twinkie from his coat pocket.

"Twinkie, Madame?" he asked her.

She stopped walking. "I'm exercising. I can't eat a Twinkie while I'm exercising."

"Save it for later."

She smiled and took the Twinkie. "Nice coat."

"Merci, Madame."

"You French?"

"Lebanese."

"I like your accent."

Uncle Ramzy removed his sunglasses and squinted. "I would like to take you out to dinner. A lobster dinner."

She laughed. "I'm married, honey. You have a good day now."

"See how easy that was," Uncle Ramzy told me as we continued walking.

"I find it kind of creepy."

"No wonder you're still a virgin."

We stood at the railing and looked out onto the water at the skyscrapers lining Windsor's shore. From his coat pocket Uncle Ramzy took out the flask he had given me. I kept it in the bottom drawer of my desk.

"You went through my things?" I asked.

"Is there a problem?"

I shook my head, letting it go. He passed me the flask. I took a swig and gave it back to him. "Did your parents ever tell you about the Pigeon Rocks suicides?" he asked.

"No," I said. The Pigeon Rocks were two towering rock pillars that rose from Beirut's shore. There was a photograph of my parents standing together on the Corniche with the Pigeon Rocks in the background.

"Before the war, the Corniche was once a hot spot for suicides."

The highest point of the Corniche, Uncle Ramzy continued, was in a neighborhood called Raouché, where a small stretch of the promenade overlooked the Pigeon Rocks. Despondent souls would climb over the railing, walk a few steps onto the cliff, and jump into the sea, crashing into rocks on their way down.

"Your mother," he said. "She saved me from jumping off the Corniche."

I turned to him. "When was this?"

"Maybe a year before you all left Beirut."

I wanted to ask him what had prompted him to consider suicide, but I trusted that he'd tell me when the time was right. "I'm glad you're still here," I said. He rose on his tiptoes and kissed my cheek.

We remained on the River Walk to watch the sunset—I put on my coat as the temperature started to drop—and then we drove to American Coney Island on Michigan Avenue and Griswold to feast on chili dogs. On our way home, we stopped to buy another bottle of vodka.

"I was worried about you two!" Mama said as soon as we entered. "Dinner has been ready for hours and I had no idea where you were."

"It's my fault," Uncle Ramzy said. "I took Amer for a drive."

Baba peered out the window. "Is that your Mustang?" he asked.

"Until the morning," Uncle Ramzy said. "Let's eat! I'm starving."

I was supposed to meet up with my friends that night, but instead I chose to stay home. The four of us spent the evening in the living room, Mama and Uncle Ramzy sharing memories of their childhood, my parents reminiscing about their university days. I listened in silence, craving cigarettes and vodka, wanting Uncle Ramzy all to myself. It was approaching one in the morning when my parents finally called it a night and went upstairs to bed. I suggested to Uncle Ramzy that we go down to the basement, where we could make as much noise as we wanted without waking them. He thought it was a good idea.

We sat on the sofa in front of the TV. Uncle Ramzy lit two cigarettes as I poured two shots of vodka. "To your health," he said, and we clinked glasses.

Field of Dreams was playing on HBO. "I like Kevin Costner," Uncle Ramzy said. "One night me and the boys watched a bootleg of *The Untouchables* in our theater. We called it a theater, but we just put folding chairs in front of a concrete wall. A guy in the back took care of the projector."

We watched Costner's character, Ray Kinsella, walk in his cornfield and hear the words "If you build it, he will come."

We barely drank as we watched the rest of the film and smoked cigarettes. At the closing credits, Uncle Ramzy poured us more vodka. I could tell the film had moved him.

"I loved Faten just as much as Ray loved his wife," he began.

Faten, I thought. The name sounded familiar, and I remembered then that Uncle Ramzy had mentioned it earlier, that night in his room after he'd shown me his scar.

He had met her during the early years of the civil war, he told me. Occasionally, following his late-night shifts, he'd leave his cowboy hat and Kalashnikov in his room and go to a patisserie for breakfast. The patisserie was in Jal-el-Baher, a few streets up from the sea. He'd sit at a wooden table to eat a croissant filled with thyme and sip on a Nescafé as French music played on a transistor radio. He loved spending these quiet moments there because it seemed a world away from the war and the killing he had done. He imagined he was a cosmopolitan man in Paris on his way to the office.

One day a new waitress served him. Her black frizzy hair sprung from her head like the fronds of a palm tree. She had big hazel eyes. He was afraid her beauty would make him stumble over his words, so he just silently stole glances at her. But on his next visit, he found the courage to start a conversation and learned that her name was Faten. Originally from Cairo, she had come to Beirut to work and send money back home to her family. Her Egyptian accent charmed him, and there was something about her that put him at ease.

When she asked what he did for a living, he told her the truth. He was afraid that Faten wouldn't want to keep speaking to him, given that he was a militiaman, but instead she brought him a slice of mille-feuille on the house.

Soon they began to take walks together on the Corniche. One day they climbed over the railing and sat down on the rocks. They took off their shoes and plunged their feet into the water. A fisherman standing a few feet away cast his line into the sea.

"Once the war is over, what do you plan to do?" Faten asked.

"We could open our own patisserie," he said. "Faten and Ramzy's. How does that sound?"

Every now and then Uncle Ramzy paid for a room at a two-star hotel so that they could spend the night together. The musty room came with a kitchenette, where Faten treated him to mloukhieh with rabbit meat, her favorite dish. Uncle Ramzy was used to eating mloukhieh with chicken. He had never tasted rabbit before. In Egypt, Faten explained, they made the dish this way. Here in Beirut, you couldn't find rabbit at the local butcher's, but she knew an Egyptian butcher in town who got special shipments of the meat from Alexandria. It was an expensive treat, which she could only afford once or twice a year. When she brought out the ingredients in the hotel room, Uncle Ramzy offered to help her make the stew, cleaning the mallow leaves, dicing the onions, peeling garlic cloves, boiling the rice on the stove, and toasting pita bread. Since there wasn't a table in the room and the floor was filthy, they sat on the edge of the bed to eat.

"It was the most delicious meal I've ever had," Uncle Ramzy told me. "The rabbit melted in my mouth. But that's not why it tasted so good. You understand why it tasted so good?"

"Yes, Uncle. She sacrificed so much to make it."

"Over the next year and a half, she managed to make the dish seven times. To save her money, I bought the meat from the butcher. We had plans to marry."

"What happened to her?"

"She was stopped at a roadblock on her way to work. The enemy checked her ID, saw that she was Muslim, and slit her throat. She had nothing to do with the war—she wasn't even Lebanese—but still they killed her."

"Allah yerhama," I said, not knowing what else to say.

"When I found out that she had been killed, I wanted to kill myself. But like I said, your mother saved me." He poured us more vodka and downed two consecutive shots. "I had other lovers after Faten, but I never fell for them. I was still in love with her. I still am. Since her death, I've made rabbit stew each March 22, the day she died. It's my tribute to her. I've never missed a year."

"March 22," I said. "That's this Monday."

"Prepare yourself for a feast."

We drank down the bottle, wanting to kill the melancholic mood.

"Let's eat some Twinkies!" I said. We stumbled upstairs to the kitchen. I tore open the box. "We need milk," I said. When I tried pouring it into two glasses, I missed the mark completely. The milk spilled over the counter and onto the floor. We both cracked up. Feeling dizzy, I tried to steady myself by placing my hand on the counter, but I knocked over the glasses and they shattered. Moments later, my parents entered the kitchen, both in their pajamas.

"What's the meaning of this?" Baba yelled at me.

"Want a Twinkie?" I giggled.

"Are you drunk?"

"No!"

"Ramzy, what's going on?" Mama demanded.

"We're having a late-night snack."

"It's nearly five in the morning."

My jaw suddenly began to twitch. My tongue felt like sandpaper. When I opened my mouth to ask for water, I vomited on the floor.

◆

I WOKE UP ON Saturday afternoon, my head pounding, to knocking on my bedroom door.

"Come in," I said, rubbing my eyes.

Baba opened the blinds slightly to allow some light into the room. He sat by my feet.

"Is anyone else home?" I asked.

"Your mother is spending the day with your uncle. They need to return the Mustang. Now about last night."

"Please, I feel like shit."

"I'm not here to lecture you. I was once your age, you know. I had my own share of hangovers. As for your uncle, I know you admire him, but he's not necessarily a positive influence."

"He's had a difficult life."

"So have we."

"He nearly killed himself. Do you know that?"

"I remember that time."

"If I make him happy, then I don't see any problem."

"Ramzy doesn't make the best choices."

"Like what?" I wanted Baba to leave my room, not liking where this conversation was headed.

"I'd rather not say."

"You mean him joining the militia? It takes a brave man to fight."

"What's he told you about his militia experience?"

"He was a sniper. He fought for years, risking his life."

"Hmm. And you believe him? That he was actually a fighter?"

"He's got a scar to prove it."

"You mean the one on his abdomen? When he was suffering from appendicitis and ended up going to a third-rate doctor for surgery. That scar?"

A sickening feeling constricted my throat. If Uncle Ramzy had fabricated his fighting days, had he also fabricated Faten? Had he been telling me lies this entire time? Why would he do such a thing? He didn't need to lie to impress me. Or was he simply lying to himself to cope better? I didn't have the heart to ask Baba whether Faten was real. She seemed real to me, and I wanted to keep it that way.

"We've been supporting your uncle for all these years," Baba said. "Sending him money every month."

"The Mustang he rented. Was that your money?"

"All his pocket money comes from us. We bought his airline ticket, too. A long time ago I told your mother to cut the funds, that Ramzy needed to grow up and learn how to take care of himself, but she always made excuses. There was a war and jobs were hard to come by, and Ramzy was trying his best, but he was unlucky. You know how much your mother adores him. She'll do anything for him."

Baba's information felt a thousand times worse than my hangover. He stood up, saying he'd fry eggs for me, but I couldn't stomach any food, not after what he had shared.

In the evening, I heard the front door open. Mama's and Uncle Ramzy's voices drifted up the stairs. When Mama came to check on me, I told her I needed to rest.

"Don't let anyone come in," I said. "I'm going to sleep through to the morning."

When Uncle Ramzy came upstairs and entered my room without knocking, I pretended to be fast asleep.

"Captain?" he whispered too loudly. "Captain, are you awake?"

I ignored him.

On Sunday, my parents made plans to take Uncle Ramzy to Port Huron for the day. They thought walking on the lakeshore, breathing the fresh air, would do him good, because he seemed to be depressed. At breakfast, he had remained quiet and sullen. I thought I knew the reason why: it was the eve of the anniversary of Faten's death.

I declined to join them, mentioning all the schoolwork I had to do. When they returned in the evening, I remained in my room, studying. But then Uncle Ramzy came in, entering with barely a sound.

"Captain," he said.

I turned around from my desk. He looked like he was about to weep. I waited for him to say something, but he just stood there.

"Did you enjoy the lake?" I asked, my heart softening.

He nodded. He sat on my bed, shoulders slouched, looking down at his hands. "Tomorrow's the day," he said. His somberness appeared too real to be an act. Was it possible that he had simply exaggerated his stories? It was something we were all guilty of. If he hadn't been a sniper during the war, maybe he had done something else involving the militia. But I wasn't prepared just yet to give him back my trust.

"Do you still plan to make rabbit stew?" I asked.

"I'd rather die than not make it," he said.

◆

THE ICY COLD RETURNED on Monday morning. Snow flurries swirled down from the gray sky, sticking to my clothes as I walked to school. It continued to snow throughout the day. On my walk back home, a black Corvette ZR1 pulled up at the curb. The window slid halfway down. Uncle Ramzy was behind the wheel in his fur coat, wearing his leather gloves. Another rental, I thought, paid for by my parents. Opening the passenger side door, I saw a metal cage on the seat. A cage with two rabbits inside, one snowy white and the other brown. Alive.

"Get in, Captain! It's cold as a sisterfucker."

I pointed at the cage.

"Just put it on your lap," he said.

"Where'd you get the rabbits?"

"The pet store. Get in!"

I set my backpack on the floorboard and rested the cage on my lap.

He stepped on the gas. "I visited all the butcher shops in town. No one sells rabbit meat. Neither do the grocery stores."

I looked down at the rabbits. "You can't do this. They're pets."

"Not for long."

At the house he removed something from the trunk and came around to my side. He was carrying a canvas sack on his shoulder. I remained seated, not wanting to give up the poor rabbits to my uncle.

"I've got this all planned out. A guy at the hunting store gave me excellent instructions. I wrote them down."

"You mean you've never done this before?"

"No. We'll do it in the garage; don't want to attract the neighbors' attention."

When I didn't move, he took the cage from me and brought it to the detached garage at the end of our driveway. Finally I stepped out of the car and joined him.

Uncle Ramzy closed the garage door after me, and then pulled the flask from his coat pocket and passed it to me. I took a swig and handed it back to him.

"I have homework to do. A lot."

He glared at me. "Don't be a pussy."

"Don't fucking call me a pussy."

"Then be a man."

Uncle Ramzy removed a tarp from the sack and spread it on the floor. He looked around the garage and pulled out a plastic bucket and a shovel, then dragged over a ladder. He opened the ladder in the center of the tarp and tied two thin pieces of rope to its crossbeams. Beneath the crossbeams he placed the bucket. He took out a utility knife, a cleaver, and a rag from his sack and placed them beside it.

"This is our butcher's station."

"Fuck this," I said, and opened the door to leave.

"Captain, please!"

I turned around.

"I need your help, Amer. I can't do this alone. I'll never ask you for another favor. I promise." His eyes moistened. "I'll die if I don't eat the stew today."

I hesitated, and then closed the door.

"We really should slaughter the rabbits halal style," he said, "but I can't use the knife because, well—"

I understood. Slitting the rabbits' throats halal style would remind Uncle Ramzy of the way Faten had been killed.

He picked up the shovel. "We'll bash their heads in over the tarp. I'd prefer to use a gun, but that would be too noisy." He opened the cage and took out the white rabbit and gave it to me. I removed my gloves and petted the trembling animal. He took the free ends of the ropes, tied each one around the rabbit's hind legs, and let it hang upside down. It began to jerk and swing from side to side.

"A shovel won't work," he said. He walked around the garage and found a pile of bricks in the corner. He brought two back and got down on his knees in front of the rabbit. Holding a brick in each hand, he opened his arms wide. The rabbit was twisting and turning.

"Please don't," I pleaded.

He remained focused on the task. "Hold the rabbit still."

I walked around the ladder, got on my knees, held the rabbit's torso and closed my eyes. I kept my eyes closed until I heard the bricks fall on the floor. The rabbit was writhing in my hands, still alive. Uncle Ramzy was sitting on his ass.

"What happened?" I asked.

He broke down into sobs. I let go of the rabbit and maneuvered around to him on my knees and embraced him. He buried his face in my chest; I stroked the back of his head. Sniffling, he said he couldn't do it; it reminded him too much of the times he'd line his enemy in his scope and pull the trigger. He drank from the flask. "What if I hold the rabbit?"

I was about to protest when I saw how sad and desperate he looked. We exchanged positions.

"Pass me the flask," I said. He passed it over and I took three swigs, feeling a burn in my chest. As Uncle Ramzy held the rabbit, his eyes closed, I brought the bricks a foot apart from the rabbit's head on either side and, before I gave myself more time to think, I smashed them together. I heard a squealing sound. The rabbit began twitching.

"Do it again," Uncle Ramzy said.

I did it again. This time the rabbit stopped moving. We untied its hind legs. Its eyes were open; blood oozed from its snout. Uncle Ramzy removed the brown rabbit from the cage and tied it up. I killed the rabbit on the first attempt.

"Now what?" I asked.

Uncle Ramzy dug into his back pocket, withdrew a folded piece of paper, and opened it up. "Now we skin them. Let's start on the brown one since it's already strung up."

He slid out the blade of the utility knife. "I'll tell you what to do."

"Why don't you do it?"

"The sight of blood—it makes me queasy."

"But you fought in a war. You *killed* people."

"And I have nightmares because of it." He gave me the knife. "Start by making a small cut in the back. Be careful not to cut into the flesh."

I pulled up the fur on the rabbit's back and made an incision through it; a small pocket opened. I slid my index and middle fingers of both hands inside the pocket, touching skin and flesh, and ripped outward with all my might, the fur sliding off down to the hind legs and to the head, unveiling pink, glossy flesh. Uncle Ramzy turned his back to me and threw up.

"Next step," I said.

He was bent over, his hands on his knees, coughing out his lungs.

All the fur was off the rabbit except for its hands and feet.

"Uncle," I snapped.

He turned around, bile hanging from his chin. He avoided looking at the rabbit.

"Read the instructions," I shouted.

"Twist off the head or chop it off."

I twisted the head and pulled it off; a tendon remained, which I severed with the knife. In a quavering voice, Uncle Ramzy continued reciting step-by-step instructions, his back to me. I cut off the rabbit's anus and pulled out a string of intestine. I wiped my hands with the rag and cleaned the blade and closed it. I slid out the gut hook and made an incision at the base of the rib cage and cut down, blood pouring into the bucket. I tore the skin open, thrust my hand inside, and scooped out the intestines and dumped them into the bucket. I cut farther up the chest and removed the heart and lungs. My hands and coat sleeves were covered in blood. I untied the rabbit's hind legs, put it on the tarp, and chopped off its limbs with the cleaver. I then went outside to hose down the carcass. In methodical silence, I skinned and gutted the second rabbit. The bottom of the bucket was filled with gore. Uncle Ramzy finally turned around. His face was yellow. I gave him the cleaver. "Butcher the meat."

♦

I'M NOW A MARRIED man with three children in their late teens. We live in a colonial house in West Dearborn. I've been a vegetarian since the day I killed the rabbits in my parents' garage.

All these years later, I'm haunted by how I felt while killing and gutting them. I enjoyed it. It came naturally to me. I can still hear the sound of fur slipping off the carcasses; the wet, gurgling sounds my hand made as I thrust it into the cavity; the plop of organs in the bucket. On that snowy day in late March, I wondered, with growing horror, if I was capable of committing a terrible atrocity. Uncle Ramzy had exposed a part of me that I never knew existed, a part I was terrified to uncover further. Because of this I distanced myself from him.

A week and a half after the rabbit butchering, Uncle Ramzy returned to Beirut. We reunited that summer when my family and I traveled to Lebanon, but by that point I had already lost my patience with him. It didn't matter to me anymore if he had told me lies or not.

On the night of March 22, the anniversary of Faten's supposed death, Uncle Ramzy feasted on rabbit stew. When Mama asked where he'd purchased the meat, he said he had put in a special order at the butcher's. My parents found it delicious, and both had second servings. Uncle Ramzy slurped bowl after bowl. It was the look on his face that I remember so well, as if one moment he was about to break into hysterical laughter and the next into tears. Both euphoria and loss. He was drunk on the stew. When he saw that I wasn't eating, he made me a bite from his bowl, a chunk of meat resting on the mallow leaves dripping with broth. He stood up and reached across the table, the stink of his underarms wafting over me, and told me to open my mouth. "From my hand," he insisted. I refused.

Acknowledgments

Twenty years ago, when I was an MFA student in creative writing, I often heard from professors and publishing industry representatives that the old days of the editor-writer relationship—where the editor works closely with the writer, page by page, word by word—were over. At the time I was disheartened, as I craved such a relationship. I wanted someone to care about my work as much as I did; someone who understood what I was attempting on the page and could help take my fiction to another level. With this book I found the editor. Eternal gratitude to Elizabeth DeMeo from Tin House for believing in my work and treating it with such grace and thoughtfulness. This story collection is out in the world because of you.

Big thanks to the rest of the amazing team at Tin House. It's been an absolute joy and honor to work with so many wonderful and talented people including Becky Kraemer, Craig Popelars, Nanci McCloskey, Beth Steidle, Jae Nichelle, Phoebe Bright, and Nicole Pagliari. Thank you to Erika Stevens, Meg Storey, Alyssa Ogi, and Masie Cochran for your thoughtful feedback.

Thank you to my Michigan family for your love and kindness, and for putting up with my bad jokes: Nader Seif, Wejdan Azzou, Diana Abouali, Maysam Seif, Andrew Shryock, and Sally Howell. Another thanks to Sally, an extraordinary historian and storyteller, for sharing your expertise on the Arab American community in the Detroit metropolitan area.

Thank you to Dr. Matthew Stiffler for directing me to research material on the Arab passengers on board the *Titanic*.

Thank you to Professor Peggy McCracken and the Institute for the Humanities at the University of Michigan—Ann Arbor for providing the space and time to work on my collection. Thank you to my 2020–2021 cohort, especially Linda Gregerson, Anna Watkins Fisher, and Aaron Stone for reading an early version of my story "Money Chickens."

Thank you to Janet McAdams, Sarah Heidt, Sergei Lobanov-Rostovsky, Pashmina Murthy, Piers Brown, Wendy Singer, and David Lynn for your friendship and support.

Thank you to David Bowen for your encouragement and sage advice.

Thank you to Siwar Masannat, Soham Patel, Carol W. N. Fadda, and Sean Conrey for your love and support.

Over the course of my writing career, I've been fortunate to have studied with Jaime Manrique, John McNally, Nicholas Christopher, Alan Ziegler, Nathan Englander, Lis Harris, Edith Grossman, Liam Callanan, Mauricio Kilwein Guevara, George Clark, and Valerie Laken. Special thanks to Valerie, Jaime, and John for your enduring faith in me.

Thank you to all the editors from the literary journals who have provided homes for my stories, and who have championed the work of BIPOC writers. Special thanks to the stellar teams at the *Arkansas International*, the *Common*, *Michigan Quarterly Review*, the *Georgia Review*, and *Prairie Schooner*.

Thank you to the gifted writer and editor, Jennifer Acker.

Thank you to my beloved friends and family in America and Lebanon.

Thank you to Cleo Cacoulidis, a true sister in every sense of the word, for always being in my corner and reading every word I send you.

Thank you to the Yaacoubs for your support.

Thank you to Imad, Keyan, Maya, and Ramsey for all your love.

Thank you to my rock star sister, Jana Zeineddine, for paving the way for me. I forgive you for breaking my toe when I was one. I know you didn't mean to throw a skateboard at me.

Thank you to my mother, Wafaa Al-Awar Abou-Zeineddine, for your love, guidance, and generosity.

Thank you to my late father, Ragheb Zeineddine, for your unwavering support. I miss you terribly.

Finally, thank you to my wife, Rana, and our daughters, Alma and Mira. You three make every day a gift. Thank you, Rana, for always believing in me. Without you I'd be lost.

© Austin Thomason, Michigan Photography

Ghassan Zeineddine was born in Washington, DC, and raised in the Middle East. He is an assistant professor of creative writing at Oberlin College, and co-editor of the creative nonfiction anthology *Hadha Baladuna: Arab American Narratives of Boundary and Belonging*. He lives with his wife and two daughters in Ohio.